# CANDLELIGHT REGENCY SPECIAL

# CANDLELIGHT REGENCIES

# THE
# PAISLEY
# BUTTERFLY

*Phyllis Taylor Pianka*

*A CANDLELIGHT REGENCY SPECIAL*

Published by
Dell Publishing Co., Inc.
1 Dag Hammarskjold Plaza
New York, New York 10017

Dell ® TM 681510, Dell Publishing Co., Inc.

ISBN: 0-440-17105-9

Printed in the United States of America

First printing—December 1980

*To my husband, Edwin,*
*who is everything to me*

# CHAPTER ONE

Lady Margaret Battersby Spence pulled the worn, rust-colored manteau closer about her shoulders as she hurried down Bond Street toward the bookstore. It had taken an uncommonly long time at the chandlery. She hated being late to open for business, even though it would likely be well on toward noon before her first customer appeared. One of the promises she had made herself when she took the tremendous step of going into trade was that the job must be done right if it were to be done at all.

The ormolu clock on the wall chimed the hour as she turned the key in the lock. She had no more than hung her manteau on the coat-tree and exchanged her rust bonnet for a white mobcap when the door opened. She looked up in astonishment.

"Alvira Simpson! What a pleasant surprise. It's been ages since I've seen you." Margaret hoped the words sounded more cordial than she felt. It was the first time she had seen Lady Alvira since Margaret had received the news that she was a veritable pauper.

Lady Alvira closed her sunshade and slid the satin loop over her wrist. "Indeed, Margaret. It has been far too long. I told Papa this morning that I simply must make it a point to call on you at your new . . . establishment." She curled her mouth around the word as if it might contaminate her somehow.

Looking around the low-beamed room, she walked to a shelf and perused the books until she finally saw a binding which attracted her attention. Then, pulling it from the shelf, she casually leafed through it and marked the place with her finger.

"It must be dreadfully difficult for you, having to live like this." She spread the book facedown on the table, and Margaret was amused to see Alvira's chaperone, who had followed her into the store, unobtrusively reach for a bookmarker and put it in the book before placing it properly on the table.

Margaret exchanged a look with the woman and her smile spilled over to Alvira. "Truthfully, Alvira, I am rather enjoying the challenge of being on my own. The shop demands a great deal of time but it is beginning to pay for itself."

"Come now, Margaret. I'll venture I spend more on fripperies than you can earn in a month."

"Without a doubt you are right, Alvira." She felt her temper beginning to simmer and she reminded herself that nothing would be gained by trading words with a potential customer, particularly an influential one. She went to a shelf and selected a beautiful leather-bound volume.

"Have you read Byron's *English Bards and Scotch Reviewers*? Of course it has been out for a while, but it is well acclaimed in literary circles. I also have Jane Austen's latest book if you are interested. They are sometimes difficult to find."

"No, they hold no interest for me. Have you a back issue of *Ladies' Quarterly*? I seem to have misplaced one of my periodicals and would like to get another. There was a certain embroidered gauze frock that appealed to me, and I thought to have my dressmaker copy it."

Margaret stooped down to search a bottom shelf for

the stack of out-of-date magazines. Finding them, she started to rise when Lady Alvira stepped too close and her slipper caught in Margaret's hem. As she stood up, the dress tore from hem to thigh, exposing a wide expanse of petticoat. Margaret had all she could take.

"Really, Alvira. Must you be so careless? You've ruined the dress beyond repair."

Lady Alvira was taken aback. "I'm sorry. It was an accident, but why are you so distraught? The dress is ancient, Margaret. I can remember your having worn it . . . why it must have been five years ago at a committee meeting for the protection of chimney sweeps."

"Nevertheless, it was one of the few presentable gowns I have left." Even though it was true, Margaret cringed the moment she said it. Of all people, she hated to have Alvira know the extent of her financial straits.

Alvira's face took on a grim set. "I had no idea you were so poor." She turned to her maid. "Lucy. Go to the carriage and bring in the clothing we were taking to the charity box at St. Stephens'. I'm sure Margaret won't mind wearing my castoffs. We are almost of a size."

Margaret ached to throw them back in her face but she bit her tongue and tried to show her gratitude. Indeed, she was hard put to know which was harder to take, Alvira's look of smug triumph or the chaperon's obvious pity.

As Alvira started to leave, she turned abruptly. "Dear me, I nearly forgot. I simply must show you my latest acquisition." She slid her shawl down her back and touched a jeweled hand to her brooch.

"It's an Austrian rosette of enamel, silver, and garnets. A friend of mine brought it to me from America. Isn't it lovely?"

Margaret smiled as she looked at the gaudy bauble. "It looks just like you, Alvira."

Alvira studied her closely, as if pondering the tone of her voice. Then, apparently satisfied, she smiled. "Yes. I believe it does. He said he chose it especially for me."

As the women left the bookstore, the chaperon glanced back and shook her head in resignation.

Surprisingly the gowns were almost new and some of them were quite presentable. By removing quantities of gold braid or a bunch of silk flowers or beading, Margaret was able to put together a fairly decent wardrobe. Although they were hardly the sort of gowns Margaret would have chosen, she was grateful to have them.

Nearly a week later Margaret, wearing her least favorite of Alvira's gowns, was working at her desk, her back toward the door. She was so completely absorbed in the inscriptions she was drawing for the nameplate to a book that she didn't hear the door to the bookstore open.

As she dipped the pen into the inkpot, she was suddenly engulfed in strong arms which lifted her from the chair and turned her around. Before she knew what was happening, she was being thoroughly and competently kissed.

Margaret had never before been kissed by a man with a moustache. It took more than a little willpower for her to free one hand and slap him resoundingly across the face.

He let her go more hastily than she had expected, and he stepped back, rubbing the back of his hand against his cheek.

"What the devil? . . . I . . . I do most heartily beg

your pardon, miss. I mistook you for another," he said as he swept off his high-crowned hat in a low bow. "It was the gown. It never occurred to me that there might be two of them in that particular shade of green."

Margaret laughed despite herself. "It is rather awful, isn't it?"

"Well . . . I . . ." He grinned broadly. "In truth . . . it reminds me of a caterpillar I once stepped on as a boy. I might add that on you anything would look delightful."

Margaret sobered. There had been no need to make this man feel at ease. He had enough self-confidence to put the Prince Regent to shame. She smoothed the yellow fichu over the bosom of the apple-green dress.

"You have no need to make amends, sir. Is there something you wished to see by way of publication? We carry five of the eight daily London newspapers, or perhaps you wish to see our books. There is a new tome which carries the complete works of Mr. Shakespeare."

"I promised my mother I would take her a book of Mr. Shelley's poems. Would you have such an item?"

Margaret pointed to a corner. "You will find them against the wall in the next aisle with the other books of poetry. Browse through them if you like, and if I can be of service, please let me know."

He grasped the lapels of his waistcoat in either hand and nodded. "Then don't stray far because there is no doubt you can be of service."

She turned quickly to her desk to hide the sudden color which flooded her face. What gall! He must have thought . . . Could he have known that she enjoyed the kiss fully as much as he appeared to savor it? The thought sent a surge of heat through her body.

Indeed! That sort of nonsense was a thing of the past as far as she was concerned. It had to be that way now that she was on her own.

She sat down at the desk and busied herself with cleaning the quill pen. For a moment while she was in his arms, she had been carried back in time to her coming out. It had been a carefree time of youthful vanity catered to by an adoring family, a time of girlish kisses stolen behind the tall hedges of the yew maze, a time of confidence in the knowledge that her future was secure as the promised bride of the viscount of Pendergast.

Less than a year later her parents were dead, as was her future as the viscountess. When it became known that her father had greatly overextended his fortunes to the point where his debts could scarcely be covered, all the fops and dandies of the *beau monde* turned away from her as if she carried the pox. The viscount sent his regrets by way of a messenger and a week later was betrothed to the daughter of an earl. The fact that his wife had grown as fat as a pig and he had gambled away most of her money went a long way toward compensating for Margaret's loss.

She dusted the manuscript with drying powder, then blew it aside before cutting the page to the proper size. Thank heaven she wasn't bitter, as most of her former friends had expected her to be. If truth be told, she rather liked this new life. Educated as she was, she had always been something of a curiosity among the other debutantes. True, she had also been trained in proper behavior among Polite Society and she could play simple melodies on the pianoforte as well as the rest of her cohorts, but her father had insisted that she be trained in languages and history as well.

She sighed. Fortunately her father had won out against her mother, or she would be in dire straits today. There was barely enough money from the sale of the estate to pay for the inventory of books. It had taken a loan from the lending bank to provide enough funds to rent the bookshop. Hopefully she would be able to repay the money before the end of the year.

This time she heard the door open. She turned quickly and rose to greet the man who approached.

"Mr. Muth. How nice to see you."

The tall, sad-eyed man nodded his head in greeting. "A good morning to you, Lady Margaret. I've come about the rental on the room."

Margaret couldn't keep the concern from her voice. "I trust everything has been satisfactory, Mr. Muth. If not . . ."

He smiled, drawing the skin taut across his bony face. "Indeed, it is most satisfactory. The books are exactly what we were looking for. I only came to give you the rent which is due."

Margaret slowly let out her breath. It was the rent money the group of intellectuals paid for the use of the back room that kept her solvent. She sat down to make out a receipt, then handed it to him. "Thank you again. I can't tell you how pleased I am that your friends care as much as I do for these valuable books. In truth, it is difficult to tell that the books have been used. Should you care to borrow others, I would be happy to make them available."

"You are most generous. I shall let you know if we require additional books for our research." He pocketed the receipt and, bowing, bid her good-bye.

Margaret turned to find the man with the moustache watching her. His face wore a speculative look and she found herself resenting it.

"Is there something you wanted, Mr. . . ."

He smiled quickly, and it transformed his face into the teasing facade which was more familiar to her.

"Why yes, I believe there is." He handed her two books. "I hope these will appeal to my mother. Would you agree?"

"Not knowing your mother, I could hardly judge, but if she is partial to Mr. Shelley, it would seem likely she would also enjoy the works of William Wordsworth and Robert Burns."

He nodded. "I shall have to trust your judgment as to that. I hope you are right. I have my reputation as a gift giver to consider."

She laughed. "Indeed. I saw the brooch you presented to Lady Alvira. It *was* your gift, wasn't it?"

He had the good grace to turn red. "You must realize, Lady Margaret, that I don't choose the gifts for myself. I try to select what pleases others. To that end I am rarely wrong."

Margaret grudgingly gave him credit. "I'll have to admit that she was inordinately pleased with your selection."

He threw his head back and laughed. "It was a hideous bit of trash, wasn't it?" he said as he settled on the two books and handed them to her.

Her smile was answer enough. She wrapped the books and handed them to him along with the coins in change. "I hope your mother will enjoy them. In three weeks we will receive another shipment of books. If there is anything which might interest you, I would be happy to let you know when it is available. Of course I would need your name and address."

He inclined his head. "You needn't bother. I rather think I shall be coming in again . . . quite soon."

"As you wish." She watched him as he went out the door and continued to walk down Bond Street. There was a supremely confident air about him that irritated her. But what plagued her more than anything else was the fact that she was attracted to him. She would have given up her supper of parsnip pie and kippers if she could have seen his carriage, but short of going outside and making a fool of herself, there was no way that could be accomplished.

It was another week before she saw him again. By that time she was certain that he had changed his mind about visiting the bookstore and his arrival caught her off guard. He recognized her momentary discomfort, and it obviously amused him.

He bowed low as he greeted her, and she dropped a curtsy. Her voice had a decided edge to it as she spoke.

"I see that you have not returned the books. I trust your mother enjoyed them?"

"Indeed. But then she enjoys whatever I select for her to read."

Margaret inclined her head. "And yet you found it necessary to ask my advice. How interesting."

He laughed. "Touché. You have a fine wit, my lady, but has no one told you that it is humility, not wit, that succeeds in the trades?"

Margaret avoided an answer. "Are you then an expert in the field of merchandise?"

"Should I choose to be, my lady, I would be an expert. As it happens, my interests lie in another direction."

His gaze swept her figure from head to foot without the least ounce of subterfuge. "I see you have forsworn the apple green for the brown velvet. May I be so bold as to say it is far more becoming to you than it was to Lady Alvira Simpson."

Margaret was both shocked and angered by his impudence. It was bad enough to wear cast-off clothing without having it called to her attention by a stranger, particularly one whom she would have liked to impress.

She drew herself up to her full height, folding her arms in front of her. "In one instance you are correct, sir. It does take a considerable measure of boldness to discuss my attire. In the future I would appreciate it if you confined your remarks to less personal subjects."

She saw the confounded, amused twinkle in his eyes and made a supreme effort to hold her temper as she showed him where the latest literary arrivals were shelved.

Sitting at her desk, Margaret watched him when she was sure his back was turned. He was obviously of the nobility. Had his arrogant manner not vouched for this, the elegant cut of his trousers would. Like all men of fashion, he had discarded the style of breeches for the new, reportedly more comfortably cut, loose trousers. Following the lead of Beau Brummell, this man chose to rely on expensive material and a perfect cut rather than bright colors to attract the eye. His dark blue trousers, matched by a blue waistcoat, were set off by a ruffled high cravat of the snowiest white.

As he reached to a high shelf for a book, she saw that the length of wrist exposed was a deep tan which matched the ruggedly healthy color of his face. It was apparent that he had spent a great deal of time out of doors. Was he one of the rare landowners who actually spent time in the fields instead of parceling his land out for others to work? She discarded the idea. No, his hands were too soft for that. She remembered the feel of them against her face and the thought sent the blood rushing through her veins.

His voice broke into her reverie. "Have you a copy of *The Morning Post* for today?"

She stood up suddenly, nearly spilling a stack of books onto the floor, but he caught them just in time, brushing her hand with his fingers. She pulled back as if burned.

He grinned. "Easy there. It wasn't my intention to unnerve you."

"I am not nervous."

"Oh? I wouldn't have thought you naturally awkward. You strike me as having been well trained in the graceful arts."

She gave him a look and walked quickly over to the table where the newspapers were kept. It was as if she had to think about her every movement lest she engender another comment from him. If only he would pay his money and go! But no. To be truthful about it, she didn't want him to leave. He angered her beyond belief, but he excited her, and it was the first time in her life that she could say that about any man.

He came again later that week, but this time there was an underlying seriousness in his humor, and Margaret found it hard to understand. He kept looking at her as if he wanted to say something, but he never managed to put it into words. While he was perusing the books, she went upstairs to her flat and returned with a kettle of water which had been heating over the coals in the fireplace.

"Would you care to join me at tea? I have just brewed a fresh pot."

"Thank you. I'd like that very much." He moved aside a stack of manuscripts to enable her to place the tray on the table, then held her chair. "I have been looking at your calligraphy. You have an extraordinary talent with the pen and brush. It's an art few people have mastered." He picked up a sheet of parchment and ran his fingers over the fine lettering. "How did you chance to become so proficient?"

Margaret was human enough to respond to his flattery with a faint blush. "Thank you for your kind words," she said. "I once had a tutor who was a frustrated artist. He wanted to become another Gainsborough, but the women he painted looked like caricatures of themselves."

He grinned his appreciation, and Margaret felt a curious delight at having amused him. He leafed through several pages of her work with a reed pen.

"You must have had to learn a great deal about the various types of script. This, for example, is totally different from the others."

"Um, there are many variations of text. Old English text alone is represented by church text, cloister text, black text, german text . . . to name a few. Different styles of pens or brushes aid the calligrapher in creating such lines as the Roman cursive, the minuscule, the uncial, and the half uncial. Most of these letters date back to the early days of the Roman Empire."

Motioning him to sit opposite her, Margaret was acutely aware of the domestic picture they depicted. It was only with the greatest self-discipline that she was able to keep her hand from trembling as she filled his cup with the steaming hot brew.

He accepted it with practiced grace and bent his head to sniff the aroma. "Your skill with the pen is equaled only by your ability as a brewer of tea." He smiled. "Am I wrong or do I detect a modicum of spice?"

"Cinnamon and a hint of extract of orange peel. I fear it is an extravagance on my part, but it is the one luxury I refuse to do without. I hope you like it."

"If I disliked it, my mother would disown me. She, too, is partial to the more exotic teas both for pleasure and their curative powers. She insists there is nothing like lemon and honey in a cup of tea to rid the system of impurities."

"Your father. Is he still alive?" she asked.

"Unfortunately, no. He died some ten years ago.

Forgive my impertinence, but I find myself wondering about your family. It is obvious that you are of the nobility. I would have known even had I not heard someone call you Lady Margaret."

"My father was the earl of Chandleford. He and my mother have been dead now for several years. They were my only relatives. I have been quite alone now for the last four years."

"You should not stay here in this place with no one to look to for companionship."

Margaret viewed him with guarded speculation. "And what do you suggest?"

He laughed. "Nothing that should merit such a wary expression, although if truth be told, such thoughts may have crossed my mind more than once in the past weeks. It merely occurred to me that you could let a room to a woman who would afford you a measure of company."

Margaret wrinkled her nose. "I tried it for a week when I first came here, but the woman was partial to snuff. After that I vowed to make it on my own."

"But you do on occasion rent the downstairs room."

Margaret's look was quizzical until she remembered that he had been in the bookshop the day Mr. Muth had come to pay his rent.

She nodded. "Yes, I have been most fortunate to let the room to a group of intellectuals, a half-dozen or so men who come here to use my reference books in their study of the ancient languages."

"How often are they here?"

"Once a week at the most."

"Indeed. I find it fascinating. Do they allow others to join them?"

"I really don't know, but if you like, I can speak to Mr. Muth tonight and offer your name."

"Yes. That would be kind of you."

She was about to prod him into giving his name when a customer came in to purchase a periodical. Before she could finish, he had gotten up from the table, dabbed his moustache with the napkin, thanked her with a slight bow, and walked out the door.

Margaret's irritation knew no bounds. Whenever she began to like the man, he did something completely outrageous and spoiled the whole thing. She gave the customer his change with a minimum degree of cordiality and stacked the dishes on the tray. One of these days she would even the score with her elusive stranger, providing she ever saw him again.

The thought that she might never see him left an empty feeling in the pit of her stomach that she found difficult to explain. Margaret considered herself a sensible girl. She had done a great deal of growing up in the past four years and she wasn't prone to romantic daydreams. Still . . . this man, with his thatch of sun-bleached chestnut-brown hair, his taunting deep blue eyes, and his rugged good looks, had worked some kind of spell over her and she didn't want to lose him.

Whoever he was, he must be a close friend of Lady Alvira because it was she whom he thought he was kissing that day in the bookshop. Despite herself Margaret felt a twinge of envy. He was too good for Alvira. She cringed at the idea of them together. Admit it, she thought. You can't abide the prospect of him with anyone.

## CHAPTER TWO

As usual on the nights when the group of intellectuals was present in the room belowstairs, Margaret retired to her private quarters so as not to disturb them. On these nights she frequently sat with a book by the window, burning the candle far past her normal bedtime. She enjoyed watching the carriages come and go in the mews behind the bookstore, curious to see if there was anyone she might recognize. There never was. Several of the men walked to the meeting, giving her cause to assume they couldn't afford carriages.

She had just heard the faint chiming of the clock from downstairs when a commotion began with the sound of scuffling interjected with loud voices. A moment later there was a pounding on her door and a voice ordered her to open at once. She was reluctant to do so, but when the voice said he was the constable, Margaret did as she was told.

The heavyset, uniformed man pushed his way into the room, brandishing his club, while a smaller man stood at her side to make sure she didn't attempt to leave.

She was frightened and angry. "What is the meaning of this?" she cried. "Just what is going on?"

The man at her side fixed her with cold eyes. "I thought you'd guess, mum. We're onto yer. We know all about the meetings you've been 'olding downstairs, you and yer mallet-wieldin' Luddite friends."

"There must be some mistake. Those men are students of ancient languages. They come here to study and share information."

"Aye. I'll wager they share information, all right. Like where they'll move next, breakin' up the knitting looms and burnin' the manufactories. We've been watchin' them for quite a spell now and we've got 'em dead to rights."

They refused to listen to her pleas of innocence, and when they finished searching her flat, they escorted her downstairs and into a black, enclosed wagon where the students were waiting under guard.

Not ungently she was handed into the wagon and told to sit on the bench beside the others. Her hands were not bound, as were those of the other prisoners. When her eyes became accustomed to the dim light, she looked beseechingly at them until she found Mr. Muth at the front end of the wagon. His eyes appeared even more haunted than usual.

"I'm terribly sorry about this, Lady Margaret. I'll try to tell them . . ."

" 'Ere now. None o' that. You were told to keep silent. There will be plenty o' time to talk in front o' the magistrate."

Margaret leaned her head back against the side of the wagon and closed her eyes. Dear heaven, what would happen now? Surely they must know that she was innocent of any wrongdoing. And what of the men? She knew a little about the Luddite revolts up in Nottingham where the workers had rebelled against being forced to use wide frames instead of the narrow stocking frames which produced better quality. The workers were forced to hold secret meetings because the Combination Act penalized workmen who united against their employers.

According to the London *Times,* the movement had spread farther north to the textile industries of West Riding and Lancaster, where workers protesting against the use of the new, mechanized power looms had begun to destroy them with huge hammers.

She studied the men on the bench across from her. They didn't appear violent. Rather they wore looks of resignation and defeat. Did they know what was in store for them? Would she, too, be subject to the same punishment? She knotted her fingers together to keep them from shaking.

Margaret had no experience whatsoever with the constabulary. Would they let her speak to her solicitor, or would she be thrown into a cell with the others. She shuddered. Worse yet, would she be kept among strangers? Despite having come from the shelter of a loving home, she had heard horror stories of the inhumanities of life in the prisons. Never had she dreamed it could happen to her.

The next few hours were like a nightmare. She was held under guard in a small room without the slightest clue as to what was taking place. Unable to turn off her active imagination, Margaret pictured the most dreadful things which might happen. Just when she had reached the point where she could no longer bear the waiting, she was summoned before the magistrate.

The questioning took less than an hour but it seemed longer. He apparently knew all the facts surrounding her entrance into the trade class and even professed to have known her father. After having elicited all she knew about the men who rented her room at the bookstore, the magistrate told her that because of those who came forward to vouch for her integrity, she was to be released and was free to go home.

Margaret nearly fainted at the news. It was a miracle that the authorities were willing to take the word of Mr. Muth and his friends concerning her innocence. She would always be grateful. A short time later the magistrate ordered a Bow Street Runner to see her to a carriage and safely home. Just as they were leaving the compound, Margaret looked up and saw the familiar figure of a man leaving the magistrate's office. In the dim glow of the gaslights she could have sworn that it was the stranger who had been calling at the bookstore.

During the ride home she had time to think about it, but she would rather have shut it out of her mind. It had to have been him. Hadn't he been in the bookstore when Mr. Muth came to pay his lease money? Hadn't he questioned her overlong about the meetings in the back room?

The knowledge of his involvement in her arrest seemed to settle like ice around her heart, and it was all she could do to fight back the tears.

Somehow she managed to get through the night. She had no more than opened the shop in the morning when a messenger arrived at her door.

She recognized the footman who attended Mr. Darchester, her solicitor, and invited him in.

"Does the message require an answer?" she asked as he handed her a sealed document.

"Yes, your ladyship. I believe Mr. Darchester is expecting a reply. If you would be so good."

Margaret sat down at her desk and broke the seal on the document. It was a message informing her that he had information of the utmost importance and would see her at her earliest convenience. He urged her to make use of the carriage which he put at her disposal with the hope that she would come to his office at once.

Margaret asked the footman to wait while she went upstairs for her cape and reticule. Her solicitor's strange request, combined with the happenings of the night before, succeeded in shaking Margaret's composure to the foundations. Was she still under suspicion, in spite of her release from custody?

Her nerves had reached such a state by the time she arrived at Mr. Darchester's office that she was hardly coherent. It was apparent from the first that he had heard of her "interrogation," as he called it.

"Please don't refer to it as 'arrest', your ladyship. It is far less of a blemish on one's character to be simply questioned." He stirred his heavy bulk uneasily in the chair and slid his square-rimmed spectacles down his nose as he peered over the top. "That is not to say that you were in no great danger. Had it not been for some timely intervention, plus the fact that the magistrate had been a friend of your father, things would not likely have gone so well with you."

"Then am I still under suspicion?"

"I would like to say emphatically no, but it would be wise for you to avoid any contact whatsoever with the Luddite element. The first thing you must do is close down your bookstore."

Margaret shook her head. "Impossible. I depend entirely on my income from it to survive."

He cleared his throat and the rumble sounded ominous to her ears. "I'm afraid you have no choice, my dear. The moneylenders have called in your markers. They have in turn been paid off by a gentleman who insists that the bookstore be closed at once."

"But they can't do that!" She stood, slamming her reticule onto the top of his desk. "I was just beginning to make it pay. I simply must be allowed to continue on in the business."

He shook his head in sympathy. "I fear that is not possible. His grace was adamant in that respect."

"His grace?"

"Yes. His grace, Peter Featherstone Carrington, the Duke of Waldenspire. He is the man who bought up your loan."

Margaret slumped down in the chair. "But why would he do such an unkind thing? I have never met the man."

"As to that, I couldn't say. But this I do know. He is eager for you to come to work for him."

"Never! I'd rather starve than go begging to him for anything."

"I wouldn't be too hasty, Lady Margaret." He handed her a letter emblazoned with the crest of the House of Waldenspire. "Before you turn him down, I suggest you make note of the figure he has offered to pay."

Margaret scanned the letter, then caught her breath. "But this is more than I make at the bookshop in a year's time. And all I have to do is draw the inscriptions for his collections of antiques?"

The solicitor smiled. "That might not be as simple as it sounds. His grace has a rather extensive collection, so I understand. It will entail working both here in London and at the ducal estate in the country. I trust you won't find it too unpleasant living at the duchy?"

Margaret made a face. "That could depend on the duke. I'm sure I don't have to remind you, Mr. Darchester, that even though I have been forced on my own, I still have a reputation to consider."

"I doubt that you have to worry on that score . . ." He began to bluster when he realized how it sounded. "That's not to say that many men would not find you attractive, but the duke is informally betrothed to a

Swedish noblewoman. Also, the dowager duchess is always in residence at the estate. She should be quite acceptable as an unofficial chaperon." He shifted again in the chair.

"May I inform the duke that you accept his generous offer of employment?"

Margaret bit the inside of her cheek. "It doesn't appear that I have a great deal of choice."

He withdrew a bundle of coins from his drawer. "In that case I am instructed to give you this, which should enable you to pay any recent bills and take care of whatever is necessary toward the immediate closing of the shop. You have no need to account for the money, and it will not be deducted from your salary. As to the books and furnishings, they will be sold and your account credited with the amount which, if any, is over and above the amount of your debt."

He waited for Margaret to signify that she understood, then continued. "The duke will send his carriage for you at ten o'clock in the morning exactly four days from now. Is that satisfactory?"

Margaret was too numb with shock to do anything but nod.

The solicitor's voice was uncommonly gentle. "Do you have any questions, my dear?"

"The duke. What is he like?"

"I confess, I have never met the man but receive my instructions through his solicitors. He is reported to have spent a considerable length of time in the colonies . . . that is to say, America, and I gather that he is a bit of an eccentric, but his moral reputation is no better or worse than the rest of the nobility."

Margaret made a face as she rose to leave. "I suppose his generosity entitles him to a degree of eccentricity."

He rose and bowed. "May I wish you every success in this endeavor, Lady Margaret."

"Thank you for your kindness. One day, when I have again accumulated enough funds to open another bookstore, I may again have to call upon your services."

"That will be my pleasure."

Four days later Margaret stood inside the entrance to the bookstore with her trunk and valise packed and ready to go. She took a look around the shop and felt a sudden pang of regret. This was all that remained out of four years of her life. Soon it would be gone—auctioned off to the highest bidder or sold in bulk for a pittance of its true value.

For the second time in her life she had been forced to undergo a dramatic change in circumstances. But she had survived before; she would do so again. This time, at least, she had a position waiting for her.

The grate of iron-rimmed wheels against the cobblestones shook her from her reverie. The carriage had arrived. While the liveried coachman remained atop his high seat, the boy hopped down from the rear of the carriage to hold the team's heads.

Margaret noted with approval the blue-black enameled coach emblazoned in gold with the stag and the spear crest of the Carrington line. As she watched, two footmen in dark blue and gold velvet livery descended and unfolded the step to enable her to enter the carriage.

They greeted her without the least bit of condescension, in spite of the fact that her baggage was worn and battered, her cape and bonnet a sure indication of genteel poverty. Their master was either well loved or a strict taskmaster. She wasn't eager to know which best described him.

As the carriage pulled away from the bookstore, Margaret turned and looked back. She had been content in her life as the proprietor of the bookstore, even though it had been a constant struggle to keep ahead of her debts. Now she was forced to begin yet another life. The thought suddenly occurred to her that she had not the slightest idea where she was being taken. A few years ago she would have been content to sit back and wait for someone to direct her life. Now, with her newly acquired sense of independence, she felt a need to know what was happening.

Leaning over to the side of the carriage, she pushed open the window and spoke to the footman.

"Exactly where are we going?"

A look of surprise crossed his face. "Why, to the residence of the Duke of Waldenspire. I thought you knew, my lady."

She waved it aside with an impatient gesture. "Yes, of course. But just where is the ducal residence?"

His face brightened. "Just off Hyde Park, your ladyship, on King Street. We'll be there before the clock strikes another hour."

Margaret thanked him while at the same time thinking that she really was in no great hurry to meet her employer. For the past four days she had searched her memories of her debutante days for the slightest recollection of the Duke of Waldenshire. Somewhere in the back of her mind she dimly recalled a man of more than average height, with hair of a sandy-brown color. She shook her head. No, the duke must surely be a younger man if he were, as her solicitor said, betrothed to a Swedish aristocrat. Still one never knew. Marriage between an old man and a young woman was not uncommon.

All she could ask was that he permit her to do her work and collect her salary with a minimum of attention from the duke himself. With a little luck she would receive her instructions from an intermediary such as the comptroller for the estate.

The carriage followed a route up Bond Street to Bruton, where they passed through the corner of Berkeley Square and turned onto Mount Street. To the right was Grosvenor Square, founded years ago by Mary Davies. To the left was St. George's Burying Ground. When the carriage turned to the right on Park Street, Margaret caught a glimpse of the avenue of trees in Hyde Park.

She felt her stomach tense as the carriage drew to a stop at a gate in front of a great, white mansion set back from the street just far enough to afford a wide graveled drive and a narrow, sculptured garden. It was larger than she had expected. The duke was evidently a man of considerable wealth. She breathed a prayer of thanks for her training in social graces at the Mary Catherine Academy for Young Ladies. At least she would know how to conduct herself.

Then it suddenly occurred to Margaret that she was coming here as an employee, not as a guest. That was an entirely new situation. She had never been trained for servitude, but one thing she knew, she shouldn't be arriving at the grand entrance but would be expected to present herself at the servants' door. She tapped on the window.

"I think there is a misunderstanding. The driver should have entered by the servants' gate. I am here as an employee, not a guest."

The footman shook his head. "Her grace was most explicit, your ladyship. She instructed us to deliver you to the grand entrance." He stepped down from his perch, opened the door, and affixed the steps. Then he bowed deeply and offered his hand. "If you please, miss. I'll see that your baggage is taken in at the back."

There were no steps leading to the wide, lacquered doors. The short walk was flanked on each side by huge marble baskets filled to overflowing with riotous blooms of red, pink, and white geraniums. On the handle of each basket was perched a pink marble butterfly. The butterfly was repeated again in the solid bronze door knocker. Margaret lifted it and let it fall as melodious chimes echoed and reechoed as if coming from a cavernous depth.

She had waited less than a minute when the door swung inward and she was greeted by a tall, dignified butler in blue and gold livery. He presented a silver salver on which she placed her calling card.

"Welcome to Walden House, your ladyship. The dowager duchess will receive you in the salon, if you will come this way, please."

She stood for an instant looking around her at the impressive array of sculptures displayed among large tubs of palm trees, some of which were a good twenty feet tall. But her eye was attracted to a tapestry some ten feet wide and a good fifteen feet high. It depicted a forest scene of mythical animals. Once again the butterfly appeared to be the overriding theme. She wanted to see more, but the butler was waiting beside the door to the salon.

"If you will make yourself comfortable, Lady Margaret, I will inform her grace that you have arrived."

Margaret managed a smile. Comfortable, indeed. She felt as if she were again waiting for the verdict in the magistrate's office. Had she another choice, she would leave before the duke or his mother had a chance to interview her.

She sat primly on the edge of the Hanoverian love

seat, folding her gloved hands on her lap. The damask cover was cool against her back. Indeed the entire room, with its soft green and ivory decor, gave one the feeling of being cool and relaxed. While green was not her favorite color, she found the muted tones of the draperies and the Greek key pattern in the rug to be most attractive. A touch of pale gold in the two velvet chairs placed beside the fireplace mellowed and warmed the green.

Margaret smoothed the coil of dark hair beneath her bonnet and settled her skirt to cover her ankles. She was infinitely conscious of the careful mending she had worked on the jacket and wondered if she had chosen wrong in wearing her own costume. The gowns given to her by Lady Alvira were in far better condition, but they did not reflect her personal taste, and today she needed all the confidence she could muster. Anyway, it was too late now. She heard the sound of voices outside, and the door opened.

The woman, tall and regal in appearance, came forward with her hands extended. "My dear Lady Margaret. How delighted I am that you have come to stay with us for a time."

Margaret made her curtsy and managed to say the appropriate things, but her eyes were drawn to the dignified, rather stern-looking man with a crown of white hair. He looked every inch the duke, but somehow he wasn't quite what Margaret had expected. For one thing he was much older than she had pictured. She forced a bright smile as the dowager duchess moved to present her.

The woman reached over and patted Margaret's
hand. "I'm sure my son would wish you to consider
yourself a guest, rather than a servant, Lady Margaret.
He has left instructions that you are to have the free-
dom of the house, and in this I most heartily concur."

Margaret was more than a little surprised by their

## CHAPTER THREE

The dowager duchess clasped her hands together and
smiled. "Lady Margaret Battersby Spence, May I present my dear friend and solicitor, Mr. John Trembe."

Margaret was taken aback. So this man was not the
duke after all. She extended her hand and he bowed
over it with practiced grace.

"I am honored, your ladyship."

Margaret murmured her reply and was immediately
directed to a chair facing the duchess and Mr.
Trembe. The duchess fluttered a porcelain-handled
fan in front of her face.

"His grace has afforded me the pleasure of welcoming you to Walden House, Lady Margaret," she said.
"He regrets that he is detained but will meet you in
the library before dinner. In the meantime I will show
you to your rooms and allow you an opportunity to
rest, if you so desire."

"Thank you. You are most kind. As to resting, I am
quite ready to begin my duties whenever it pleases his
grace."

The woman reached over and patted Margaret's
hand. "I'm sure my son would wish you to consider
yourself a guest, rather than a servant, Lady Margaret.
He has left instructions that you are to have the free-
dom of the house, and in this I most heartily concur."

Margaret was more than a little surprised by their

cordiality, particularly when one considered the fact that for all practical purposes she was here against her will. Had not the duke seen fit to call in her marker, she would still be operating her bookstore. This, however, was not the time to make a scene. The duke held the answers to her questions, not his charming mother.

A half hour later Mr. Trembe took his leave and the dowager duchess escorted Margaret to her suite on the second floor.

"I hope you will find the rooms to your liking. My own suite is directly across the hall. I have assigned Corrine to be your abigail. She is at times impertinent, but the girl has a way with the curling tongs that is hard to equal."

"It is quite unnecessary to provide me with an abigail, your grace. I have learned to care for my own clothing and am quite capable of doing for myself."

"I am simply following my son's instructions. Surely you don't object to being looked after?"

Margaret wanted to reply that she didn't need a keeper, but she vowed to save her remarks for the duke.

The bedchamber and its adjoining rooms were decorated in ivory and pale turquoise. Margaret caught her breath at the perfection of the decor. The sitting room boasted a large oval Oriental rug with a background of ivory. The detailing around the edge was in dark turquoise and in the middle was a stylized flower design intermingled with turquoise and pink butterflies. Two chairs, upholstered in pale turquoise velvet, were placed on either side of the fireplace and on the far wall an ivory lacquered desk held an abundance of writing paraphernalia. Tables and lamps for reading were located strategically around the room.

The bedchamber was a haven of femininity. Yards

and yards of ivory silk were suspended over the walnut poster bed from a coronet held aloft by three silver butterflies. The silk draped down to blend with the silken coverlet which overlaid a skirt of turquoise velvet. In the corner of the room was an elegant-looking chaise lounge which was covered in a similar turquoise velvet. At the foot of the chaise was folded a comforter of pale pink satin.

Most delightful of all was a tiny room set aside for one's personal care. It boasted a basin set in a marble stand which held a water pitcher for one's morning ablutions, a china chamber pot complete with a padded lid silencer, and an enamel hip bath which could be moved to the fireplace on cold days. Margaret had never seen such extravagance, and she found it increasingly difficult to believe that the duke intended for her to be treated with such consideration.

The duchess chuckled softly. "From the expression on your face I perceive that you are not displeased."

"In truth, I have never seen anything quite so lovely. It has been years since I have been so thoroughly pampered."

"Yes, my dear. I've heard of your . . . financial distresses and, at the risk of embarrassing you, I must tell you how deeply I respect your independence and determination. A weaker woman might have turned to a protector in order to survive. I thank a kindly providence that I was not tested as you were."

"Please don't make me out to be a martyr, your grace. Although my first reaction to poverty was one of terror, good sense finally took over, and I confess that I rather enjoyed the challenge . . . that is until most recently." Her voice faltered on the last words, and the duchess made a hasty attempt to change the subject.

"I see that your bags have been brought up. Corrine

will be in shortly to unpack and hang your gowns in the armoire. In the meantime I shall give you some time to yourself to freshen up. When you are ready, you may join me downstairs in the library. I thought you might enjoy a tour of the house and then you may rest before your interview with the duke."

Margaret felt the tension leave her shoulders once she was alone. She moved toward the tall, Empire mirror and surveyed herself from head to foot. Had it not been for the hopelessness of the situation, Margaret would have laughed aloud at the contrast between her shabby clothing and the luxury of her surroundings.

The duchess had said that she was considered a guest in the house. Surely they would not expect her to accompany them while they entertained bona-fide guests. To say the least, she was hardly presentable. She would have to make her feelings clear to the duke.

She took a few minutes to smooth her dark hair into a neat bun at the back of her head. She sighed. At least her figure and skin were good. As to her clothing, who would notice once she began her duties? Doubtless she would be secluded in a corner of some room where no one would even see her. She pinched a bit of color into her cheeks, then went downstairs to meet the duchess.

A footman standing at attention at the foot of the winding staircase escorted Margaret to the library when she inquired where to find it. As they approached the open door, she heard voices and looked up at the footman.

"Is the duchess entertaining? I shouldn't care to disturb her."

"No, my lady. I believe she is expecting you." He motioned her to precede him and stopped just outside the doorway.

"The Lady Margaret Spence," he said with as much

pride as if he were announcing Prince George himself.

The duchess eagerly came forward as Margaret was announced. "Good news, my dear. The duke has come home earlier than expected. Come, you must meet him."

Margaret had seen the tall figure silhouetted against the window as she entered the room. For a moment he had seemed familiar to her, but the lighting was such that she couldn't accurately identify him. As he approached, her eyes widened in disbelief. There, standing before her with a look of amusement stamped on his face, was the stranger from the bookstore.

Only her rigid training saved her. She managed to curtsy properly and to say the right things. He gave no indication that he had ever seen her before, and she was too numb to do anything but follow his lead.

The duchess chattered on so rapidly that she effectively covered any blank spaces in the conversation. After a while she stood and pulled her shawl over her shoulders.

"Peter, my dear, if you and Lady Margaret will excuse me, I shall leave the two of you to discuss your work."

They both rose and acknowledged her curtsy as she left the room, closing the door behind her.

Margaret's shock at seeing him and discovering he was the duke had given way to anger. She confronted him, her hands clenched at her sides, her eyes blazing.

"Of all the unmitigated nerve! I might have known it was you who was responsible for dragging me here."

He grinned. "I trust you have not been unduly mistreated."

"It was a plot from the beginning, wasn't it? You planned the entire episode right from the first day we met."

He stood, his legs spread wide, his arms folded across

his chest as he studied her. "I should be careful of that word 'plot' if I were you. There are those who still suspect you of having been involved with the Luddite mob."

"Am I to assume that you are one of those misguided people?"

"Hardly. If I had the least suspicion that you were involved, you would this minute be resting behind bars at Newgate Prison."

"Do credit me with a modicum of intelligence, your grace. I am well aware of the part you played in the arrest of the students."

He raised an eyebrow. "As to their arrest, I confess to being responsible in that I discovered their meeting place, quite by accident, I might add. I had no idea that you would also be taken for questioning, but I did my best to remedy that."

"What are you saying?"

He shrugged as she fixed him with a questioning stare. She clasped her hands tightly in front of her to keep them from trembling.

"Are you telling me that it was you who came forward in my defense?"

"In all fairness, the Luddite men also vouched for your innocence."

She folded her arms in front of her, then paced across the room and back. "That explains a number of things. I wondered why the magistrate would accept their testimony that I had no part in the conspiracy, if indeed there was one."

He looked at her without comment. She stopped her pacing, and, much subdued, paused in front of him and met his eyes.

"It appears I am in your debt for having been spared a prison sentence."

He smiled. "If that is meant as an apology and a thank you, let's say no more about it."

She started to protest that he still had a number of things to answer for, but he stopped her.

"Unless the day has overtaxed your energies, I would like to discuss the work you have been hired to do."

It had entered Margaret's mind that his intentions may not be strictly honorable. Since the onset of her financial distress a number of men had offered to set her up in a private house, but she would be no man's doxy. She nodded, and there was an edge to her voice when she spoke.

"By all means. I have been waiting four days to hear just what is expected of me in return for your over-generous stipend."

"Did I detect a note of rancor, Lady Margaret? But never mind. Come over to the desk. I should like to show you something."

She tucked her hands into her sleeves and followed him to the massive teakwood desk from which he extracted a large, leather-covered tome.

"Lady Carmina Rosanna de la Cruz, an ancestor of mine from the Mariposa branch of our family, the Castilian side, began a collection of replicas of butterflies many generations ago, and succeeding generations of our family have added to it. The first one was reported to have been a gift from Eleanor of Castile, the wife of Edward the First."

He opened the book, and Margaret moved closer to read the documentation surrounding the acquisition of the gold and emerald butterfly brooch. When she had finished, he leafed through the parchment pages.

"You will find here the records of other gifts and purchases for the collection. If you like, I will later show you the various items, some of which are kept on

display and the others which are stored in the vaults."
He closed the book with proper caution.

"Some of the original owners took care to see that
the purchases were recorded and inscribed in the book,
but as the collection passed from generation to generation, the owners were more concerned with the purchase than with recording the information. What I
would like to do is copy the style of handscripting used
in the book and record the history of each item in the
collection which has not been previously listed. Do you
feel capable of duplicating that type of calligraphy?"

Margaret drew the book toward her and opened it.
She studied it carefully for several moments before responding.

"This appears to me to be a variation of the Carolingian minuscule which is a type of Roman lettering
used by scribes and monks during the time of Charlemagne. I would have to use a reed pen for this particular work, but yes, with a few days practice I think I
can master the style."

"Excellent. I knew from the moment I saw your
work that you were more than capable."

"I shall need a large table, preferably by a window
where the light is good."

"Of course. If you will follow me, I will show you to
my study, where much of the collection is on display."

He bowed for her to precede him down a long corridor to a room at the rear of the house. It was not an
overly large room, but it was built for exactly the purpose for which it was used. One wall was lined with
books, while another was covered with glass compart-
ments in which were displayed models of sailing ships.
A third wall featured a large bay window flanked on
each side by many-drawer chests which proved to con-
tain a large portion of the collection of butterfly replicas.

He pulled out a drawer and selected a gold plate which was encrusted with butterflies composed of various precious jewels. In the center was the Carrington crest and the date 1632.

"This plate was a gift to one of the Waldenspire dukes by Charles the First." He picked up a tiny silver butterfly which was attached to a fine gold wire. "And I am told that this trinket was stolen from the ear of an Egyptian dancing girl by one of my more uninhibited ancestors."

He spent the next hour telling her about the history of some of his treasures. Finally he closed the drawers. "I fear I must have bored you. Few people find the collection as stimulating as I do."

"On the contrary, your grace. I was entranced." She wandered to the far side of the room. "Do you also collect models of ships?"

He laughed. "In a way, yes. My family has been involved in shipbuilding for as long as I can remember. These are but a few vessels which were produced by our line. This one"—he pointed to a large three-master—"is the *Mariposa*, one of our larger butterflies."

She smiled at his jest, remembering that "mariposa" is the Spanish word for butterfly. "Do you often sail on your ships?"

"Not often, but I have just returned from America on this ship. I was on a diplomatic mission for the Regent in the hope that we might forestall war with the Americans."

"Was the mission a success, if I may ask?"

He shrugged. "It is too soon to tell, but I have hopes. If there is anything Britain does not need, it is another war." He appeared to settle within himself for a few moments, then he abruptly pulled himself out of it and smiled. "I thought perhaps we might remove the pedestal and fern from the bay window and place your worktable there, where you would have light from three sides. Do you think that would be satisfactory?"

"Quite satisfactory, I'm sure . . . but the room is your study. Would I not be disturbing you?"

"I think not. I am rarely at home these days."

Margaret had mixed feelings of relief and disappointment. In the brief time she had spent with the duke, she had once again begun to think of him as the charming, if sometimes irritating man whom she had met at the bookshop.

There was no denying his physical attraction. Even now, as they spoke of the work he had planned for her, Margaret was actuely aware of him as a man. It had been a long time since she had thought of anyone in that particular way, and it was disturbing to her in light of the fact that her prospects were so limited. She tried to focus her mind on the subject at hand.

"I should like to begin my work as soon as possible. Could you have the table waiting for me in the morning?"

"Of course. I presume the dowager duchess has informed you that we consider you a guest in this house?"

"Yes. That is most generous of you, but surely you do not expect me to be present when you are entertaining others?"

"Would that be such an ordeal?"

"Hardly. I quite enjoy such socializing, but need I remind you that my wardrobe, handed down as it is for the most part, is not presentable in such surroundings?"

"Don't concern yourself on that score. No doubt the duchess will see that you are provided with a new wardrobe."

Margaret was aghast. "Really! I do beg your pardon, your grace, but I could never permit such a thing."

"Indeed? I thought all young women were more than eager to receive any manner of gift."

"Then perhaps you have been socializing in the wrong circles." She almost bit her lip at her audacity, but she had thrown caution to the wind when she had seen the amused expression on his face.

He strode toward the door and held it open for her. "I fear I have kept you too long. If you will excuse me now, I shall see you in the salon for a glass of sherry before dinner." He bowed.

Margaret made her curtsy and then departed as quickly as possible. She could have sworn she heard him laughing as she scurried down the corridor toward the stairs.

It was a relief to return to the safety of her rooms away from his mocking gaze. She threw herself across the bed and buried her face in her arms. It was all coming back to her, the subtle attraction she had felt for the stranger in the bookshop. But he was a stranger no more. Peter Carrington was not only the duke, but, for the present, he was in control of her future. The thought of being in his power sent a shiver of anticipation down her spine. There were still a number of unanswered questions. For one, why had he gone to the trouble of bringing her here? Not simply to draw the inscriptions for the butterfly collection. There were any number of calligraphers in London, and most of them were more talented than she.

Margaret rolled over on the bed and stared at the three butterflies suspended over her head. It was lovely to be in such splendid surroundings. She must take care not to grow used to them, because the day would soon come when she would have to leave. The thought of it caused a heaviness inside her, and she had to admit that it wouldn't be the house she would hate to leave behind. Irritating as he was, the duke held a fascination for her which she had not known with another man.

She sat up on the edge of the bed and surveyed her face in the mirror. She looked tired and drawn. A touch of rouge would help a little, but what she really needed was a little more weight. She had become very thin during the last few months.

The abigail had seen to it that her gowns were hung in the armoire. One was freshly cleaned and ironed, and Margaret took it as a subtle suggestion that she wear it to dinner that night. She spent the rest of the day resting and tending to her toilette. Corrine knocked on the door an hour before dinner and asked if she might help her dress. Margaret sighed. She would have rather looked after herself, but it was expected that she allow the girl to assist her.

"Thank you for pressing my gown, Corrine. It is so worn that I doubted anything could improve it."

"Aye, miss. A bit o' coffee on the pressin' rag goes a long way toward takin' the shine outa the cloth. Will you be wearin' the jacket wot matches the brown skirt?"

"Yes, and the cream-colored fichu."

"You should be wearin' blue, my lady. The dark colors are not good for you."

"I know, but all my lighter colors have worn beyond repair. I fear I shall have to do something about my clothing before I leave here."

"Don't fret, miss. Your face and figure can carry the day, no matter wot's on your back."

Margaret laughed. "I hope you're right, Corrine, since there is no other way."

\* \* \*

As she went downstairs to the salon, Margaret felt exhilarated and excited in anticipation of seeing the duke. As she approached the door to the small salon, Margaret was greeted by the sound of tinkling, silvery laughter. She had not expected there would be others dining with the duke and his mother. Squaring her shoulders, she entered the room. The duchess came to greet her, and the duke straightened long enough to smile in her direction and make a token bow. She made a curtsy, but her heart wasn't in it. Indeed, the only thing she wanted to do was flee to the sanctuary of her room.

The woman to whom the duke was talking was without a doubt the Swedish noblewoman to whom he was reportedly betrothed. In all her life Margaret had never seen such an exquisitely fragile woman. Her hair, like silken wheat, was caught loosely at the back and formed in a cloud about her head. Her blue eyes smiled up at the duke, and from where Margaret stood, it appeared that he was drowning in them. The thought was almost too painful to bear.

# CHAPTER FOUR

The dowager duchess, perhaps sensing Margaret's discomfort, came toward her and took her by the arm, as if welcoming her into their circle.

"Do come and join us in a bit of sherry, Lady Margaret. You must meet our guest."

The duke detached himself from the blond woman's side and bowed. "Lady Jordice Lucretia Peterson, may I present Lady Margaret Spence."

The woman returned Margaret's curtsy and regarded her with wide blue eyes. When she spoke, her voice was so soft and gentle that Margaret had to concentrate on her every word.

"Ah, then you are the one whose skill with the pen will record the Carrington history. I envy you your talent, Lady Margaret. Ja, I fear I was blessed with nothing, save womanly talents." She smiled impishly. "I shall have to find a brave, strong man to take care of me."

Margaret smiled. "I am told, Lady Jordice, that that in itself is a talent."

The dowager duchesss snorted in a most unladylike way as she moved aside to permit the butler to offer Margaret a glass of sherry. Margaret accepted the wine and touched it to her lips. She wished fervently that she had kept silent. What on earth had possessed her to speak with such an acid tongue? It was not like her

46

to be hateful. She ran her finger around the rim of the glass.

"Is this your first trip to England, Lady Jordice?" she asked.

"Nej. It has been many years, but I came here as a child when my father was an emissary for the king. The country is very beautiful and London is an experience to cherish."

She had resumed her chair and the duke bent over her in a protective way.

"We have hardly begun to show you the city," he said. "Tomorrow we shall visit the Royal Academy of Art. According to Benjamin West, they have agreed to permit John Constable to put his landscapes on display. Later in the week we are invited to a rout at Stafford Hall Pavilion."

Lady Jordice clasped a tiny, jeweled hand to the bodice of her fashionably cut gown. "So many plans. I fear I shan't know what to wear on such a splendid occasion. Perhaps Lady Margaret can advise me on what is the current rage." Her gaze swept over Margaret's brown velvet dress, which had been out of vogue for several years. "In Sweden we are somewhat behind the times where styles are concerned."

Margaret forced a smile. "I doubt that you need concern yourself with being out of style, Lady Jordice. Rather than looking to me for advice, I suggest you consult a recent issue of *Ladies' Quarterly*. Although the latest fashions from France are not readily available because of the war, the *ton* usually manages to duplicate them."

Lady Jordice looked at her with wide, admiring eyes. "You are so clever, Lady Margaret. Ja, I envy one who is able to forgo womanly vanities to pursue a career."

Margaret pursed her lips as she felt the heat bring a flush to her cheeks. Fortunately for her the dowager duchess chose that moment to change the subject. A short time later the butler announced that dinner was served. There was an awkward moment when the duke made an effort to see each one of them to the table, but, once there, the footmen seated Margaret and Lady Jordice while the duke seated his mother.

Apparently the household had spared no expense in entertaining Lady Jordice. The ivory damask cloth which covered the long, narrow table was set with plates and tableware of what appeared to be solid gold. Hothouse flowers—violets, primroses, and lilies—spilled from footed vases and were reflected in crystal goblets by the light of a hundred candles affixed to a great chandelier.

The duchess wore a sedate gown of midnight blue which, while making no statement of its own, set off her cap of white hair to perfection. The duke, like Margaret, was wearing brown, but unlike Margaret, his attire was of exquisite fabric, cut by the finest tailor. His ruffled neckcloth of ivory and rust was hemstitched so expertly that it defied description.

Next to the comparative drabness of their attire, Lady Jordice sat among them like a flower. Her satin and gauze gown of buttercup yellow was a subtle echo of the glory of her hair. Her abigail had created a magnificent coiffure studded with pearls and sapphires which were just a shade darker than the blue of her eyes.

Margaret noted grimly that even the girl's skin was just short of perfection. The thought did little to stimulate her appetite. As course after course of rich food was brought in by the footman, Margaret longed for the simple meals of thin soup and black bread which had often been her fare. At least there had been no emotional conflict other than the need to survive.

She had been aware for some moments that the

duke was watching her, and she made a superhuman effort to sample the elegant-looking dishes. The jellied salmon was light and well seasoned, but, when the roast of beef was brought in along with the inevitable boiled potatoes, her stomach rebelled and she put her fork down. The duke sipped his wine and regarded her over the rim of the goblet.

"Our food does not appeal to you, Lady Margaret?"

"On the contrary. Your food is excellent, as you are surely aware. It is simply that I am unused to such a large repast, and my hunger is easily satisfied."

Lady Jordice helped herself to another portion of butter, which had been pressed into a tiny butterfly mold. "Papa tells me that butter and other rich foods are ruining my skin, but I fear I am too weak to refuse them." She smiled prettily and lowered her eyelashes against her incredibly creamy cheeks as she looked up at the duke.

The effect wasn't lost on him. He shook his head. "Far be it from me to disagree with your father, Lady Jordice, but, to save my soul, I find no fault with your skin."

Idiot! Margaret thought. Why do you think she mentioned it? It was almost more than she could bear, watching the duke so thoroughly taken in by a bit of blond fluff. Fortunately the meal drew to a close before Margaret felt forced to communicate her feelings. Afterward she pleaded fatigue and asked to be excused.

She was washing her face in preparation for retiring when someone tapped on the door. Margaret pulled a dressing gown over her shift and walked into the sitting room.

"Who is it?"

"Eleanor Carrington. May I come in for a moment?" the duchess asked.

"But of course," Margaret said as she opened the door. "Please come in and sit down, if you wish."

"I shan't keep you but a moment. I merely wanted to apologize for our guest's behavior at dinner. She is a lovely child, as a rule, but when she feels threatened . . . Well, then she's a foreigner, too, and one must take that into consideration."

"Threatened? I don't understand, your grace."

"Come now. Don't be so modest. You surely must know what effect you have on men."

Margaret studied the woman's face for a moment, then laughed. "Your grace, if I may say so, I think you delight in saying the most outrageous things."

The wrinkled face dimpled, then broke into a wide, pixie grin. "I fear you've found me out. You are most astute for a woman. Does this come from having to fend for yourself? If so, I recommend it. None of this coy mincing about for me, girl. I like a straightforward, honest exchange. Don't you agree?"

"Most certainly. If one can't be honest, there is little virtue in one's existence."

The duchess clapped her hands and laced her fingers together. "Well put, my girl. With that thought in mind, when are we going to get rid of those ghastly gowns you've been wearing?"

Margaret drew in a sharp breath. "I beg your pardon?"

"Please do not dissemble. A woman of quality such as yourself can hardly be unaware of their unsuitability. I want to have an entire wardrobe made for you, and I want to start tomorrow."

"Thank you, but I can't allow it."

"Don't be muzzy-headed. Of course you can. Nothing would give me more pleasure than to dress you the way you should be dressed. I've always wanted a daughter." She sighed and leaned her head back against the love seat. "If truth be told, I had several girl children, but they died before they drew their first breath. Fifteen children . . . that's how many I carried. And Peter was the only one to survive."

"I'm dreadfully sorry. But at least you have him. In truth, what more could you ask for? He is intelligent, handsome, witty . . ." Her voice trailed off as she saw the expression on the duchess's face. "I . . . that is to say . . . the duke is quite presentable, and his affection for you is most apparent."

"Indeed. Yes, I make it a habit to thank my maker for the blessing of my son. But back to your wardrobe. I shall expect you to accompany me on various excursions while you are living here. Consequently it is imperative that you dress accordingly."

"Very well. If it is that important, I will visit a dressmaker and select some fabrics, but they shall be at my expense."

"Indeed? Well, we shall see. I shall order the carriage for tomorrow after breakfast."

"I'm sorry. I promised the duke I would begin work on the inscriptions in the morning."

"Oh, fiddle." She rose. "We will discuss it over tea and scones in the morning."

Margaret smiled as she closed the door behind her. She liked the peppery duchess. It was nice to be part of a family circle once again, even if she was there as an outsider. Not that the duchess was anything like Margaret's mother. Indeed she was just the opposite. Margaret hardly remembered her mother in any way except as a loving servant. Meek and quiet, her whole concern had been the comfort of her husband and daughter. Margaret missed her dreadfully.

If truth be told, the duchess was more like Margaret's father. He had trained her early on to ask more of herself than she could easily do. He had also placed great value on being honest with oneself.

Margaret removed her fichu and placed it in the clothespress. The suggestion of a new wardrobe was sorely tempting. She loved beautiful things. It crossed her mind that the duke had never seen her in an attractive gown. She gave an impatient shrug. And if he had, what would it matter? One could hardly begin to compete with Lady Jordice.

The thought nagged at her until she finally fell asleep. The next morning she awoke refreshed and with a firm resolve to concentrate on her work and the prospect of once again having sufficient funds to open a bookshop.

Breakfast was laid on the sideboard in the small dining room when she went downstairs. The duke was seated at the table with a copy of the *London Post* propped against a silver candelabrum. He rose as she entered.

"Good morning, Lady Margaret. I didn't expect to see you for yet another two hours."

"Indeed? But it was my understanding that I was to begin my work this morning." She saw an amused twinkle in his eyes as he looked down at her.

"Morning comes earlier for some people than for others. Lady Jordice says that one is hardly human until the clock strikes the noon hour."

Margaret stifled a sharp retort. "As a member of the working class I cannot permit myself the luxury of such a philosophy."

He grinned. "I'll wager you were an early riser even before it became a necessity."

She laughed despite herself and turned toward the sideboard. "I'll give you one for that, your grace. The

dawning has always been my favorite time of day."
She helped herself to a small portion of freshly sliced
peaches from a crystal bowl, then lifted the cover of a
bun warmer and selected a crusty, hot scone. Placing
them on the table, she returned for a cup of steaming
chocolate topped with a dollop of heavy cream. The
duke looked at her in speculation.

"I hope you don't plan to limit yourself to such a
small repast. The fried pilchard is hot and quite
crisp."

"Thank you, but I'm not hungry enough for fish.
This will do nicely. May I refill your cup?"

"Thank you." He smiled as he moved the newspaper and laid it alongside his plate.

She unfolded the napkin and placed it on her lap.
"Please don't let me interrupt your reading."

"I've never liked breakfasting alone. The war with
Napoleon and the problems of Parliament could not
begin to compete with your companionship."

Margaret's face took on a rosy tinge, and he laughed
when he saw it. "I fear I've embarrassed you." He
studied her face for a moment, increasing her discomfort to a marked degree. "You blush very prettily,
Lady Margaret."

"I must admit that I am unused to casual flattery.
In truth, I do not much care for it." She dusted her
lips with her napkin. "Whenever it is convenient for
you to give me my instructions for the work you wish
done, I am most eager to begin."

He raised an eyebrow. "Much as I hate to disap-
point you, I was under the impression that you were to
accompany my mother to the dressmaker this morning."

Margaret gave a tiny sigh of irritation. "Indeed, we
discussed it, but I assumed that my work would come
first."

"Of course, if it distresses you. I shall not order you to accompany her, but·it would give her a great deal of pleasure. To me that is more important than the cataloging of my collection." He leaned an elbow on the table and rested his chin on his hand as he studied her. "Since you were hired as an artist, not a companion, I would not fault you for refusing."

"And since you put it that way, you knew I couldn't possibly refuse." Her smile took most of the bite from her words.

He grinned. "That was my intention. I rather suspect that your abigail has your clothing already laid out for you."

"I wonder, your grace. Do you always manage to get your way?"

"Always."

Their gaze met for a moment, and neither of them chose to break the spell. But in that instant Margaret knew that beyond doubt, the time would come when their wills would cross, and it would take all her courage to stand up to him. It was a small triumph that he was the first to look away.

To Margaret's disappointment Lady Jordice elected to accompany the duchess and Margaret on their visit to the dressmaker. They were escorted to a private sitting room when they arrived at Madame Marie's shop on Bond Street, and, when the two younger women were seated on damask-covered French Provincial chairs, the duchess took Madame Marie aside and engaged in a whispered conversation. A short time later a maid in a pearl-gray uniform with immaculate white collar and cuffs brought in a selection of bolts of fabric.

Margaret felt extremely uncomfortable in a faded gown of striped cambric, but she knew no recourse to the excursion and was determined to see it through with her head held high.

They sorted through a veritable mountain of fabric. Margaret selected two serviceable bolts of cotton with the intention of making them, or if necessary having them made, into gowns, but under pressure from the duchess she agreed to a single bolt of Japanese silk in a heavenly shade of blue. Lady Jordice ran her hand over the material with a gesture of respect.

"Ja, this shade of blue is divine. I think I shall buy enough for a ball gown. It is the same color as my eyes. Do you not agree?"

Margaret thought she saw a rather grim set to the lines around the duchess's mouth, but the woman smiled and patted the girl's arm.

"Perhaps you're right, Lady Jordice. I believe it would be more becoming to you than to Lady Margaret."

Margaret felt something curl up inside of her. She hadn't thought the duchess capable of such treatment, and it hurt more than she cared to admit. She forced a smile and pushed the fabric aside.

"I'm certain you are right. In truth, I would have very little occasion to wear anything so festive."

The duchess made a sound and signaled to Madame Marie, who disappeared into another room. They waited but a few moments, then she returned with the most elegant gown Margaret had ever seen. It was a pale peach brocade with lace inserts, dyed to match, at the sleeves and bodice. Accompanying the gown was a delicate rust-colored silk parasol and matching shawl, gloves, and purse. The duchess motioned Margaret to stand. Margaret began to protest that the gown would cost more than half her salary, but the duchess silenced her with a look. The dressmaker held the gown up to her and nodded her head vigorously.

"Oui. It ees as I thought. The gown ees perfect for her ladyship. Do you not agree?"

The duchess nodded, her enthusiasm shining in her eyes. Lady Jordice fingered the material with something approaching reverence.

"Ja, it is splendid. I should like to try this on."

"The gown is far too long for you, Lady Jordice," the duchess said quickly. "Besides, I can tell from her expression that Lady Margaret has decided to take them."

"Them?" Margaret asked weakly.

"Of course," the duchess beamed. "You would want to buy the others, too. Bring them out, Marie."

There were four gowns in all, each designed to emphasize a woman's femininity to the fullest, yet each cut so subtly that they exuded an aura of innocence. Margaret loved them all and would have been hard put to choose.

She ran her fingers over the mint-green silk. "Perhaps I could afford one of them."

Lady Jordice held the gentian-blue faille, which was hand painted with designs of wild flowers along the hem. "I must have this one and the ivory. They could easily be shortened to fit."

The duchess reached for it and held it below Margaret's chin. "Nonsense. It would ruin the lines. Don't you agree, madame?"

"It would seem a shame, however . . ."

The duchess cut in with an impatient gesture. "You are right. It would be a shame. It would also be unforgivable to buy only one when the four would complement each other so outstandingly."

Margaret swallowed hard and tried to control her voice as she fingered the peach ensemble. "Could you tell me the price, please?" She tried to keep from gasping as the woman mentioned a figure that was quite beyond her reach. She shook her head. "I'm sorry. I simply cannot afford to pay so much for one gown."

The duchess assumed a look of surprise, then turned to the dressmaker. "But of course you meant the price to include the entire wardrobe?"

The dressmaker, who seemed to be receiving silent messages from the duchess, nodded slowly. "Oui. As I told her grace, the gowns were ordered by the Princess Caroline, but she has regretfully changed her mind. Since it is difficult to find one whom they would fit so perfectly, I would be pleased to offer them to you . . . at my cost."

The duchess let out a long sigh and smiled at Margaret. "You see? It is not every day that one is able to dress like a future queen. I simply cannot permit you to say no, Lady Margaret."

Lady Jordice's eyes glittered with greed. "I'm sure you intend to be kind to Lady Margaret, but you must consider that she will have little opportunity to wear the gowns. Indeed, she would look most ridiculous dressed like a princess among her musty books and newspapers. On the other hand I would be glad to double the price for the gowns." She placed an arm across the dressmaker's shoulders and lifted a worn palm in her small hand. "It is inhuman to force a woman to work so hard for such little money. The fabric alone is worth far more than you are asking for the gowns."

The dressmaker pulled away slightly. "I am indeed sorry, mademoiselle. I have given my word and cannot go back on it."

The duchess sighed. "It's settled, then. See to it that the gowns are sent out this afternoon, Marie. I'm weary of shopping and wish to go home, but I shall be in to see you in another month or so and we will see to redoing my entire wardrobe."

The dressmaker's eyes sparkled. "That will be my pleasure, your grace. Thank you for your generosity."

Lady Jordice decided against the blue silk after all, and the trio left the shop a short time later.

The state carriage with the Carrington crest emblazoned on the door seemed to take forever to return to the estate on King Street. As they passed St. George's Burying Ground, the duchess leaned over to Margaret.

"If you really would like to please me tonight, wear the blue faille with the border of wild flowers when you come down to dinner. It should look smashing with your hair and coloring."

Margaret nodded. "If that is what you wish." It occurred to her that the duke was expected to dine at home tonight. Was that why the duchess wanted her to wear the new gown? She rubbed her gloved finger against the palm of her hand. It had been years since she had dressed up to please a man. The thought set her blood to racing.

# CHAPTER FIVE

A cold collation of pheasant in aspic, spiced herring, sliced pork in a delicate sweet sauce, cheeses on a mahogany board with a crystal cover, thin-sliced buttery bread, and an assortment of fresh fruit in a footed compote were waiting for them on the sideboard when they returned home.

A few minutes after the women met in the dining room, they were joined by the duke. He looked at them with an amused tolerance.

"I assume you completely divested Madame Marie's fine shop of all her latest fripperies?"

Lady Jordice shrugged her delicate shoulders. "Lady Margaret managed to find some dresses, but nothing there excited me. Alas, I fear I am far too selective in what I choose to wear. But as Papa says, I have my position to consider." She pirouetted on the ball of her foot. "You will simply have to accept my wardrobe with all its imperfections, Peter, dear."

He ran a finger around the top of his neckcloth. "I have the distinct feeling that whatever imperfections you have experienced, Jordice, you have learned to rise above them."

Margaret was surprised to see that Lady Jordice took his comment as a compliment. She would have wagered a guinea that the duke had not meant it as such. He turned to Margaret.

"If my mother can manage without your company

this afternoon, I would like to show you what needs to be done to begin work on the collection."

Margaret nodded. "By all means. I look forward to getting started on the work."

Lady Jordice laid her hand on the duke's coat sleeve and pouted as she smiled up at him. "You promised to take me riding in Saint James's Park. I hope you have not forgotten, Peter."

"Yes, I remember. Five is the fashionable hour for riding in the park. No doubt you will prefer to take the air when the rest of the nobility will be there to exchange greetings?"

"Ja, that sounds good."

With the rest of the day apparently well organized, they settled down to their repast. Afterward Lady Jordice and the duchess drifted off to their rooms to rest or freshen up, while Margaret followed the duke to the study at the end of the hall.

An oak trestle table inlaid with bone and mother-of-pearl in a marquetry design had been moved into the alcove formed by the bay windows. The duke bowed Margaret to the chair, which was placed in front of it, then seated her with as much formality as if he were seating royalty.

"I think you will find all the supplies you need. If not, kindly ring for the footman and he will fetch them for you. You will find cards with each of the items to be registered. I would like to suggest that you make the inscriptions on parchment sheets. When they are completed, we can cut them to fit the book, then later they will be bound in their proper order. Otherwise you would have to organize them in chronological order before you begin your art work."

She nodded. "An excellent suggestion. Also it is less difficult to work on a flat surface. Before I begin, I would like to go to my room and fetch the guide book

I will use for the Carolingian script." She started to rise, but he put his hand on her shoulder, easing her down.

"The maid will go after it. You must learn to let others do for you."

She looked up at him, acutely aware of the warmth of his hand through the thin fabric of her dress. He was so close that she could see the tangle of hair in his thick eyebrows. For a moment she had an almost irresistible urge to run her fingertips across them to smooth them into place. Instead she traced a quick tongue over her lips and moved slightly so that he was forced to remove his hand. An hour later, after he had gone, she could still feel the pressure of his hand against her shoulder blade.

She saw him twice more during the afternoon. The first time he stayed for nearly an hour, discussing the various pieces of the collection and how they had come into the possession of the Carrington family. He was solicitous of her comfort and the thought that he might be distracting her.

"Does it disturb you to have someone watching over you while you work?"

"Not if you will forgive me for not looking up when we speak to each other. I find your company most pleasant." She turned pink when she realized what she had said and tried to hide her expression in her work, but he appeared not to have noticed.

The second time he came in he was dressed in soft doeskin trousers and a rust-colored velvet jacket. He held his high-crowned beaver hat in his hands, along with his gloves and walking stick.

"I've left orders for Thomas to look in on you from time to time, since I know you are loath to summon a footman. Should you like refreshments or anything else, please don't hesitate to ask."

"Thank you, your grace."

He bowed. "I shall see you at dinner."

She inclined her head and smiled as he left the room. Dinner, indeed. She would wear the blue faille, as the dowager duchess had suggested. For that matter she might even enlist the services of Corrine to concoct a new hairstyle. The thought sent her fingers flying, and she had to force herself to slow down lest she ruin the letters.

Corrine proved to be even better with the curling tongs than the duchess had led Margaret to believe.

"Saints be, your ladyship," she marveled. "Your hair is as fine as the fur on a kitten's belly. It'll be a right good pleasure to work with it." She brushed and combed it until it glistened like a raven's wing. Heating the curling tongs over the globe of a lamp, Corrine proceeded to shape and bend the curls until they satisfied her. After a time she handed a mirror to Margaret and waited for her opinion.

Margaret was amazed at her own reflection. She turned to look at her abigail, surprise lighting her face. "It's lovely, Corrine. I hadn't realized until now what could be done to improve my hair. Thank you so very much."

The girl shrugged. " 'Twas nothing, your ladyship. I simply followed the latest style. You hair is full enough to wear wi' a crown o' curls at the top."

"I like the large curl hanging down at the side. Since I am tall, I need something to minimize my height."

The maid looked quizzical until Margaret explained. "To make me look shorter."

The maid laughed. "Indade, miss. I know a ha' dozen short girls would give a year o' life to be tall as you."

"Which proves we are never satisfied." They both laughed as they walked into the bedroom where Margaret's new dress was laid out on the bed. Corrine stroked the painted border with her hand.

"Aye, it's bonny enough for a queen, wouldn't you say? I can't see the princess turnin' back such a fine gown."

Margaret smiled. No news traveled faster than gossip on the servant grapevine. "I'm grateful that she did, or I never would have been able to purchase them. I was able to buy the four gowns for the price of one." She remembered that the sum was still considerably more than she cared to spend, but it would have been foolishly miserly to forgo the offer when she so desperately needed decent clothing if she continued to socialize with the nobility.

An hour later, when she dressed for dinner, Margaret nearly wept with gratitude when she saw her reflection in the mirror. She had never looked so . . . so beautiful in her life. She thought it particularly strange because she had never considered herself pretty. Whether it was the dress or her new coiffure or a combination of both, something had given her a special glow, and she was astounded by her own appearance.

To her surprise the dowager duchess seemed not in the least amazed by the transformation. When Margaret went downstairs to the small salon, the duchess turned and clasped her hands together in a gesture of triumph.

"Now then, don't you consider that a bit of improvement?" she asked.

Margaret laughed as they both appreciated the understatement. "I confess, I didn't think it was possible." She shook her head when the duchess offered her a glass of sherry. "I shan't need anything to bolster my spirits tonight, your grace. I fear I am already walking on the clouds."

"And well you might, my dear. The Prince Regent himself would be hard put to find a more fetching companion. What a shame that we shall have to dine alone tonight."

"Alone? But I thought that the duke . . . he said that he would join us for dinner." She tried without success to keep the disappointment from her voice.

"I know, Lady Margaret. But the coachman delivered the message that Lady Jordice asked to visit friends of hers in Bedford Square, and she and the duke had been invited to stay to dinner." She laid her hand on Margaret's arm. "I had hoped, my dear—well, never mind. We shall make up for it tomorrow night. Peter and Lady Jordice will be attending an assembly at Stafford Hall Pavilion, and we have been invited to accompany them."

"Must I go? Really, I feel very much out of place, under the circumstances."

"It would please me if you were to join us."

Margaret forced a smile. "Then of course I shall accept."

After that the duchess instructed the butler to serve their dinner in her sitting room. The two women spent an intimate evening talking of their past experiences. It seemed that the duchess could never hear enough about Margaret's venture into the world on her own. It occurred to Margaret that perhaps the duchess was seeking the courage to break out of her own mold, but the idea was ridiculous. What could the woman want beyond what she already had?

Margaret found it impossible to sleep after she left the duchess. She lay wide awake on the feather bed long after Corrine had completed her duties and retired. It had been hours since Margaret had heard the duke's carriage enter the gate, but still sleep eluded her. She felt confined, unable to breathe, and she longed to spend the night cleaning or scrubbing floors, as she had on countless nights at the bookstore when her active mind had been unable to yield to her weary body.

Throwing the coverlet aside, she reached for her dressing gown and pulled it over her nightdress. The room lay in half-light as the first glow of dawn filtered through the windows and, as she started downstairs, she rejected the idea of lighting a candle. She walked cautiously, clearly defining the edge of each stair with the toe of her slipper before she stepped down.

Reaching the end of the stairway, she turned down the hallway leading to the French doors which opened to the garden. It was darker here, with no illumination save at the end of the corridor, and she had failed to remember the urn and pedestal which stood near the wall. Fortunately she had been walking slowly or she would have knocked them over when she bumped into them. As it was, the only damage was to her foot. She let out a gasp of pain, but her cry turned to one of alarm when she was grabbed from behind by someone apparently hidden in a doorway.

Margaret would have fought if she could have gotten her arms free, but she was held by an immovable force. She stopped struggling the moment she heard his voice.

"What the devil is going on here? You know that all servants are required to quit this wing after midnight. Quietly now, who are you and what is your position here?"

He slowly took his hand away from her mouth so that she could reply.

"I'm sorry, your grace. I only meant to get a breath of fresh air."

He turned her around in his arms to face him. "Lady Margaret? Is that you?" His voice held a strange quality of wonder, and she had to struggle to still the beating of her heart.

"Yes . . . I . . . I'm sorry for having disturbed you. I . . . I couldn't sleep."

"You sound breathless. Are you all right?"

Despite her efforts, she couldn't control her voice. He was holding her so close, almost in an embrace. And heaven help her, she wished it were so. She began to tremble, and for an instant she wondered if she might faint.

"I said, are you all right, Lady Margaret?"

"It's my foot," she lied. "I bumped it on the pedestal."

"So that was the noise I heard. Come, let's have a look at it."

"No, please. It's nothing at all."

"Don't be silly. You could have broken a toe." With that he picked her up and carried her to the study, as if she weighed nothing at all.

Only one candle was burning in the room, and he placed her on his desk next to it. Then he knelt down and removed her slipper. Dressed as she was for bed, Margaret wore no stockings and the touch of his warm hand against her bare foot sent tremors of fire along her spine. He was jacketless. His shirt, open nearly to the waist, revealed a dense thatch of dark hair which curled upward toward the depression at the base of his throat. She swallowed, forcing herself to look away. He stroked her foot, seeking out each joint, each bone, to test for tenderness.

"Tell me where it hurts," he ordered.

"I . . . please. It's nothing. It was the surprise more

than anything which caused me to cry out. I didn't mean to disturb anyone."

"I don't think you've broken anything. Do you think you can walk?" he asked as he eased her foot into the slipper.

"Certainly. Truly, I am not injured. I should return to my room."

He circled her waist with his hands and lifted her down. "And miss the sunrise? I thought you said you wanted some fresh air. Join me in the garden. There is a place by the wall where one can see the sunrise over the trees." He took her hand and held it firmly, lacing his fingers with hers. Margaret knew she should have demurred, but at the moment she wanted nothing more than to see the sun come up over the garden wall.

She felt the need to make casual conversation to quiet her racing pulse. "Do you often rise early to greet the dawn?"

"Only when I have trouble sleeping. It seems we both danced with the devil last night, Margaret."

He laughed in response to what he apparently thought was her unasked question. "Danced with the devil. Haven't you heard the expression? It's when one has too many things on one's mind to permit sleep. I suppose it was meant to imply a guilty conscience."

"No. I didn't mean . . ." She thought she had stopped in time, but he was alert.

He threw his head back and laughed. "Aha. So that's it. You are disturbed because I used your given name without your title. Forgive me, Margaret. I've wanted to call you that since I first met you. I am not, as you will see, overly fond of pomp and circumstance. Besides, having held your naked foot in my hand should entitle me to certain privileges." Even in the dim light she could see the mischief in his eyes.

"I beg of you, your grace. Please do not speak of it again. You would cause me nothing but embarrassment. Indeed, if anyone saw me here dressed as I am, I should be unable to look at them again without feeling shame."

He pressed her hand between his wide palms. "Then it shall be our secret. I vow I would never seek to bring shame on such a lovely head." He pulled her close, as if trying to see her face, and for an instant Margaret was sure he meant to kiss her. She could feel his strength and the heat of his body, and for one giddy moment she felt an overwhelming desire to surrender to her need for him.

They both pulled back at the same instant. Margaret hugged her dressing gown closer about her. "Forgive me," she said. "I think it best if I return to my bedchamber." He started to say something, but she shook her head. "Good night, your grace."

"Good night, Margaret. Sleep well. We'll share the sunrise another time."

Somehow, even before her head touched the pillow, she knew she would sleep very well indeed.

When Corrine drew back the draperies a few hours later, Margaret could have sworn only minutes had passed. But with her usual ability to rebound, she was up, washed, dressed, and finishing her breakfast by the time the duchess arrived on the scene. Moments later the duke came into the dining room, causing the duchess to look up in surprise.

"Peter! Don't tell me that you have just come downstairs."

"And pray tell, why not?"

"You never sleep late except when you are ill. You aren't taken with a fever, are you?"

His tone was dry. "Hardly. My only complaint is that I'm famished." He nodded toward Margaret, and she returned his unspoken greeting with a shy smile.

The duchess filled a plate and seated herself at the table. "You might like to know, Peter, that I have decided to accompany you and Lady Jordice to the party at Stafford Hall Pavilion tonight. Lady Margaret will also be joining us."

Margaret thought she detected an overlong pause before the duke answered.

"Indeed? That should make for an interesting evening."

"I perceived it so. You don't imagine that Lady Jordice will object, do you?"

"Certainly not. I'm sure she will be delighted with the company. She has often told me how entertaining her visit has become since Marg . . . Lady Margaret took up residence in the house."

"Indeed?" The duchess's voice mirrored her astonishment. "I had not thought her to be so generous with her compliments."

"You must realize, Mother, that she is a foreigner and therefore must be forgiven her outspokenness."

Apparently the duchess had been unaware of his slip. Margaret held her breath as their conversation continued. Surely he would not go so far as to use her given name in front of others. She shot him a warning look, and he had the grace to turn pink. No, it was not his plan to be so bold. She sighed and leaned back to sip her chocolate.

The rest of the day passed without incident. As soon as breakfast was dispensed with, Margaret secluded herself in the study with the Carrington collection. The duke stopped in twice to inquire as to her progress. One of those times Lady Jordice was with him.

She had a propensity to handle things, and Margaret breathed a sigh of relief when the precious porcelain butterflies were safely put away.

They talked about the assembly for that evening and, true to the duke's estimate of her character, Lady Jordice seemed to be pleased that Margaret would be joining them.

"Which gown will you wear tonight, Lady Margaret?" she asked.

"I hadn't thought about it. I think perhaps the peach with the rust cape."

"Ja, it is an elegant dress. It should make quite an impression." She waved her fan. "I must go now. Peter has promised to take me for a drive. We shall see one another tonight. Ja?"

Margaret nodded. "Yes, tonight."

Corinne had just finished Margaret's hair and was ready to assist her into her dress when the dowager duchess rapped on the door and came in without waiting for an invitation.

"Good. I see you have not dressed. Which gown will you wear?"

Margaret motioned to the bed. "The peach one."

The duchess puckered her mouth. "Would you mind wearing the ivory brocade?"

"Is this one not suitable? I . . . I thought . . ."

"It's not that. I'm sure you have excellent judgment in such things. Please grant me this one request."

"But of course. Each dress is lovely in its own way. I shall be happy to wear whichever you choose."

Margaret learned the reason an hour later. As she came out of her suite and stood at the top of the stairway, she caught a glimpse of Lady Jordice wearing a vibrant shade of red in a most fetching gown. Next to her Margaret, in a pale peach gown, would have faded into insignificance. As her hand grasped the stair rail, she breathed a grateful thanks to the duchess, who had saved the evening.

Margaret had just begun her descent when the duke strode though the grand foyer and happened to glance upward. He stopped short, then stood very, very straight as Margaret continued to walk down the stairs toward him. As her foot reached the landing, he bowed deeply and offered his arm.

"Margaret, you look lovely. I had no idea until now how beautiful you really are."

# CHAPTER SIX

As Margaret placed her gloved hand on his arm, she noted with an unconscionable sense of pride that the duke looked unusually handsome in his dark blue coat and well-cut trousers. His cravat was a creamy, ivory white, fastened in place at the ruffles by a diamond and ruby stickpin. His voice was husky as he spoke.

"I fear I shall have to watch you closely tonight, Margaret, or someone will steal you away."

They turned the corner of the hallway and saw Lady Jordice through the open door of the salon. Despite herself, Margaret could not keep the edge from her voice.

"I doubt you will have the time or the inclination to supervise my movements, your grace."

Before he could venture a reply, Lady Jordice saw them and turned to greet them. As she looked at Margaret, her eyes narrowed into thin blue lines.

"Ja, Lady Margaret. So you are finally ready. Did you not tell me you had planned to wear the peach-colored gown?"

Margaret nodded. "Yes, I did, but a last minute whim persuaded me to change my mind. I trust that it does not distress you?"

"Ja, and why should I care which gown you select? It seems to me that you would have wanted to wear something that gave a little color to your face, but then I forget that you are not overly concerned with your appearance." She placed her hand on Margaret's arm. "Peter and I are so pleased that you could join us tonight. I hope the party will not wear you down. You do look tired, doesn't she, Peter?"

He quickly looked at Margaret's face. "Tired? I wouldn't have thought so. Lady Margaret, have we been too demanding of your time?"

"Not at all, your grace. I have never felt more energetic. If indeed I look tired, then I must attribute it to a normal flaw in my appearance."

He handed her a glass of sherry, then looked down into her eyes. "I've heard it said that he who speaks of the pearl as being flawed is surely a blind man."

Margaret felt the color rise to her face. She was saved from having to respond when the duchess joined their group. She took one look at Margaret in her ivory gown, then looked at Lady Jordice in her flaming red satin. When she looked back at Margaret, her face was expressionless, but she managed a sly wink when she was sure no one else was looking.

Once the duchess joined them, they departed immediately for the Stafford Pavilion which was only a few minutes away by carriage. A huge crowd of guests had already arrived and, when Margaret heard the music from the ballroom, she felt as if she were once again the young debutante who had danced until her feet were numb. There were many familiar faces, for the most part people whom she hadn't seen since her financial setback.

The house was more splendid than she could have envisioned. Grecian in design, its rooms were interspersed with tall pillars and statues of nude centurions and dancing ladies. Margaret particularly liked the atrium, where a reflecting pool set in the center of the room mirrored the skylight above, which sparkled with stars amidst the darkness of night. Marble benches had been placed at random among potted palm trees and tubs of flowering shrubs, and white lilies grew in profusion in the shallow water.

It was obvious from the start that Lady Jordice had no wish to share the duke's attention with Margaret. She soon managed to separate herself and the duke from the rest of his party. But Margaret was far from being alone with the duchess. They had no more than arrived when she was approached by Sir Wendell Gifford, whom she had seen frequently during her coming out. He was wide-eyed with admiration.

"I say, Lady Margaret. You've been away far too long. It's not at all the thing to deprive the *beau monde* of your delightful company."

Margaret was tempted to tell him that it was not she who stopped attending parties; it was the *beau monde* who stopped inviting her once she became poor. Instead she smiled prettily and fluttered her fan.

"Indeed, sir. That is most kind. Having been missed makes the return all the more sweet."

He took her hand in his and looked into her eyes. "This time we shall not let you run away. Have I your permission to call?"

Margaret was suddenly caught without an answer. Since she had reached her majority, she didn't need permission, yet she was a guest, or, in truth, an employee of the Carringtons, and she felt disinclined to take advantage. She looked at the duchess, who nodded and spoke.

"I'm sure her ladyship would be happy to receive callers on Thursdays," she said. "She is for the present living at Walden House on King Street."

He bowed. "I am quite familiar with the estate, your grace. It will be my pleasure to leave my card."

After that it seemed as if Margaret was constantly

surrounded by men. The dowager duchess tactfully drifted to one side, on the pretext of inspecting some valuable porcelain, while Margaret proceeded to hold court. It occurred to her that she had never been quite so popular, even when she had made her curtsy to the queen. The fact puzzled her.

Dark-haired, olive-skinned Count Dantoni stood out among all her admirers. In his quiet, Continental way he made the young officers and noblemen seem like so many schoolboys. He touched his lips to her hand with barely discernible pressure, but to Margaret it set an alarm bell ringing in her head. He was not a man to be trifled with. While the bucks and fops of the *ton* might be content with the chase, this man was out for the prize, and the devil take the consequences.

Had she been younger, she might have swooned at a single glance from Count Adolfo Dantoni, but her womanly instincts had matured enough to allow a degree of insight into the ways of certain kinds of men.

She dropped a curtsy as she acknowledged their introduction. "In answer to your question, Count Dantoni, we haven't met before because I have been hard at work running my bookshop."

He raised an eyebrow. "How enchanting. But did I misunderstand? I thought you were introduced as Lady Margaret. How can it be that a noblewoman is involved with trade?"

She laughed. "It is a simple matter of keeping bread on the table, Count Dantoni. Either one works when one is poor, or one does not eat. I do enjoy food, so you see . . . ?" She spread her hands in a helpless gesture.

"Madre mia. How is it that these Englishmen have not come to your aid? Had I known, I would have thrown my fortune at your feet."

She smiled. "I doubt, sir, that I could have returned your generosity."

He studied her from the tip of her head to the toe of her slipper, then threw his head back and laughed. "That, your ladyship, would have been my least concern. But since food is so important to you, might I beg to escort you to the table so that we may fill your plate?"

Margaret looked around and saw no sign of the duke or Lady Jordice. Seeing the duchess approach, she smiled at the count. "I presume that your invitation also includes her grace, the duchess?"

"Only if it must."

"Then I shall be pleased to accept for the two of us."

The focal point of the entire assembly appeared to be the dining room. While it was usually the custom for a gentleman to fill a lady's plate, here at the pavilion the desire to view Chef Armand's latest creation was so intense that the ladies elected to choose their own food.

The duchess grasped Margaret's arm. "I wouldn't have believed it, my dear, but the chef has outdone himself again. Have you ever seen such table decorations in your life?"

Margaret could safely say she had not. The ivory damask-covered table stretched for thirty feet across the center of the great dining room. Massive candelabra hung from vaulted ceilings, which had been painstakingly illustrated with frescoes of Grecian gods at play in their own Valhalla. Directly below the nave of the dome, a birdcage constructed of living flowers rose almost fifteen feet above the table. One could see perhaps ten varieties of colorful and exotic live birds flying from perch to perch within their floral prison.

The count leaned toward the ladies and placed his

hand next to his mouth as he whispered, "With this great crush of humanity, we should be grateful for the heady scent of the roses. Now that you have seen the table, may I be allowed to fill your plates?"

The duchess folded her fan and let it fall to her wrist. "No indeed. I've been told there is everything from glacéed pineapple to hart's tongue and plover's eggs. I want to decide for myself what is palatable. And you, Lady Margaret?"

She hastily agreed. Hungry as she was, she had no desire for such exotic food, but the fresh fruits and thinly sliced cheeses looked delectable.

They had filled their plates and found a comfortable table when the duke approached. His face was tight with anger as he faced his mother.

"Your grace, I must say that I was appalled to see you standing in line at the serving table like some shopkeeper. Were you so famished that you could not wait for me to serve you?"

The duchess looked from her son to Lady Jordice, who clung to his arm like a fragile red flower.

"I perceive that you are a bit miffed, Peter. Have you not heard that given the proper surroundings, it is quite correct for a woman to serve herself, so long as she is escorted by a man?" The duchess's voice sounded faintly amused.

His face turned a dull red. "I've heard it is true in some circles, but I would not have thought that you, of all people, would risk being called common."

Lady Jordice leaned her head against his arm and batted her lashes at him. "Peter, dear, we must consider your mother's position. No one would have the temerity to call her common. Why don't you summon the footman for some wine to go with the dinner?"

He ran his finger around his neckcloth and bowed. "If you will excuse me."

Once the duke and Lady Jordice rejoined them at table, the rest of the dinner became considerably more restrained. Even an outsider would have realized from the start that there was no love lost between the duke and Count Dantoni. Aside from the fact that the count was an obvious womanizer, Margaret found his company quite entertaining, as did the duchess. Only Lady Jordice held herself aloof from the conversation, and that was perhaps due to the count's having failed to compliment her appearance. She was not used to being ignored.

They all breathed a sigh of relief when the music began in the adjoining ballroom, and they had an excuse to separate. After the duke and Lady Jordice excused themselves, the count turned to the duchess.

"Your grace." He bowed low and kissed her hand. "May I request the pleasure of the next waltz?"

She shook her head. "Thank you, Count Dantoni, but I would not presume upon your generosity. I'm sure that what you really want is a turn on the floor with Lady Margaret." She was speaking to the count, but Margaret was certain the duchess was looking across the room at another man. Margaret had no time to single him out, because the count had taken her hand and was leading her to the dance floor.

He was an accomplished dancer, so much so that he literally took Margaret's breath away. They circled and whirled until she felt as if her feet barely touched the floor. At the same time she was aware that he held her considerably closer than was considered good form. She felt compelled to protest, but he only laughed.

"My dear Lady Margaret. How can one such as you, who has flouted Polite Society by going into the trades, be perturbed by a simple waltz? Is it not a tribute to the music that we danced as one? Holding you at arm's length would have been a desecration."

Before she could respond to his argument, they were dancing again, and she felt young and giddy as she gave herself over to the spell of the music. A few dandies attempted to spirit her away, but the count managed to keep her in his arms. Margaret looked across the room at one point and was surprised and delighted to see the duchess dancing with her solicitor, Mr. Trembe. Even from that distance Margaret was aware of their feelings for each other. She was glad for them, but wondered how pleased the duke would be if he happened to see them together.

Thinking about him seemed to summon him up, because when the dance ended, the duke was at her side.

His voice was intense, and there was no refusing him as he spoke to the count. "If you will excuse us, Dantoni, the next dance is mine."

To the count's credit, he stood his ground. "If that is the lady's wish."

Margaret barely had a chance to stammer before she was whirled onto the floor. The duke held her stiffly and at arm's length, a fact which added nothing to the grace of the dance. Twice they bumped toes, and it occurred to Margaret that it was like dancing with an angry bear. Once they were on the other side of the room, the duke pulled her off the floor.

"What do you think you're accomplishing by making such a fool of yourself?" he demanded angrily. "I trust you are unaware of Dantoni's reputation and that is understandable, considering your absence from society, but even you, Lady Margaret, must be aware that he was holding you scandalously close."

"I saw no harm," she replied with some asperity. "Other couples were dancing in much the same manner. In truth, he is a fine dancer and I rather enjoyed it."

He swore softly. "Perhaps this party was a poor choice for your reentry into society. Come." He danced her onto the floor, as if he were afraid to touch her, and came to a halt where Lady Jordice, the duchess, and Count Dantoni waited in silence.

The duke released her and made a perfunctory bow. "If you are ready to depart, Mother, I believe we shall make our excuses."

The duchess looked up in surprise. "But it is early."

Lady Jordice clasped her hand to her forehead. "If you will forgive me, your grace, I fear I have a dreadful headache."

The duke shot her a look of gratitude. "I'll see that the carriage is brought around," he said.

While he was gone, Count Dantoni managed to get Margaret aside. "Now that we have found each other, my lovely one, we must see each other again soon. Perhaps tomorrow . . . a ride in Hyde Park? I have a lovely new Park Phaeton with a team of four matched bays."

Margaret was ready to refuse but, remembering the look of anger on the duke's face, she smiled sweetly and fluttered her fan. "Tomorrow I will be indisposed, Count Dantoni, but if you will extend the invitation to the following day, I shall be pleased to accept your kind offer."

He bowed. "Your wish is mine to obey. I will call for you at five."

He stayed only until the duke returned and then took his departure. Lady Jordice stared at his back, at the duke, and then at Margaret.

"I really can't see what you find attractive about the man, Lady Margaret. He seems rather . . . a womanizer."

The duchess snapped her fan and slipped it into her reticule. "And what man isn't, given the chance?" she replied testily. "Count Dantoni happens to be one of the richest men in the country. In addition to his huge estate here, he has a castle and three villas in Spain."

Lady Jordice looked properly impressed. "Ja . . . I had no idea. Since he did not seek to dance with the higher nobility, I assumed that he was . . . as you might say . . . down at the heels, in spite of his elegant dress." It was plain from the tone of her voice that she was disappointed not to have been told earlier that he was a man of considerable substance.

The ride home was accomplished in comparative silence. For some reason even Lady Jordice and the duke seemed to be at odds with each other. She sat like a statue on her side of the carriage, while he sulked on the far side. Instinctively the other women remained silent as well. Just before the carriage turned into the drive, Lady Jordice thanked the duchess for her hospitality and announced her plans to leave in the morning to spend a few days at the Emery estate. The duchess was obviously taken by surprise but chose not to question the abrupt decision. For her own part Margaret settled back in her seat with a sigh of contentment.

Late the next day Margaret was alone in the study. She had just begun work on a delicate porcelain butterfly vase made by the Dresden artisans of Germany. The piece, dating back to 1733, had been a gift of Augustus the Third. Just as she began the flower wreath which encircled the letter D, the duke walked in and came to stand behind her.

Margaret found it most disconcerting to have the duke bending over her as she worked. He was so close that his breath, like a caress, disturbed the hair at the base of her neck. Finally he moved away and paced the room with nervous, purposeful strides. It was plain to see that something bedeviled him. Was he already missing the lovely Jordice?

Margaret turned to look at him. "Will Lady Jordice return here before she journeys back to her home in Sweden?" she asked.

He stopped pacing. At least she had caught his attention. He came over and sat down on the edge of the table. "You aren't overly fond of Lady Jordice, are you, Margaret?"

So now she was Margaret again. He had gone to great lengths to use her title in front of the duchess and Lady Jordice.

"Well?" He seemed to insist on an answer.

"I can't see that my feelings are of any consequence. She is one of the most beautiful women I have seen."

"When you come to know her better, you will realize that she is also a fine woman. Her moral character is without a blemish."

Margaret could sense that he wanted her approval, and she felt a brief moment of compassion. "I am sure, your grace, that she has many fine qualities. The Swedish are noted for their gentleness of nature. No doubt, she finds it difficult to adjust to our way of life."

"She seemed to have adjusted quite well at the pavilion assembly." He spoke as if he were thinking aloud.

"It was a splendid party. I haven't enjoyed myself so much in years."

His voice hardened. "That was evident from your behavior. You were as giddy as a schoolgirl with her first beau."

Margaret was taken aback. "Indeed? And how would you know? You were hardly in evidence most of the evening."

He chose to ignore her jab. "One in your particular

position should be especially aware of how quickly gossip spreads through a crowd. I would have thought you would be careful not to encourage idle talk."

Margaret's voice was tight with controlled anger. "One in my 'particular position' learns early on that people will find something to gossip about whether or not anything exists. As long as I live up to my own standards, my conscience is clear."

The duke's mouth was set in a thin line below his moustache. "And will those standards allow you to make a fool of yourself on the dance floor? You came dangerously close to having two successive dances with the count, which as you know, is the limit society has set. If I had not stopped you from dancing again, the *ton* would have demanded your immediate betrothal. To make matters worse, you did not dance with anyone else."

Margaret raised an eyebrow. "How quickly you forget. Unfortunately my sore toes have a vivid memory of our having danced together. In point of fact, the two of us made more of a spectacle than Count Dantoni and I."

Getting up quickly, he strode across the room and back, at the same time swearing at the perversity of all women. "You know very well that I wasn't including myself. I could hardly forget our disastrous attempt on the dance floor. It's Dantoni I object to. He has a way of dancing that makes it appear as if he and his partner are participating in . . . in . . ."

Margaret was appalled. "Really! I object most strongly to your criticism. The duchess made no such comment. Count Dantoni and I danced very well together." She scrutinized his face. "I find myself wondering if perhaps the evil is only in your mind."

His face was dark with anger. "It was not only my

mind, Lady Margaret. Jordice was aware of it too, as I'm sure were many other guests."

Margaret decided it was time to put an end to the unpleasant discussion. She tried to calm her voice as she pulled the inkpot toward her and started to dip the pen.

"I regret that you feel this way, your grace, but my private life is my own. I do not choose to disgrace your family and, truthfully, I cannot believe that I have done so."

He turned away. "Be that as it may, it's over and done with. As long as you have nothing more to do with Dantoni, we shall say no more about it."

Margaret took a deep breath. "That may not be quite as simple as it sounds. I have an arrangement to go riding with him in the park tomorrow."

"Then you will have to extend your regrets."

"No, your grace, I cannot do that."

He whirled around and came toward her. "You would deliberately defy me?"

"If I must."

He made a sudden move as if to strike her, and she ducked. His hand bumped the inkpot, sending a spray of black ink over the top of her gown at the shoulder.

Margaret gasped and jumped up. "Dear heaven! Look what you've done! My shawl and dress are ruined."

He grabbed a clean cloth and began rubbing at the ugly dark stain. "Perhaps if we work fast we can remove it before it has set." He rubbed harder and succeeded in removing a large amount of the stain from the dark blue gingham, but, as he worked intently, he slipped his hand inside the neckline of her gown, and his knuckles grazed the softness of her bare shoulder.

Margaret felt a tremor of fire begin at her neck and travel the length of her spine.

## CHAPTER SEVEN

Margaret caught her breath and put her hand up to stop him. Their gazes met, and for a time all motion was suspended as they stared into each other's eyes. Margaret was the first to turn away.

"Please. Don't be concerned. The gown will be all right."

He picked up the shawl and pleated it between his fingers, as if desperately in need of something to do with his hands.

"I'm afraid the shawl is ruined beyond repair. Forgive me, Margaret. I didn't mean to . . ."

She laid her hand on his arm. "Don't say anything else, your grace. We've already said too much today. I'd very much like to get back to my work."

He knotted the shawl in his hands and squeezed it into a ball. His face was closed, and there was a whiteness around his mouth which contrasted strangely with the darkness of his moustache.

"Is it a compulsion that drives you to work, or is it merely a means of escaping from an unpleasant situation?"

Margaret backed away from him, fighting for composure as she smoothed her dress into place. "I would not like to think of it in either context, your grace. Although it is true that I am forced to work in order to survive, I enjoy what I do and take pride in the fact

85

that I need look to no one for help." She turned away from him and arranged the parchment in front of her.

"And have you no wish to marry and have children?"

Margaret sighed and turned toward him once again. "There was a time when I would have married because it was expected of me. However, circumstances have changed. Since then I have come to realize the importance of finding the right man to father my children. I no longer feel compelled to marry for the sake of security. If this makes me seem less feminine, as Lady Jordice has indicated, then so be it."

His gaze was focused on the basket of anemones. "You're different from other women, there's no doubt about that. As to your being unfeminine, the attention you received last night at the pavilion should have silenced any questions on that score."

"I urge you not to make too much of it. Some of the men who spoke to me were old friends whom I hadn't seen since I left my former home. It was not as if they were courting me."

"Is that also true of Count Dantoni?"

She paused, searching for the proper words to avoid another scene. "I can't in good conscience say that the count is an old friend. Last night he was most considerate of my comfort, and I confess to enjoying my conversations with him. He is an accomplished dancer, another fact which added to my enjoyment of the evening."

"And you insist on seeing him again?"

"I have given my word that I would."

"Even against my orders?"

She gazed at him without blinking. "I don't think you will order me not to see him, your grace."

"And if I did?"

She saw perspiration begin to bead on his forehead. "I would consider your advice, then make my own decision."

"Damn your independence, Margaret. Damn it to hell." Still clutching the shawl, his hands were knotted into fists as he strode from the room.

It was several minutes before her legs stopped their trembling. She pressed her hands together to steady them before attempting to take up the reed pen and begin work.

The rest of the day passed without incident. The duke had disappeared, and she didn't see him for two days.

Margaret chose the peach dress to wear when Count Adolfo Dantoni called to take her for a drive in the park. Corrine had shaped her hair into a fashionable twist with the curls combed to one side of her bonnet which was tilted at a saucy angle toward her right eye.

The duchess nodded her approval. "Fetching, my dear, most fetching," she said. "Are you absolutely certain you wish me to accompany you? I'm sure I don't have to remind you that etiquette does not require you to be chaperoned."

Margaret's laugh was dry. "One of the few benefits of growing older, I suppose. In truth, I look forward to having you along. I don't look upon you as a chaperon, your grace, but as a friend." Margaret saw that her remark had pleased the duchess, who fluffed her hair and settled her own bonnet into place.

"I thank you for that, Margaret, if I may be so bold as to address you by your Christian name."

"I would be honored, your grace."

The woman smiled wickedly. "Apparently my son has also chosen to overstep the bounds of formality."

She waved her gloved hand as Margaret started to protest. "It was not intended as a criticism, my dear, only as a comment."

Margaret was saved from responding when the maid announced that Count Dantoni was waiting with the carriage.

He was wearing a pearl-gray jacket with black piping at the collar and cuffs. His loose trousers were of a matching material, cut with an eye to compliment his narrow waist and slender hips. Margaret was fascinated by a great ruby ring which he wore on his index finger, but the duchess was impressed by his open phaeton carriage lacquered a vivid Chinese red. The cushions, which faced each other, were upholstered in expensive black velvet.

The duchess nodded as he assisted her onto the seat opposite Margaret and him, which permitted her to face forward. "A most unusual carriage, Count Dantoni," she commented. "I doubt that I have seen one quite like it."

"Do you disapprove, your grace?"

"Not at all. Red is the color of happiness."

He smiled. "It pleases me to hear you say so. Beau Brummell has led me to believe that the color red is so ostentatious that its use should be limited to the demi-rep."

She laughed. "I can hardly fault his taste in wearing apparel, but one's carriage is another story. I wouldn't, however, recommend this carriage for a secret rendezvous. It is bound to become the center of attraction wherever you go."

"I beg to disagree, your grace. In the presence of you and Lady Margaret, the carriage will go completely unnoticed."

It soon became clear that they would not be allowed to proceed uninterrupted. At the fashionable hour of five the park was crowded with strollers, horsemen, and carriages of all make and manner. If the count were out of favor with the duke, he certainly made up for it by his popularity among the older women of the *haut ton*. His Continental way with the ladies won over not only the dowagers with daughters of marriageable age, but widows with an eye out for an eligible bachelor. Those who had formerly cut Margaret dead after her slip into poverty now went out of their way to speak to her. Her sense of humor saw the ridiculous side, and she was amused, rather than angered.

Their excursion to the park was the first of several forays into society during the next four days. Margaret made it a point to include the duchess wherever they went, not so much to protect her reputation but because the duchess enjoyed herself so thoroughly.

The duke was not impressed with the new trio, nor did his temper improve when Margaret began to share her time with other men of the *beau monde*. He confronted her late one night after her return from a concert at Vauxhall Gardens.

Looking at the clock on the mantelpiece in the small salon, he shook his head. "I wonder at your energy, Lady Margaret. You seem bent on driving my mother to an early grave."

Margaret was horrified. "Surely you don't mean that? I know we have been extraordinarily busy, but it was at her choice. In no way have I encouraged her social activity."

"Would she have said 'no' if you had?"

"I . . ." Margaret shook her head. "In truth, I know she would not. I'm sorry, your grace. I shall try to be more considerate of her age."

"Of whose age?" the duchess demanded as she came into the room. "Did I hear rightly, Peter? Were you suggesting that I am too old for routs and parties?"

He mumbled something inaudible and turned away in embarrassment as the duchess, hands on hips, confronted him.

"In the future, please address your criticism directly to me." She turned away, smoothing her fichu against her small chest. "It occurs to me that you have been in a dreadful state these past few days. Is it because Lady Jordice has failed to return on schedule?"

He gave her a grim look. "That has nothing to do with it. If indeed I seem to be in a temper, Lady Jordice is not involved in the slightest degree."

"No? I would have thought your intentions were rather serious in that vein."

Margaret felt her senses quicken at the sudden turn of conversation. She stole a sideways look at the duke, who seemed to be having trouble with the fit of his cravat. He ran his finger around the top edge.

"My intentions, whatever they are, are between Lady Jordice and myself. My frustrations lie in quite another direction. Suffice it to say that I regret having spoken of your activities. My only concern was for your well-being."

"Indeed?" She spoke as if she doubted his word and he shot her a look. She continued unscathed.

"In that case, my dear," she said, "suppose we plan an evening at home tomorrow night, just the three of us? Something festive like a cozy dinner by the fire."

He smiled indulgently. "I thought you might have suggested a grand evening at a masque ball or a visit to Brighton to attend the theater. It takes surprisingly little to satisfy you, Mother."

She shot him a triumphant look. "Those outings were next on my list. We shall take them in order."

Margaret was relieved that the discussion of her newly acquired popularity was laid to rest. She found it hard to reconcile the duke's position as an employer with his obvious attempt to act as a guardian. With the duchess on her side, she need not be concerned, but his attitude was nevertheless profoundly irritating. She was too fatigued to fence with him tonight, and when the opportunity arose, she said good night.

The next afternoon a messenger arrived with the news that Lord Perceval had been assassinated in the House of Commons. The duke, who had been reading at his desk in the study while Margaret worked at her calligraphy, left immediately for a consultation with Lord Liverpool and several other members of Parliament.

The duchess was distraught when she heard the news. "Such a tragedy. Of all times for this to happen. The empire is still in a state of upheaval since the Marquess Wellesly resigned as foreign secretary."

"But surely Castlereagh can manage the job?" Margaret inquired.

"Indeed. But at this time we need things on an even keel. With the American embargo on shipping which was enacted in April, it can only be a question of time before we're at war with them."

"It is hard to perceive that they would declare war on us."

"Peter thinks they well might. But come, enough of this. I have no idea what time he will arrive home tonight. Are you up to waiting for him, or would you prefer to dine as usual?"

"I'm quite willing to wait. Whatever pleases you is fine with me."

"Good. Then we shall wait. I rather suspect he will be tired and ill-tempered after a few hours spent trying to put things into some kind of order. Why don't you put on a pretty gown after you finish your work for the day and join me in the library?"

Margaret continued to draw letters until the light

had completely faded. It was tedious, exacting work, but the pleasure it gave her to see the beautiful, hand-drawn inscriptions was well worth her painstaking care. She had added many pages to the collection of manuscripts which would later be incorporated into the leather-bound volume.

Most fascinating of all was the collection of butter-fly replicas. Even those of comparatively little value Margaret handled with as much care as if they were equal to the diamond, ruby, and sapphire coronet which would be worn by the future duchess of Wal-denspire. It was one of the items which were kept in the vault in the little room adjoining the study where she worked.

Margaret had given in to her female curiosity one day while she was alone and placed the coronet on her head—but only for an instant. As she stared wide-eyed at her reflection in the study window, she had the strangest urge to cry. Hurriedly she took it off and slipped it back into its velvet box, then replaced it in the small vault where the valuable items of the collec-tion were temporarily stored. She often thought about the exquisite work of art, with its countless diamonds and the three butterflies set with rubies and sapphires. Admittedly it wasn't the jewels which appealed to her; it was their significance. One day the coronet would probably belong to Lady Jordice. The thought was not one on which she cared to linger.

Before dressing for dinner, Margaret allowed herself the pleasure of a long, relaxing bath in the hip tub. Corrine had added oils and a scent to the water, an almost forgotten luxury where Margaret was con-cerned. While she closed her eyes and let the water soothe her, Corrine went to the armoire.

"Would you be wantin' the blue dress tonight, miss?" she asked.

"No, the family is dining alone." She chewed her lower lip. "Wait, Corrine. Do let's choose the blue gown with the wild-flower border. Her grace particularly wanted this to be a pleasant evening."

"Aye. 'Tis a sad day for the Commonwealth when a nob gets struck down in the light o' day." She slanted a look at Margaret. "If this don't serve to cheer 'is grace, nothin' would, short of a miracle."

Corrine disappeared while Margaret toweled herself dry. When the abigail returned, she carried a spray of fragrant honeysuckle. A short time later she had brushed Margaret's hair away from her face and fastened it at the back of her head with a circlet of flowers. With the tip of her comb she freed a few strands of hair above each ear and twisted them into ringlets. Margaret surveyed the results in the mirror.

"What a delightful idea, Corrine. Such a change from the fancy curls and fripperies women wear to parties. I couldn't be more pleased."

Corrine nodded, hands on hips. "Aye, it's right becoming to you. It gives you the little-miss-innocent look that sets the men to pantin'."

Margaret laughed. "I assume you speak from experience?"

Corrine giggled. "In me own way, I could say so. Only wi' me it's plaits not flowers. When I ties me 'air in braids, Jessup Grover, the fine-lookin' new stablemaster, gets to breathin' like he's about to expire."

"Are you fond of him?"

"Mebbe so, then again mebbe not. I'm in no 'urry to set me heart on one man. Like you, the name 'old maid' holds no fear for me."

When she realized what she had said, her hand flew to her mouth. "Beggin' your pardon, miss. I didn't mean to call you an old maid."

Margaret smiled. The term had never bothered her

before, but suddenly it hurt more than she dared show. "Don't apologize, Corrine. I'm well aware that my single state has placed me in the spinster role. No doubt I've been called worse names."

She was glad when her abigail had finished and left her to go downstairs alone. She was just at the top of the stairway when the dowager duchess came out of her rooms.

She looked up in pleased surprise. "My dear Margaret, how lovely you look. Didn't I tell you that Corrine has a true talent with the curling tongs? I'm so pleased that you dressed for dinner. The duke has arrived and will meet us in the library."

Her voice took on a casual tone. "Mr. Trembe has consented to join us tonight. I hope you will be pleased."

Margaret studied the woman's face. "Pleased? Beyond a doubt, but not as pleased as you, I daresay."

"Whatever do you mean, child?"

"Only that you seem to have gone to a great deal of trouble to dress for a quiet dinner at home."

The duchess smoothed the skirt of her heliotrope lace over a white gauze dress. "Simply an attempt to brighten a gloomy day, Margaret. You needn't make something out of nothing."

Margaret smiled. "Yes, your grace. If you say so." She saw the duchess quickly hide her smile behind the ivory inlaid fan which was held to her wrist by a thin gold chain.

The duke and John Trembe arose as they entered and exchanged greetings with the women. It occurred to Margaret that the duke lacked much of his usual energy and sparkle, and her heart went out to him. The duchess searched his face.

"What is the news from Parliament?"

The duke drew a deep breath and flattened his

palms on the marble surface of a refectory table. "Liverpool is being asked to form a new administration."

She frowned. "Will it have a chance, do you think?"

He shrugged. "Not with the support he has now. He needs time to unite the Tory party." He straightened and, for the first time, really looked at Margaret.

"My compliments, Lady Margaret. You look even more lovely than usual."

Mr. Trembe lifted his glass. "A toast to both lovely ladies. I daresay, Peter, the two of us are truly honored by their presence."

Because of the lateness of the hour, they wasted little time over sherry before ordering dinner served at a table set before the fireplace. It was a simple meal of crusty venison pie, fresh vegetables drenched in butter, and the inevitable potato. Sweet apricot tarts topped with thick Devonshire cream completed the meal as they sipped strong tea mellowed with a dollop of milk.

The duke stretched his long legs in front of him after the table was cleared away. "This was a pleasant evening, Mother. It reminds me of when I was a boy and you used to play for us on the pianoforte."

Mr. Trembe took her hand in his. "Eleanor, my dear. I didn't know that you were a musician. Play something for us, won't you?"

She blushed until her face matched the pink of her shawl. "I couldn't. It has been years . . ."

They insisted and she finally agreed. At first the stiffness of age was apparent, but, as her fingers flew over the keys, her confidence grew. Suddenly Mr. Trembe rose and bowed to Margaret.

"May I have the pleasure of a dance, your ladyship?"

Margaret rose instantly and dropped a curtsy. "The pleasure is mine, Mr. Trembe."

They circled the floor several times until the music

ended; then he bowed over her hand and saw her to the chair. "Thank you, my dear. You dance far too well to waste your talent on an old man. Out of fairness to you and to my aging heart, I will turn you over to the mercies of a younger man."

The duke looked uncomfortable. "I fear you have made a poor choice, Mr. Trembe. Lady Margaret has already been laid cripple by my attempts on the dance floor."

"Nonsense, Peter," his mother scolded. "You dance as well as most men. Don't pretend to be humble."

He rose stiffly, walked over to Margaret's chair, and bowed. There was a grim set to his lips as he offered his arm. When the music started, Mr. Trembe joined the duchess at the pianoforte and assisted with the pages of music. Margaret put her hand in the duke's lifted palm and walked into the circle of his arm.

The music began in a slow waltz tempo. Holding her at a distance, the duke was able to look down into her eyes.

"I regret that my skill cannot begin to compare with that of Count Dantoni."

Her tone was dry. "One can't have everything."

He stumbled, and his face turned scarlet as he breathed an oath. She fought to keep from smiling.

"Would you like to sit down, your grace?"

"We'll finish this dance if it kills us."

"As it well might."

"Dantoni's not that good. I know it and you know it. I've never been awkward before."

"Indeed?"

"You're baiting me, Margaret."

"Why would I do that?"

"Why indeed? Truthfully, is Dantoni as good as they say?"

"As a dancer?"

His face turned a dark red. "I'm warning you."

She cleared her throat and forced a straight face. "He dances . . . differently. Closer."

"Yes, I remember that," he said grimly. "Is this what you want?" He pulled her close until she all but gasped for breath, but she refused to protest.

As the music dipped and soared, he gradually loosened his hold until their bodies touched like a caress instead of an abrasion. Margaret felt herself respond to his commands as if she were an extension of his body. She gave herself over completely to the dance, turning and whirling like a leaf caught in the wind.

They danced as one being, attuned to the music and to the alchemy which had been generated between them. Margaret closed her eyes as she felt his lips graze the top of her forehead. She wanted the night to go on forever.

# CHAPTER EIGHT

The duchess ended one song and began another as Margaret and the duke drifted across the room. They moved with one body, so much in rhythm with each other's movements as to require no conscious effort.

Margaret's head rested against his cheek. She could feel his breath in her hair and the sensation stirred something deep inside her. It was a new feeling, a yearning so deep that it touched her very soul. At the same time she experienced a sense of contentment, a completeness she had never known before.

Inevitably the music came to an end, and the couple reluctantly drew apart. Mr. Trembe, who had taken a seat on the bench next to the duchess at the pianoforte, rose and said that that he had to be leaving. The duchess also rose and offered to see him to the door.

Once they were alone, there was a moment of awkwardness between Margaret and the duke. When he looked down at her, his eyes were lighted by a fire she had not before seen in them. He rubbed his palms against each other, then laced his fingers together, making a steeple against his chin. Margaret was at a loss to know what he was thinking. She turned to walk toward the window, where the draperies were open to reveal the blackness of the hedge against the thinner darkness of the lawn. Pressing her forehead against the window, she let the coolness of the glass chill her heated skin.

He came to stand behind her. She sensed rather than saw him. They stood there for a time until he spoke, his voice tight and barely controlled.

"Was that the way it was with him?"

Margaret turned to face him. "I . . . I don't know what you mean."

"The devil you don't! I'm talking about Dantoni."

Margaret shook her head. It was all she could do to keep her voice from breaking. "Please. Don't do this."

"I've got to know. When you danced with Dantoni, did you feel as though . . . ?"

She shook her head. "No. With him it was only a dance."

He put his hands on her shoulders. "Do you swear it?"

Margaret searched his eyes. "Why should you doubt me?" She had a feeling that he was going to kiss her, and she lifted her face.

He swore softly and, dropping his hands, turned away. "Because I want so much to believe you."

Margaret felt cheated. She had wanted to be kissed even more than she dared admit to herself, and the knowledge stung her. She folded her arms across her chest.

"Was that the way it was when you danced with Lady Jordice?" she asked.

He whirled around. "What has she to do with this?"

Margaret felt tears begin to burn at the back of her eyelids. She shook her head. If she didn't stop now, she was going to make a complete fool of herself.

"I . . . I'm sorry. If you will excuse me, I'm rather tired and would like to go upstairs."

He bowed in response to her curtsy, then she turned

and walked toward the door. As her hands reached for the twin knobs which opened the double doors, his voice, low and husky, stopped her.

"No, Margaret. With her it was just a dance."

She stood for an instant, then opened the doors and fled down the corridor and up the stairs to the safety of her room.

Corrine, who was laying out Margaret's nightdress and robe, looked up in surprise as she came into the bedchamber. "I say, miss. You're in a bit of a hurry now, aren't you? Look at you wi' your face all red and flushed. Did you have a drop o' wine too much?"

Margaret's expression must have reflected something of her feelings. Corrine looked at her in surprise.

"You don't look at all well, your ladyship. Was it something you ate?"

Margaret forced a smile. "That might have been it. Please don't think about it. I'll be fine after a good night's sleep." She managed to dismiss her abigail after a minimum of attention, then leaned her head back on the pillow and closed her eyes.

She desperately needed this time alone. Things were happening between her and the duke, and she was powerless to stop them. If truth be served, she had no desire to stop them, and the knowledge frightened her.

Margaret had no illusions about her marriage prospects. Few men would be willing to offer for her when she stood to receive nothing by way of an inheritance. True, there were quantities of suitors among the laboring class who would consider themselves lucky to have landed a noblewoman, but she was caught between two worlds. She was too well-bred for the working class and too poor to live among the nobility.

Until now it hadn't really mattered. She had been so involved with trying to make ends meet that she hadn't missed the challenge of the social world. But it hadn't taken long for her to fall back into the ways and the expectations so easily taken for granted by the nobility. If she were to consider things in a realistic way, her present situation was far worse than it had been while she lived at the bookstore. This position was at best temporary. When she finished with the inscriptions, she would be without employment and without a place to call home, unless she could save enough to manage another loan.

The gowns she had bought had taken a great deal away from the amount she intended to save. Still, Margaret could not bring herself to regret having bought them. She would simply have to rely on a kindly providence to see her through. If she were wise, she would begin now to make plans. Instinct told her that to remain in this house with the duke would be to court disaster. Remembering the way she had felt when his arms were around her, Margaret moaned softly. There was a magic in his touch which she had never felt before. Was it perhaps already too late for her to leave? She rolled over on her side. Tomorrow was bound to look brighter.

Half an hour before high tea the next day Lady Jordice arrived, bag and baggage. If Margaret had forgotten how beautiful the woman was, it came back to her with a vengeance. She was wearing a pale pink velvet jacket with a matching narrow skirt in the latest style. White lace decorated the round collar and cuffs, while the white was repeated in her gloves, soft kidskin slippers, and lace sunshade.

As if by prearrangement the duke, who had absented himself from the house since last night, arrived precisely at the same time. There was a feverish look to his face, as if he seemed intent on assuring the Swedish noblewoman of her welcome. Margaret felt sick inside but fought desperately to hide it as she greeted her.

"I hope you had a pleasant stay, Lady Jordice."

"Ja, it was nice enough. A number of my countrymen were also guests of the house, and it was as if one rout followed the other." She dimpled her cheeks. "My chaperon complained that she had no time at all to sleep."

The duke took her arm in a proprietary fashion and escorted her to the foot of the stairs. "I wondered why you chose to extend the length of your stay."

Lady Jordice patted his cheek. "Forgive me, dearest. I should have returned sooner, but I am happy to see that you missed me. I thought perhaps with Lady Margaret here you would soon forget that I existed."

Dead silence fell and suddenly Margaret could bear it no longer. Her voice was cool and dry when she spoke. "Strange that you should be concerned on that score, your ladyship. As you are aware, I am in the duke's employ, nothing more."

Lady Jordice laughed like a tinkle of silver bells. "Ja, that is so." Standing on the second stair, she bent to kiss the duke on the forehead.

Margaret left the room as quickly as she dared.

Somehow they all managed to get through tea and maintain a congenial atmosphere. Lady Jordice monopolized the conversation with her surprisingly vivid description of the mansion and the people who attended the house party. Margaret found that she enjoyed the account, despite the fact that she had hoped to be bored.

With tea over she returned to the study and her drawings for the collection. She had been working less than an hour when the duke came in and stood looking over her shoulder.

"Your work is lovely, Margaret. I particularly like the two-color effect on the capitals."

"Thank you, your grace."

He cleared his throat. "Regarding last night."

She looked up questioningly.

He turned and strode to the window. "I . . . I feel I owe you an apology. I shouldn't have . . . That is to say, I was unusually tired and upset with the assassination and all. For that reason, perhaps, I was less under control than I should have been. For that, I beg your forgiveness."

Margaret laid down her pen. "I see no need for an apology, your grace. We danced together in the presence of the duchess and her solicitor. I assumed you intended nothing sinister, and no offense was taken."

He bowed. "You are most kind. If you will excuse me then, I have an appointment."

She nodded.

When he reached the doorway, he returned and fished something from his pocket. "I'm in a rush. Would you be so kind as to place this ring in the safe? I wouldn't want to lose it, since it is quite valuable." As he placed it in the palm of her hand, the brief contact sent a shower of signals speeding across her skin.

She rose. "Of course. I'll take care of it at once." There was no doubt of its value. Margaret guessed that it was worth a small fortune with its large, flawless emerald faceted to show it to perfection. Surrounding it were five perfect diamonds, each small but of exquisite cut and quality. As she turned it in her fingers, she noticed a tiny inscription: "To J. Love Eternal." Had she not been holding it so carefully, Margaret would have dropped it. Hurriedly she placed it in the velvet tray and closed the safe door, locking it securely.

There was no question now where the duke's sentiments lay. She had almost allowed herself to believe that there was a chance for them. It had all been a dream, a foolish, immature daydream, the result of permitting her heart to rule instead of her head. It wouldn't happen again; she would see to that. From now on she would avoid the duke as much as possible. A dozen men had been pleading to court her. Well, why not? Her work occupied her daytime hours but not the nights. This might be her last chance to go places and see things before her return to the world of poverty. She might as well make the most of it.

Having made the decision, Margaret felt her problems should have been lightened, but they only weighed more heavily as evening darkened into night. She pleaded a headache and begged to be excused from dinner. Corrine brought a cold collation up to her sitting room a few hours later, but she barely tasted anything.

The next day dragged on interminably. Margaret was grateful for her work. It kept her body occupied, if not her mind. Lady Jordice, apparently suffering from boredom, came in several times to chat, and Margaret learned a great deal about the girl's life at home in Sweden, where she was supposedly under the control of an overly strict father. Away from those she thought she had to impress, Lady Jordice was pleasant, entertaining, and, although Margaret hated to admit it, rather nice. She had wanted to dislike her, but found herself drawn to her.

Late in the afternoon Lady Jordice persuaded the duchess to take her to some of the shops on Bond Street. Margaret was invited to accompany them but declined. It was pleasant having the time to work alone without constant interruptions. She worked diligently for an hour and was so engrossed that she didn't realize the duke had come home and was standing behind her. He murmured an apology for having surprised her.

"You've been working too hard. I've brought you a cup of tea and a sweet."

Margaret arched her back. "How very thoughtful." As she rose, she saw the extra cup on the tray. "Will you join me?"

He smiled boyishly. "That was my intention. I would have thought you would have elected to visit the shops with my mother and Lady Jordice."

She seated herself in a straight-backed chair and poured the tea into fragile, hand-painted porcelain cups. "They were kind enough to invite me but, if truth be told, it was no punishment to remain at home."

He nodded, and she wondered at his smile until she realized she had used the word "home." Her face turned a deep red.

"I . . . I meant remain here."

"Don't apologize, Margaret. I consider it a compliment."

She carried her cup over to the wall where the ships were displayed. He followed and came to stand behind her.

"They hold a peculiar fascination for you, don't they?" he commented. "Have you ever sailed?"

"No. My father hated the sea. We rarely traveled, except by coach. He said it was much safer. As it turned out, it was a coaching accident that killed him and my mother."

He put down his cup and lifted up the model of the schooner, the *Mariposa*. "You would love sailing. Taking a voyage on this ship is like drifting on a cloud, save for the flap of the sails and the creak of the masts. It's clean out there on the sea. None of the overpowering odor of fish or the stench of the open sewers

105

that permeates everything on a hot day in London. Even sailing a small boat is a thrill to reckon with." He put the model on the top of a glass case. "I'd like to take you one day. Would you be willing?"

"I . . . I don't know."

"Why not? I tell you, it's an experience."

Seeing the eagerness in his eyes, she smiled. "Then of course I would like to go." There was a moment of awkward silence which left her discomfited. "Is this an exact replica of the *Mariposa*?" she asked, more to fill space than for the information.

"Almost, but it lacks the lettering on the bow." He looked at her. "Could you letter the name onto the model?"

She shrugged. "I would think so. It would have to be very small, of course. The main problem would be to hold the ship on its side so that it would be steady enough to paint. I'm not sure how we could manage that without causing damage to the model."

"I see no problem there. I can hold it while you do the lettering."

"Um, I suppose, although it would take considerable time."

"Would you be willing to try it right now?"

"If that is what you wish."

"It's a perfect time for me, now while the house is quiet. Later I am committed to taking Jordice for a ride in the park, but we have a goodly amount of time until then." He showed her an example of the lettering he wished to copy and where on the model he wished the name to appear.

Margaret assembled her tools, while he arranged two chairs facing each other next to the desk. As she looked at the arrangement, she began to have second thoughts. It was tedious work at best. She had grown used to working with him in the room, but trying to work with him practically in her lap was another thing. She moistened her lips.

"I really think there ought to be a better way. Surely you have enough to do that you should not waste your time on such trivial matters."

"Nonsense. It's time I gave my mind a rest. After spending the morning with the aides to the Regent, I feel I deserve to enjoy myself."

"The new administration . . . is it working as well as you'd hoped?"

He shook his head. "Unfortunately, no. If it were put to vote now, Liverpool would surely be set down by lack of confidence. I think it's just a question of time until they vote him out." He shrugged as if to dismiss the subject and motioned to the chair. "Sit by the desk where you can rest your arm. I'll take the chair opposite you and hold the model on its side."

Margaret did as she was told. There was a scraping of chairs as she adjusted her distance from the desk and he, avoiding her knees, seated himself opposite her. It was plain from the beginning that his chair was too far away.

Margaret laughed to cover her nervousness. It sounded tinny and unnatural. She reached for her stylus, only to find that he was holding the model too far away.

"I . . . I'm afraid you'll have to bring it closer. I need the stability of the desk to support my arm."

"Right. Just a moment and I'll move closer." He grabbed the seat of his chair, lifting and moving toward her knees while balancing the model in his other hand.

"Do be careful," Margaret warned. "It looks terribly fragile."

Margaret felt her face turn red as their knees touched, but he was apparently unaware it had happened. He sat down again, only to find that they were still too far apart. Margaret was ready to call a halt, but he seemed determined.

"Now then, move your chair a tad and that should do it."

She lifted slightly and eased her chair forward, bringing herself into a perfect position to work on the model. At the same time he was able to steady his wrists on the desk. The only trouble was that her knees were between his knees. As he leaned forward, they touched. Even through the fabric of her dress and petticoats, Margaret felt the pressure of his leg against hers. She tried to force it from her mind, but it was a far greater intimacy than she was prepared to handle.

She swallowed quickly, concentrating on the work at hand. "You want the name to start about here?"

"Perfect. Can you manage?"

"I don't know." Her hand began to shake. "I really don't think this is going to work," she said, fighting back tears of panic.

He moved slightly and the pressure of his leg against hers sent fingers of fire down her side. Later she wondered if she had gasped. Whatever the reason, he looked up suddenly and saw the expression on her face. Then, slowly, as if moving through a dream, he laid the model on the desk and reached for her hands.

Their gaze held as he took the stylus from her fingers and placed it beside the model. Pressing her hands between his two palms, he lifted them to his lips.

"Margaret, Margaret," he whispered. "What are you doing to me?"

Speechless, she shook her head.

He rose and, taking her elbows in his hands, pulled her to a standing position against him. Then his arms were around her, and his mouth found hers with a hunger too great to be denied.

At first Margaret refused to yield to him. She held herself rigid, though the strength of his hands as they roamed her body commanded her to surrender. He moved closer, gathering her into the circle of his desire. He groaned, sliding his hand down the length of her back. Loosening her hair with his other hand, the duke pressed his mouth against hers until all sense of time and place melted away. She was in his arms, she loved him, and nothing, *nothing* else mattered.

Faintly she heard him speak her name. She refused to open her eyes lest reality become a dream. Placing her hands on either side of his face, she pulled his mouth against hers again, sensing for the first time the rasp of his moustache and then the softness inside. His head moved from side to side, exploring, seeking, demanding. No longer playing the timid game, Margaret gave him measure for measure, sometimes leading, sometimes following until her senses reeled.

He was lifting her. She felt her feet leave the floor and, as he leaned backward, he rested her whole weight against the length of his body. It was as if they had merged into one being, one soul, and Margaret knew that she belonged to him as surely as if he had taken her to bed. Indeed, if he had suggested such a move, she would have been his willing slave.

But he drew back. His face was haggard with unfulfilled need as he settled her on her feet and held her at arm's length.

"My God, Margaret. My dear God."

It was too beautiful to spoil with words. Tears welled up in the corners of her eyes as she looked at him. The pulse at the base of his throat began to throb and, as she reached up to touch it, he took her hand in his. Turning it over, he placed it against his mouth. The simple intimacy drove her wild with desire. She longed to have him master her, to take her as no man had done before.

He reached for the buttons on her gown, his fingers warm against her throat. One, two, three, four. Her eyes widened. He moved close again and pressed his mouth against the soft rise of her bosom where it spilled over the top of her chemise. More, she wanted more.

He shuddered once, then moved away.

Margaret searched his face. His eyes were dark with need. He couldn't desert her now. He couldn't.

# CHAPTER NINE

Margaret's mouth felt hot and dry. She ran a quick tongue over her lips as she watched him back away slowly, as if afraid to go yet afraid to stay. When he spoke, it was as if his voice were torn from his soul.

"Margaret. Forgive me."

She reached out to him, silently pleading with her eyes, but he continued to back away until he reached the door. Then he turned and walked out, closing the door behind him.

Drained of emotion, she sank down onto the love seat and, leaning her head against the back, stared unblinking at the ceiling as tears rolled down her cheeks. She felt whipped, beaten, punished, and there was nothing she could do to save herself.

He must know what he did to her. Surely he was aware that she had been willing to do his least bidding. Then why did he refuse her? Was it his idea to shame her? No! Even with her limited experience, she knew that he had wanted her almost beyond endurance. He was no saint! What little she knew of him laid waste to that notion. Even Lady Jordice . . . she blinked rapidly several times, then dried her eyes on the back of her hand as she sat up.

So that was it. He was afraid someone would come in. With Lady Jordice under the same roof, she was sure to find out, if one of the servants had seen them kissing.

Margaret straightened with a sigh. The duchess mustn't find her in such a state. It would be too humiliating. She dragged herself to a standing position, then, like a woman of seventy years, turned to the desk to resume her work. The model lay careened against the inkpot, deserted, abandoned without a thought to its value. She felt a kinship too painful to pursue as she gently returned it to the shelf.

For a while work was out of the question as Margaret attempted the delicate strokes required to make the letters. Her thoughts kept returning to the warmth of his kiss, the touch of his hands, the heat of her passion. Laying the reed pen on the table, she rested her chin in the palm of her hand. There had to be a reason for his abrupt pulling away. He was an honorable man, she was sure of that.

Margaret sat up straight. But of course. He *was* honorable. That was the answer. He would not make a commitment to her while he was officially or unofficially betrothed to Lady Jordice. He would have to settle matters with her before he could in good conscience come to Margaret.

She pressed her palms together beneath her chin and breathed a prayer of gratitude. Time . . . it was just a question of time until he would come to her, free of all his former ties. Margaret smiled. She needed something to hold onto. It was true. It simply had to be.

Margaret could not have survived the ordeal of high tea with the duke sitting in the same room. Fortunately no one came to question her absence. She would also have preferred to send her regrets for dinner, but that would have been asking too much of good fortune. Prompt to the second, she made her appearance in the dining room where the others were already sipping glasses of wine.

The footman, in his satin livery of dark blue and gold, offered her a glass, which she pretended to sip. Wine was never important to her, least of all now when her stomach was less than certain. She managed to smile and say all the right things, but she dared not face the duke. Instinct told her that he was watching her. All her being cried out to meet his dark gaze and give him the reassurance he must surely crave, but to do so would be tantamount to an open declaration of love.

The duchess had spoken, but Margaret was too preoccupied to hear. She turned to face her. "I'm dreadfully sorry, your grace. What was it you said?"

The duchess smiled. "I trust you've not allowed my son to work you too hard, Margaret. You look a little pale." She placed her empty glass on the Sheffield tray and dabbed at her lips with a lace handkerchief. "I was just saying that we have all been invited to a small gathering tonight at Hampshire House. I took the liberty of accepting for you." Seeing Margaret's distressed look, she patted her arm. "Ah, but I see I should have consulted you first." Her disappointment was obvious in her tone of voice.

"No, please believe me, it is perfectly all right. You were kind to include me."

The duchess looked relieved. "Good. Then it's settled. We shall all go in the state carriage."

Margaret was grateful for the tall urn of hothouse roses on the dinner table which prevented a direct line of vision between her and the duke. Somehow she was able to get through the meal and, on the pretext of having to prepare for the evening out, she sought the safety of her room without having to join the after-dinner conversation.

Getting dressed was an ordeal. Corrine insisted that Margaret have her cheeks rouged because of her extreme lack of color and, to save an argument, she finally agreed to a faint touch of pink. She wore the blue gown for the same reason, but this time obstinately refused the circlet of flowers at the back of her hair. They reminded her too much of the duke.

Hampshire House was a tribute to Gothic architecture. Tall spires pierced the night sky like tines of a pitchfork lifted on high. Towers and turrets, softened by ancient ivy vines, glowed in the light of a hundred torches. Inside, the grand entrance, which was large enough to have accommodated several hundred people, was decorated with tapestries of hunters in their pink coats, surrounded by horses and dogs. Interspersed between the tapestries were statues of knights in shining coats of armor. Footmen in bright green livery were so numerous as to almost outnumber the hundred or more guests.

Looking around for a familiar face, Margaret noticed Count Dantoni speaking in his intimate way to a rusty-haired dowager of indeterminate age. He looked up and nodded, his face wreathed in a smile. Margaret responded, then quickly turned away. It was better not to encourage him. It would only serve to cause trouble with the duke.

When the duke removed Lady Jordice's silk manteau and handed it to the footman, a chorus of "oh" spread over the room. She was wearing a sheer spun silver gown over another gown of a polished gold fabric which glittered in the light of the crystal chandelier. Around her neck she wore a fortune in emeralds and diamonds.

Margaret had never seen anything so lovely and so wildly extravagant. The girl was a picture of perfection. Having chosen to act the demure role that night, she enhanced her desirability. Margaret felt sick inside, but it was nothing compared to her feeling when Lady Jordice lifted her hand to her hair. She was wearing the ring, the one the duke had asked Margaret to put in the safe, the one inscribed "To J. Love Eternal."

He must have given it to her earlier that evening, after he had spent the afternoon with Margaret. The thought was too painful to bear. It was over. Her brief dream of fulfillment was gone in the flash of emerald fire on the hand of another woman. Margaret felt more defeated than she had at any time in her life. This time there would be no answer to her problem, no conceivable solution.

Standing there, uncertain where to move, she was startled when someone put an arm around her waist. It was Count Dantoni. Indeed, who else would have been so presumptuous. He looked at her in speculation.

"Hm. Forgive me my uncertainty, your ladyship. I was not sure whether to stay or run. Your eyes for a moment were cold beyond belief."

She forced a smile. "On the contrary, Count Dantoni. I was hoping you would tear yourself away from your friend long enough to speak to me."

He laughed. "I find it difficult to believe there was a single doubt in your mind. If the choice were mine, I would steal you away to my castle in Spain, locking out the world for all eternity."

The duchess had approached in time to hear his comment, and she frowned. "Lady Margaret, we are joining the Prince Regent and his party in the west wing. Won't you come along?"

The count clicked his heels and bowed. "Begging

your indulgence, your grace. Lady Margaret has just promised to let me show her the collection of ivory in the study."

Margaret considered protesting the bald-faced lie, but the prospect of being with the duke was too much to countenance. She returned the duchess's questioning gaze and nodded once.

"Of course, if it is your wish that I join you," said Margaret, "I will forgo viewing the collection."

The duchess shrugged. "Needless to say, the choice is yours. You know where to find us, my dear," she said with a lift of the eyebrows which seemed to say, "if you need me."

Margaret dropped a curtsy and the duchess took her leave. A trifle embarrassed at her part in the deception, Margaret looked up at the count. His eyes glittered with anticipation, and she felt a twinge of uneasiness at the back of her neck.

"Count Dantoni, perhaps we should go in search of the collection."

He threw his head back and laughed, then offered his arm. "As you wish, my dear Margaret, but I'll wager it will take an inordinate amount of time, if indeed there is a collection."

Margaret was appalled. "You lied. You stood there and lied to the duchess. And please don't call me Margaret," she added as an afterthought.

He lifted an eyebrow. "And did you not also lie, lovely one?"

She took his arm, too subdued to do anything but follow his lead.

It was soon apparent that they were going to the garden. Normally Margaret would have been cautious about such improper behavior, but her nerves were so tightly drawn as to ignore such warnings. Besides, the

116

hint of chill in the air did much to revive her spirits. She lifted the hair at the back of her neck and let the breeze cool her fevered skin. He looked at her with approval.

"This is much better, Margaret. The color is warm on your cheeks."

"It's rouge, Count Dantoni. My abigail insisted I was too wan to spend an evening with the *haut ton.*"

He made a face. "How distressing. I was sure that my presence was responsible for your flushed appearance. In truth, I must argue that earlier on you were exceedingly pale."

Margaret shrugged.

The path, walled on each side with yew hedges, curved to reveal suddenly a small gazebo hidden among the trees. Dantoni circled her waist with his arm and turned her toward it before the faint moon disappeared behind the clouds. It was a quaint structure, enclosed with white painted slats to permit one to see out while obscuring the vision of the outsider looking in. Clearly it was designed for intimate tête-à-têtes.

A single candle set in a niche cast soft shadows about the room, giving an illusion of movement to a marble statue of two nudes entwined in the act of love. Margaret turned away in embarrassment, only to catch Count Dantoni's expression of amusement.

"Can it be that you are offended, Margaret? A woman of your obvious experience cannot pretend innocence in the ways of love."

It was a discussion she had no wish to pursue. Like most others who knew of her independence, he would never believe her to be chaste. Indeed, to talk of such things was in itself an act of impropriety. As a virgin she was not expected to understand the needs of men until instructed in such arts by her husband when he took her to wife.

The count was not to be put off. "Come, I have waited too long for the taste of those lovely lips."

His hands were warm on her waist, and for an instant she was transported back to the study. The man reaching for her was the duke, and she yearned for him with an eagerness that appalled her. His mouth was against her hair as she lifted her arms and placed them around his neck. Crushing her body against the door of the gazebo, he covered her mouth with moist, hot lips that plundered and searched.

Their very softness made her draw back. This wasn't the duke. There was no sharp rasp of moustache against her mouth. She thrust him away.

"No! Please stop. You mustn't do this."

His voice was edged with anger. "Don't play games, Margaret. We've gone too far for such childish things."

"I'm sorry. I wasn't myself. Do forgive me, Count Dantoni. I really must go back to the house." She turned to leave and, as he grabbed her, his hand caught the neck of her gown, ripping it to the shoulder. He looked truly apologetic.

"Lady Margaret, do forgive me. I only meant to stop you long enough to talk about it."

She tried unsuccessfully to hide the bare expanse of skin. "Dear heaven, what am I to do now? Even my shawl won't conceal the damage."

He took off his jacket. "Here. Wear this."

"I can't," Margaret wailed. "That would be equally suggestive."

"Yes," he murmured. "But wait, I have an idea. I'm staying at the house for the rest of the week. You can go to my room and . . ." He saw the expression on her face. "Please. Don't jump to conclusions. You can go to my room alone. I'll send the maid up to repair the damage to your gown. A few stitches at the seam will make it as good as new."

Margaret weighed her choices. It seemed the only way out. "Very well. If you promise to let me go alone."

He bowed. "I swear, Margaret. I would never try to force you to do anything you did not profess to desire."

She looked at him, needing to believe in someone, then nodded her agreement.

Fortunately his room was located near the end of the corridor and was easily accessible by the servants' stairway. The only one they met was a dewy-eyed girl of seventeen or so who was obviously in great awe of Count Dantoni.

He spoke to her in rapid Spanish. Margaret glanced from him to the girl and back again. The girl lifted the edge of the shawl to survey the torn gown. She nodded, then spoke to the count.

Listening apprehensively to the rapid exchange, Margaret breathed a sigh of relief when the count patted her arm and, turning, went downstairs. The girl motioned Margaret to follow, and they entered the bedchamber, closing the door behind them.

By means of sign language, the maid managed to let Margaret know that she was to wear the count's dressing gown while the dress was being repaired. She helped Margaret slip it over her head, then hung it on a rod while she indicated that she would return shortly with a needle and thread.

Margaret hesitated over putting on the dressing gown. It had been worn; she could tell by the slight scent of musk and tobacco which clung to the burgundy red silk. It was bad enough being in his room without wearing his robe as well. She waited impatiently for the girl's return. Finally she appeared carrying a tea tray laden with cups and a delicate Oriental porcelain teapot tucked into a white cozy.

The girl motioned her to sit down on the bed. Tea was the last thing Margaret wanted at the moment, but, rather than try to overcome the girl's insistence, she accepted a cup and surprisingly was pleased by the warmth it generated.

It soon became apparent that the girl was no genius with the needle. Margaret made a feeble attempt to take over for her, but the girl gently eased her back onto the bed with a warm smile. In truth Margaret felt too mellow to protest strongly. She had worked hard during the day, a fact which must have accounted for the feeling of heaviness in her thighs and legs. The pillow looked enormously inviting. She pulled it from the coverlet and, placing it along the opposite side of the bed, leaned back and closed her eyes.

How long she dozed, Margaret didn't know, but when she opened her eyes, the girl was gone. Margaret's gown lay across the chair and, as she started to rise, a flood of warmth swept over her, engulfing her with the strange feeling that her feet were walking on air. There was an emptiness inside her, a need that cried out to be filled, and she was powerless to understand it.

"So, Margaret. You have awakened from your little nap. I've been waiting for you." Count Dantoni rose from the chair, not once lifting his gaze from the swell of her bosom above her chemise.

She gasped at her state of undress and attempted to cover herself.

He shook his head. "The flower of your body is waiting to be picked, my love. Don't try to conceal it."

He came toward her through a haze. One part of her

yearned to reach out to him, to feel his hands slide along the smooth skin of her body until she reached her fulfillment. Another part of her wanted to scream for help. It was as if twin devils waged battle inside of her. First one gained ground, only to lose for a moment to the other.

He touched her, sending a surge of heat through her veins. Dizziness engulfed her. She reached up to hold onto him, and he laughed deep in his throat, a sound echoed by her own voice as she lifted her mouth with undisguised hunger.

He came down on her with rasping breath and glazed eyes. But it was the wrong mouth. Even in her drugged state her body knew the difference between passion and love. It was not wise to settle for false gold. With all her strength she pushed against him until he fell across the foot of the bed.

He shook his head as if to make sense of her sudden change in mood. "Fool girl. She didn't give you enough."

Margaret tried desperately to focus her gaze. "You . . . you drugged me!"

He smiled. "It was nothing, my sweet. Just a drop of gypsy magic in your tea." He motioned to the cups. "There is still some left. Share it with me, my darling, and we will feast on the fruits of life with no inhibitions."

Margaret grabbed her gown, which had not been mended, and held it up in front of her. As he moved toward her, she backed against the wall.

"Stop or I'll scream."

He smiled and moved toward her, tracing his finger across her lips. "Are you so certain, little one?"

"I warn you, Adolfo. Leave this room at once, or I'll scream."

He threw his head back and laughed. "And what do you think that would accomplish? Our host is quite used to screams during the night when he entertains. The servant girls have quite a thirst for my gypsy tea."

Margaret's eyes brimmed with tears. "Please, I beg you not to touch me."

His eyes hardened. "But you are a woman of fire. I am no fool to be taken in by your pretending." He leaned back and looked at her, a peculiar expression in his eyes. "Or is it my body which offends you?"

She drew a deep breath and prayed for words that would stop him without arousing his anger and thus his violence. "No, I cannot truthfully say I find you offensive. We have had many enjoyable times together. But I speak truthfully when I say I am still untouched."

He shook his head. "That I cannot believe, my lady. Some man has awakened the woman in you. Your body pants from the need of him."

Her lips trembling, she faced him. "There is some truth to what you say, but I did not lie, Adolfo. I am in love with the duke but, as God is my witness, he does not know, nor shall he. When you kissed me, I pretended it was he. Although I enjoy your company, in all honesty I could never let you make love to me."

He touched his fingers to her cheek. "Such honesty overwhelms me. Only now that I'm losing you do I realize your true worth. It breaks my heart, Margaret, to have to give you up before we have had a chance to . . . to know each other. What I would give to be worthy of a woman such as you."

Much relieved, she managed a smile. "Perhaps you are a better man than you think you are, Adolfo Dantoni. The man you show to the *beau monde* is not the real you."

"I wish you were right, but I see myself through my own eyes," he said, motioning to the pot of tea. "It was something else in me, not just the drug, which prompted my subterfuge."

"You give yourself scant credit. Were I wrong, I fear my fate would have been different today."

He turned and shoved his hands into his pockets. "Then, for both our sakes, I think I had better leave while you put on your dress."

Her hand flew to her mouth. "Dear heaven. How long has it been? The duke and his mother . . . they must be out of their minds with worry."

He shook his head. "No, I had our hostess say that you had elected to take a moonlight carriage ride. She promised to see you safely home."

Margaret was appalled. "The marchioness would lie for you?"

He shrugged boyishly. "She is a good friend . . . a very good friend." With a provocative grin he slipped out the door and closed it behind him.

Five minutes later Margaret was trying to repair the damage to her gown when the duke burst into the room.

# CHAPTER TEN

Margaret gasped and held her gown up in front of her. He came toward her in three quick strides.

"Has he hurt you, Margaret?"

"I . . . I . . ."

"For God's sake, answer me before I kill him for nought."

She shook her head, wide-eyed with fear and shame for having been discovered like this. "No, he has not harmed me."

"You expect me to believe that? Look at you. You're not even dressed." His eyes were aglow with a dangerous light. "If he touched you in any way, I'll see him hanged."

She bit her lip to keep it from quavering. "No, you mustn't cause any more trouble. I . . . I came to his room willingly, but I assure you, nothing happened."

He seemed unable to pull his gaze away from the upper curve of her bosom. She tried to break the spell.

"Please, can't we go home? I'm dreadfully tired."

There was an edge to his voice as he studied her face. "As well you might be, Lady Margaret. The count's reputation boasts well for his endurance. Let me call a maid to help you dress."

"No! The gossip would surely be all over town. I'll do it myself."

He swore profoundly. "It will take forever. Here, let me do it." His hands were more gentle than she had supposed they could be. That, added to her predicament, was her undoing. She began to shake with silent sobs. When he turned her around to look at her, she saw that his hand was bleeding.

"Peter! You're hurt."

There was a note of triumph in his voice. "Not as much as your friend, Dantoni."

"You didn't!"

"Didn't I? If you want to play the game, Margaret, you have to suffer the consequences. Dantoni knows it. You are beginning to learn."

He grabbed a sheet and wrapped it around her like a shawl, then escorted her downstairs. The house was blessedly silent, and they left without meeting a soul.

The ride home seemed to take an eternity. Margaret stole a sideways look at the duke as he sat next to her. "What made you come looking for me? The count told me that the marchioness had explained away my absence."

"She certainly tried. I didn't like the smell of it from the start. The longer you were away, the less I liked it. Finally I returned and, after bribing the chambermaid, I learned that you were in Dantoni's room."

His voice hardened as he said the words, and Margaret winced. To explain everything would be to court danger for both the duke and Count Dantoni. The duke would be sure to seek vengeance for such an affront to her name. The thought strengthened her resolve to remain silent. She stirred in the seat.

"Your hand has been bleeding again. Is it terribly painful?"

He gave her a look but refused to answer. She sank

back on her seat, averting her gaze until the carriage pulled into the drive.

A sudden apprehension disturbed Margaret. "Does the duchess know that you went looking for me?"

"I tried every effort to spare her." He shrugged. "She will doubtless find out eventually."

"Thank you, your grace, for . . . for everything."

He looked steadily into her eyes, as if he were going to say something, then changed his mind. The coachman dropped the steps to the carriage, then opened the door and assisted them out. A quickly shielded glance told Margaret that he had noted her condition but was too well trained to stare. Nevertheless the news would soon be a priority item on the servants' grapevine.

The house was dark when they entered, save for a light in the entrance hall. Margaret noticed that the cut on the duke's hand was bleeding at a steady rate. She put her hand on his arm.

"You can't let it go like that. Your hand needs to be bathed and bandaged. Come into the kitchen and let me do it for you."

"No thank you. I'll manage by myself."

She was too exhausted to bandy words with him. "For heaven's sake, stop acting the fool and follow me."

She found hot water waiting in the reservoir end of the great iron stove, which was banked with wood for the night. Filling a pan with water, she told him to immerse his hand and soak it until she found the bandages. The warm water hastened the flow of blood, but it also cleansed the wound which was comparatively slight. Margaret pressed the edges of the cut together and covered it with a pad of lint. Then she bound it with a clean white cloth and straightened the kitchen while he remained to watch. Neither of them talked. There was nothing left to say. The thought brought on a desolation of spirit so intense that she wondered if she could bear it. They separated at the stairs with nothing more than a quiet good night.

It was late in the morning before she awoke. A hard yank to the bellpull brought Corrine on the run. Seeing Margaret's irritation, she put her hands on her hips. "Now don't you be wrathful, your ladyship. It was the duke hisself who told me not to waken you." She smiled impishly. "Hit weren't long ago when he left 'is own bed, so you've no call to feel bad."

Margaret tied her hair back with a ribbon and hastily washed her face. The blue gown, which she had hung over a chair before crawling into bed, had been cleaned and repaired and was on a hanger in the armoire. Margaret took it out and examined the tear.

"Did you stitch this up this morning, Corrine?"

"Hit weren't so much, miss. It was just the seam what came apart."

"Just the same, you did a very nice job, and I appreciate it."

"That must have been some party at the Hampshire House. I hear tell from the maid what works backstairs that there are some pretty fancy goings-on over there."

Margaret tried to keep her voice even. "One really can't believe everything one hears. As for the gown, I tore it in the summer house."

"Yes, ma'am."

It was plain the girl did not believe her, but at least it put an end to the conversation.

Breakfast had already been cleared away, but Thomas asked if he could get something for her, and she settled for a pot of tea and a muffin, which she took with her to the study. Thankfully the duke was not in evidence.

She sat down at the table and surveyed the work which she had accomplished. Page after page of beautiful lettering was stacked neatly in a drawer. She was particularly pleased with the addition of color she had used when drawing the illustrated capitals. Where the calligrapher in the days of Charlemagne may have used simple leaves and flowers to illustrate the capitals, she had added tiny butterflies in pastel colors. The effect was striking and still authentic enough to conform to the Carolingian style of alphabet.

She carefully returned the papers to the drawer. There was still much to be done. She longed for nothing more than a quiet week to get caught up on her work, away from the mental turmoil that had begun to plague her life.

How could she face the duke after last night? It was plain from his attitude that he disliked too much independence in a woman. Now that she had been forced to tell him she had willingly gone to Dantoni's room, his regard for her must surely have plummeted. But there had been no other choice. If he knew that Dantoni had been the aggressor, the duke would hardly have stopped short of murder.

No doubt the count deserved a good setdown. He had tried to drug her, something no decent man would even consider doing, but he was a Spaniard. Perhaps such actions were looked on differently in his country. Then too, like most men, he assumed her morals were less than perfect, since she had entered the trades.

She leaned her chin against her palm. Did the duke also think that she was no longer a maiden? His desire for her had been as great as hers for him, but he had not forced himself on her. Indeed he had drawn away. She gave a short, humorless laugh. If that were a measure of worth, then Dantoni must also qualify. He could have taken her by force during the time she lay half clothed on his bed, but he preferred to have her come to him. In her drugged state she had very nearly yielded to him. Had it not been for her sudden awareness, she might even now be . . . She closed her mind against the thought.

Still in good conscience she could not bring herself to hate the count as much as he surely deserved.

Pushing her chair back from the table, she went to the cabinet to begin work on another item from the collection. She had completed most of the larger pieces and looked forward to tabulating the small, exquisitely jeweled butterflies which were kept in the uppermost drawer. One in particular, a bracelet of comparatively little value, intrigued her, and she was eager to learn its history. It was designed with a silver circlet which expanded to slip over one's wrist. Centered on the circlet were three butterflies crafted of spun silver. They rested on a bed of flowers made of infinitely tiny diamonds and rubies.

She opened the drawer but, after searching for a considerable length of time, was unable to find the bracelet. The space where it had rested was bare, although it seemed to Margaret that some of the other pieces had been moved to cover the bareness. She rang for Thomas and asked if he had seen the duke or duchess remove it.

His voice mirrored his concern. "No, your ladyship. It is most unlikely that either of them would have taken it from the room. They rarely view the collection." He stood for a moment as he pondered what to do. "The duke is in Parliament this afternoon, but as soon as he returns, I shall ask him about it. As for her grace . . . she remains in her rooms and has said that she does not wish to be disturbed."

Margaret wrinkled her brow. "Indeed? I hope she is not ill."

"Not likely, your ladyship. She often elects to spend some time by herself."

"For the present I would prefer not to worry her about the bracelet. It is inconceivable that it could just disappear, but for the moment, until we can consult with the duke, I think perhaps we should keep this to ourselves."

"Yes, miss. I think that is wise. I shall do my best to discover what has happened to it."

"Thank you, Thomas. That will be all for now."

He bowed and left the room.

Two hours later she still had found no trace of the bracelet. Finding it impossible to concentrate on her work, Margaret went upstairs to her room to look for a reference book. Corrine was doing some mending in a chair by the window. She looked up and smiled.

" 'Ave you 'eard the news, miss? Lady Jordice is leavin' bag and baggage this afternoon."

Margaret was surprised. "Indeed? Will she be returning?"

"Aye, that I couldn't say, but cook says she 'eard 'er and 'is grace fightin' as if . . ."

Margaret interrupted. "We really shouldn't be discussing it. Besides I have something else on my mind."

"Yes, miss. I thought you looked overly concerned. Is there somethin' I could be doing about it?"

"I'm afraid not." She sat down on the edge of the bed with a feeling of complete helplessness. Good sense told her not to talk about it, but she needed to talk to someone. "The thing is . . . something, a bracelet, has disappeared and I haven't the least idea what could have happened to it."

Corrine sat down abruptly. "Could you describe it, your ladyship?"

"Of course. It was a circlet of silver topped with three butterflies and a cluster of diamonds and rubies. Why? Have you seen it?" Margaret asked with growing interest.

Corrine turned away. "No, miss. But I thought if I did, it would be nice to recognize it."

"Oh . . . yes, of course. Well, if you do find it, please let me know at once. I am greatly disturbed that it is missing."

Margaret thought she had wasted her breath telling Corrine about it; nevertheless she felt somewhat relieved. It came as a great surprise when Corrine, along with Thomas, approached her in the study early that evening.

Thomas stood at attention as he waited for her to finish the last crucial strokes of the letter L. Corrine waited a few steps behind him, as was fitting for one of lower rank.

Margaret spoke. "Thank you for waiting. What was it you wanted to tell me?"

Thomas looked around, then ordered Corrine to close the door to the study. "I wasn't sure what to do about this, your ladyship. Her grace is still indisposed, and the duke has not yet returned." He looked profoundly uncomfortable.

Margaret gave him her full attention. "Go on, Thomas."

"Yes. In regard to our conversation earlier today. Corrine has informed me that you also spoke with her about the missing bracelet."

"Yes. Perhaps I should not . . ."

He brought his hands in front of him. "Would this be the missing jewelry, Lady Margaret?"

Margaret got up and rushed to take it from his hand. "Why, yes. It most certainly is. Wherever did you find it?"

"That's just the trouble, your ladyship. Becky, one of the maids who was tending Lady Jordice during her stay, found it hidden among her ah . . . unmentionables in the clothespress. It seems that the lady has a habit of taking any number of things of little value."

"Oh, Thomas, are you certain?"

"As right as I can be without seeing it for myself. The upstairs maids have apparently been aware of her weakness for some time, but this is the first I have heard of it."

Margaret turned to Corrine. "How does it happen that you have never mentioned this in the past?"

Corrine shrugged. "Far be it from me, miss, to tell the master that 'is lady love is light-fingered. Were 'e to choose between 'er or me, I doubts that it twould be me. No, sir, I keeps me mouth shut, I do."

"And yet you chose to come forward now?"

Corrine shrugged. "Sometimes I forget to be smart."

Were the situation different, Margaret would have laughed. The duchess was certainly correct when she said the girl had an impudent streak.

"I can't tell you how much I appreciate this, Corrine. My only concern is what to do about it now. Is it your impression that Lady Jordice was planning to take it with her?"

"That she was. Becky overheard 'er ladyship tell 'er own maid to pack everything from the clothespress and armoire."

Margaret turned to Thomas. "Is it possible the duke could have given it to her as a gift?"

"Indeed, no, your ladyship. His grace would sooner part with a hand than dispose of a piece of the collection."

"Then what do you suggest we do?"

Corrine spoke up quickly, despite a warning look from Thomas. "Please, Lady Margaret. Don't tell 'is grace that Becky or me was snooping in 'er ladyship's belongin's. Hit jolly well might not sit good wi' 'im and we could get the sack." There was genuine concern in her voice.

Margaret nodded. "Yes, you could be right."

Thomas looked perturbed. "I hope your ladyship is not considering replacing it in the clothespress."

"No, not if you are certain the duke couldn't have given it to her."

"I'd stake my life on it."

"Then, there is only one thing to do. I will return it to its proper place in the study, and, for the moment at least, we will say nothing about the fact that it was ever missing."

Thomas nodded. "Mayhap that is the best way."

"Eventually the duke will have to be told, I suppose, but I doubt that this is the time for it."

Margaret thanked them for their loyalty and discretion, and they left, apparently both pleased with the outcome.

About an hour later she heard the commotion of trunks and valises being brought downstairs. It was true, then, that Lady Jordice was leaving. Had the duke recently returned home? Surely she wouldn't leave while he was away. Margaret finished the page she was working on with undue haste and went to the entrance hall to say good-bye. But she was too late. The carriage, laden to the top with luggage, was just pulling out of the drive. The duchess stood stiffly beside the door until it had turned the corner.

"Oh, Margaret, I didn't hear you come out."

"I'm sorry, your grace. I didn't mean to disturb you. I just came to tell Lady Jordice good-bye, but I seem to have missed her."

"Don't fret. She was in something of a rush." She sighed, and Margaret noticed lines of weariness on the normally smooth brow.

"You look tired. Would you like me to send for a pot of tea?"

"Indeed, yes. We'll take it in the study, if you are in the middle of work. I know how you hate to stop."

Margaret spoke to the footman, then followed the duchess to the study. They settled themselves in comfortable chairs. Margaret suspected that the duchess had something on her mind and wanted to talk. She was right. They had just begun to sip their cinnamon tea when the duchess shook her head.

"You are simply not going to believe this, my dear, but Mr. Trembe has asked me to marry him."

Margaret clasped her hands together. "How absolutely wonderful. I knew this would happen. Have you set the date?"

The duchess looked shocked. "You surely don't think I accepted?"

"Well I . . . I'm sorry, your grace. I assumed that you are in love with him. The two of you seem so devoted."

"Indeed? I was not aware that anyone had noticed our mutual attraction"

Margaret smiled. "Surely you jest. One would have to be blind not to have guessed. You do love him, don't you? If I may be so bold."

"Love . . . at my age." She looked properly abashed, but then her natural good humor took over. "Yes, I suppose I do love the dear man. Not that anything can come of it."

"But why not?"

"Well, there's Peter. I don't know how it would set with him. Mr. Trembe is, after all, a commoner."

"But the duke is quite fond of him."

"Indeed, but I would have to give up my title." Her eyes pleaded for understanding. "I've been a duchess for nearly forty years. I don't know that I care to be just plain Mrs. Trembe."

Margaret fought to refrain from smiling. So that was it. In spite of her admiration for modern trends, the duchess was nobility to the core. She spoke gently.

"I assume it is not a question of money, your grace. From what I understand, Mr. Trembe is rather well fixed."

"No, money has nothing to do with it. Of course his house is smaller than this, but it is more than adequate." She shook her head. "It's the title. I simply don't want to relinquish it, at least not until Peter is married and there is another duchess to run the house."

Margaret lowered her gaze. "It was my understanding that he and Lady Jordice are informally betrothed. Have they not set the date for a formal betrothal?"

"Not to my knowledge, and I assume I would have been told. Peter seems loath to settle down. He should have given me grandchildren by now, but either he is running around the world for the Prince Regent or he is escorting first one and then another young lady of the *haut ton*."

Margaret refilled their cups as the duchess continued.

"His father had hoped for an alliance between Peter and Lady Jordice. It would have united two of the largest shipbuilding concerns in the world. If anything, her father is even more adamant that the betrothal be formalized, but so far nothing has happened. She is rumored to have been in love with another man, who is betrothed to a princess."

Margaret carefully put her cup down on the table. So that was it. Jordice, not the duke, was delaying their marriage. If this held true, then the duke must surely be in love with her. No wonder he was so testy most of the time. No man liked to be held at arm's length once he had declared himself. She pleated the fold of her skirt between her fingers.

"Is Lady Jordice planning to return?"

"I really don't know. She was in a fair temper when she left. Apparently Peter had promised to come home several hours ago. When he didn't arrive, she packed up and left."

The door opened, and the duke looked into the room. "I beg your pardon. Am I intruding?"

"Certainly not, Peter," the duchess said. "Come in and I'll ring for another cup and a fresh pot of tea."

"Make it a brandy, and I'll agree."

She looked at him closely. "I say, you do look rather dragged out. Was it that business last night?"

Margaret caught her breath. Just how much did the duchess know?

The duke shot Margaret a questioning look and sat down, stretching his long legs out in front of him.

# CHAPTER ELEVEN

The duchess repeated her question. "Well, answer me, Peter. My abigail said you went out again late last night. I thought perhaps something happened at the palace. There's been talk that King George has been much worse these last few weeks."

He sighed and leaned his head back against the chair. "I've just come from a very long session of Parliament. Liverpool was forced to resign today on a vote of no confidence."

"Dear heaven. What will this do to the Tory party?"

"The question is, Mother, what will this do to the empire?"

Margaret was too unnerved to listen to the rest of the conversation. She breathed a silent prayer of gratitude that her reputation, as far as the duchess was concerned, was still unblemished. She stole a look at the duke. It was true; he looked dreadful. Knowing that his condition was not entirely her fault did little to salve Margaret's conscience. It had been terribly late by the time they had arrived home. He couldn't have slept more than three hours. That, added to his problems with Lady Jordice, was enough to wear him down.

He had earlier removed the bandage from his hand. It was gratifying to see that the abrasion was hardly discernible. Then, too, he went to some pains to keep from displaying his hand. It would be hard to explain away an injury of that sort. The duchess brought Margaret's thoughts back from where they strayed.

"I assume, Peter, that you know Jordice has returned to Sweden?" Her voice was gentle and it was plain that she was uncertain of her ground.

He straightened and ran his fingers through his hair. "Truthfully I didn't know she had gone, but it doesn't surprise me. We were supposed to have gone riding in the park this afternoon. She doesn't like to have her plans changed without so much as a by-your-leave. Unfortunately I was too busy to even send a messenger."

She reached over and patted his hand. "My dear, I am so sorry."

He shrugged. "Not as sorry as she will be when she faces her father. He is determined to bring an alliance between our businesses. He was counting on Jordice to cement that alliance."

He glanced over at Margaret, his eyes dark and haunted. She longed to say something which would ease his pain, but she was powerless to help him. A short time later the duchess ordered him to rest for the remainder of the day.

During the next few days it was obvious that the duke was taking great pains to avoid being alone with Margaret. Whereas before her entanglement with the count at Hampshire House the duke had worked alongside her in his study, now he sent Thomas or a footman to fetch his papers and ledgers. A few discreet questions to Thomas revealed that the duke had taken to working in his private rooms.

Neither Thomas nor Corrine had made the least mention of the incident with the bracelet. Margaret had mixed emotions. She hated keeping secrets; it was tantamount to telling a lie. But she could not in good conscience blame either of the servants for their silence. One in a position of servitude soon learned that concerning unpleasant subjects, the less said the better.

Still in a state of upheaval since her proposal from Mr. Trembe, the dowager duchess spent a great deal of time alone in her room. It was unlike her, and it worried Margaret. She wondered if the duke had been told of Mr. Trembe's offer for the duchess's hand in marriage, but good sense told her the duchess would not add her own problems to the ones he already carried.

Indeed the press of duties had apparently increased greatly during the past few days because the duke was rarely at home for dinner and sometimes it was well into the night before Margaret heard his carriage turn into the drive.

Corrine was brushing Margaret's hair one morning after a sleepless night of waiting for the duke to return. She looked at the dark circles around Margaret's eyes and shook her head.

"Sure and I can't 'elp but wonder wot this 'ouse is coming to. The duchess 'iding herself in 'er room all day, 'is grace carousing all night with that flashy Lady Alvira, and you workin' at yer table till your eyes are about to fall out. I'm fair put to wishin' the Swede was back wi' her fancy ways. At least there would be some life in the 'ouse."

Margaret tried to keep her voice steady. "The duchess needs to have some time to herself. She is not as young as she cares to pretend, and who are we to judge the duke? He works exceedingly hard, keeping an eye on the shipbuilding concern and at the same time holding his seat in Parliament. Not many noblemen would be so conscientious. He is entitled to relax at night. Besides, Corrine, one can hardly lay fact to rumor."

"Rumor, indade, is it?" She placed her hands on her hips as if to emphasize her words. "I 'ave it on the best authority, that bein' the maid at Gresham Place, that 'is grace is friskin' these nights wi' a half-dozen young women, most often wi' the Lady Alvira."

Margaret felt something inside her begin to shrivel. "How he chooses to spend his time is really none of our concern," she said. "I really do not wish to discuss it, Corrine." Corrine sniffed and hurried through the business of combing Margaret's hair with uncustomary haste. When she finished, she placed the combs on the dressing table and left without waiting to be dismissed.

Her solitary breakfast over, Margaret went to the study to resume work on the collection. She had eaten little. Strange how food could lose its savor because one was forced to dine alone. If the duke were eating breakfast these days, he must have elected to eat in his chambers rather than face her across the table.

She had delayed starting her work for as long as possible and was hard put to understand why. Working with the pen and brushes had been a source of pure joy to Margaret, and she had made great headway in the past week. Indeed at this rate it would not require many days to complete the inscriptions.

And that was the trouble. She simply did not want to return to her old life. It wasn't the poverty she minded. During her stay at the mansion, she had come to care deeply for the dowager duchess. And then there was Peter. She mentally chastised herself for using his Christian name. The thought of never seeing him again was almost too much to bear. She loved him; it was as simple as that. Given time she would no doubt recover from her loss, but the pain would always be there in her heart. No man could ever take his place.

She walked over to the glass case and picked up the

model of the *Mariposa*. Running her finger across the smooth hull, she remembered the night he had held her in his arms and kissed her as if for him she had been the only woman in the world. The recollection stirred her blood.

She smiled. They never had managed to paint the ship's name across its bow. Well . . . that was only one of the things left unfulfilled. She turned as she heard the door open, and the duchess entered the study.

"I knew I'd find you here, Margaret my dear."

"Your grace. How marvelous to see you out and about so early. I trust you are feeling more yourself?"

She wrinkled her nose. "In truth, what I've done is stopped wailing over my predicament."

Margaret looked at her with interest. "If you will forgive my asking, have you then made a decision concerning Mr. Trembe's offer for your hand?"

"My decision is not to make a decision. Mr. Trembe has kindly consented to give me as long as I want to make up my mind. Dear heaven," she smiled, "I hope we both live long enough to see that day."

Margaret laughed. "At any rate it is wonderful to see you looking so well."

"I wish I could say the same for you. The smudges under your eyes suggest that you've been working in the coal mines at Leeds. I really must have a talk with Peter. He has no right to work you so hard."

"Please. You musn't say anything to him. He is not to blame. Besides, I haven't seen him for days."

"Indeed?" The shock in her voice was profound. "But what is going on? Has he not taken his meals with you in the dining room?"

"He is rarely at home these days."

"Well, we shall see about that." She leaned on the

141

case and looked at the model Margaret had been holding. Her short burst of spirit apparently vanished, she took Margaret's hand in hers.

"It's time we did something new. Tell me. Have you ever been to the docks to see the ships come into harbor?"

"No. My father hated ships."

"A pity. You've missed so much. The docks aren't a place for ladies to go unaccompanied by a man, but Mr. Trembe has asked me to go to the office down at the wharf to sign some papers for the company. I'd like you to go with me."

Margaret readily agreed. "I'd like that. Ships have always fascinated me."

"It's settled then. I'll ask Peter to accompany us."

Margaret started to protest, then thought better of it, but the duchess caught the expression on her face.

"You seemed upset when I said that Peter would join us. Has something happened between the two of you?" Her face took on a dark flush. "Surely he hasn't . . ."

"No! No, your grace. Never! In no way can I fault his behavior toward me."

"Then I fail to understand your reaction." She blanched. "Oh, Margaret, my dear. Have you gone and fallen in love with him?"

She was so obviously distressed that Margaret could not bring herself to tell the truth. She forced a smile. "Nothing so serious as all that, your grace. The duke and I have had words." Seeing the curious look on the duchess's face, she continued. "He does not approve of my friendship with Count Dantoni."

"Is that all? Dantoni comes from one of the finest families in Spain. Oh, I'll admit he does have a bit of a reputation." She laughed. "I'll amend that to say a considerable reputation with the ladies. But I find him comparatively harmless. Indeed I've heard tell that he's helped more than one nobleman out of their financial straits after a night at the gaming tables at Watiers Club. I'll have to have a word with Peter."

"No, please. I wouldn't want him to think I went to you for assistance."

"Well, perhaps you're right. Give him time, my dear. He will mellow as he comes to know the count."

After the duchess left to send a messenger to inform Peter of her plans, Margaret sank down on the chair. She had all but lied to the duchess. That, added to the knowledge that she might be forced to spend the afternoon with the duke, was enough to set her stomach churning for the rest of the day.

Apparently the duchess's word was tantamount to law where the duke was concerned. A scant hour later his carriage arrived at the mansion, and he instructed Thomas to have the maid lay an extra plate for the noon meal.

The duchess looked full of vigor and enthusiasm as they waited for the carriage to be brought around. Mr. Trembe had arrived earlier and planned to ride in the coach with the three of them. It touched Margaret to see the devotion for the duchess shining in Mr. Trembe's eyes. She wondered if the duke were aware of Mr. Trembe's offer for the duchess's hand.

As for the duke, he acted cool and somewhat aloof. When they boarded the carriage, he took great care to see that the duchess was seated alongside Margaret, leaving him free to sit next to Mr. Trembe. He tried to give the impression that he wanted to talk business with the solicitor, but the conversation soon became generalized.

"You'll notice," Mr. Trembe pointed out, "that the new sections of warehouses at the East India docks are even now filled to overflowing. Had Parliament not convinced the city to go along with the dock-building program, an unbelievable amount of trade would have gone begging."

Margaret could not have imagined anything so grand in design. The river was packed with ocean-going ships of all manner—schooners, whalers, giant East Indiamen, tea clippers, and a light, swift-looking galley which the duke told Margaret was called a galliot and was said to have originated on the Mediterranean. There were hundreds of small vessels dealing in all manner of trade, from wine, sugar, and tea, to coffee, timber, silks, and ivory.

The duke laughed dryly. "And I'll venture to say that more than half of them are involved in smuggling or illegal trafficking of one kind or another."

"Aye, no doubt you are right, your grace," Mr. Trembe said. "But it was much worse back in the last century when we had open quays and unguarded wharves. The problem is the rapid growth. The world looks to London for its shipping and no other country will ever equal her in power."

The duchess laughed. "I hope you are right, John. Our economy depends on it."

"Oh look," Margaret nearly shouted. "Isn't that the *Mariposa*? She seems to be leaving port."

The duke gave her a quick look as if he, too, were remembering the ship's namesake. "Yes, the tugs are taking her out of the pool and into the channel. When she hoists sail, she'll be on her way to Germany."

They watched as the schooner slowly inched its way between the forest of tall-masted ships anchored at the quay or waiting to be guided to their berths. The wind had freshened from the south, making the navigation even more tricky. Finally the ship turned toward the channel, and the crew scrambled onto the rigging to set the sails. Margaret could have spent hours watching the traffic on the Thames, but the carriage moved on until it drew to a halt in front of the shipyard owned by the Carrington family.

The office of Carrington Shipbuilders was on the second floor of a sturdy but unpretentious brick building. While the driver stayed with the carriage, Mr. Trembe escorted the duchess, and the duke was left to offer Margaret his arm. Since he made no effort to start a conversation, Margaret saw no purpose in making idle chatter; so they walked in silence.

The office was a man's place, decorated throughout in heavy woods with polished floors studded here and there with small, braided rugs. Margaret was ushered to a chair against the wall, while the three of them entered a separate area for the signing of the contracts. It took less than an hour. When they finished, the dowager duchess spoke to the duke.

"Mr. Trembe has promised to show me his new method of keeping books. I know it holds no interest for you, Peter, so why don't you take Margaret for a stroll along the wharf? There is so much to see, and women have few opportunities to come here."

For either of them to have refused would have been awkward. The duke made a perfunctory bow and gave Margaret his arm.

"Very well, Mother. If you will excuse us, we will return within the half hour."

She waved them off without another thought, and they made their way across a small courtyard to the docks. Loading was going on at a feverish pace from warehouse to waiting ships.

"Are they always in such a great hurry?" Margaret asked.

"Only when they are trying to catch the tide," the duke answered. "You will notice that some of the ships are being unloaded. Those newly purchased hoists are specially contrived to aid in unloading heavy cargo. Over there you can see them unloading heavy mahogany logs onto that dray as if they were matchsticks."

"There must be an army of men working here."

"Indeed. Some say there are over two thousand dockmen and overseers here at these docks alone. Even with the wars, our shipping business is unequaled by any other country."

"You like being down here, don't you?"

"Yes, I do. However I have had to choose between diplomacy and shipbuilding. Mr. Trembe handles the legal matters, and my overseers handle construction matters, so there is really no excuse for my interference. Besides they do a far better job than I could hope to do."

"You like Mr. Trembe, don't you?"

"He is most respectable."

She frowned at his use of the word. "I was referring to his personality, not his morals."

"Indeed? Can the two then be separated?"

"Most certainly. That is not to say they have to be."

"I would hope not.

"From what I have seen, Mr. Trembe is a gentleman in every sense of the word."

He really looked at her for the first time that day. "I have the distinct impression, Lady Margaret, that you are pleading his cause."

Margaret felt her face go pink. "Was it that obvious?"

He nodded. "And your reason?"

"I don't believe I care to state it, your grace."

"As you wish. Permit me to make a suggestion, if you will. I would advise you not to set your cap for him. My mother has become overly fond of the gentleman, and she would be a frightening competitor."

Margaret stared at him. "Truly! You can't for a moment imagine that I had romantic intentions toward the man?"

He raised an eyebrow. "If I am to judge from your past behavior, I would be hard put to give the response you seek."

"Don't be absurd." She studied him closely. "How long have you known that your mother and Mr. Trembe were seriously attracted to one another?"

"Longer than the duchess has, I suspect. She pretends to be a liberalist, but she is nobility and she always will be—even if she marries the solicitor."

"Would that upset you, your grace?"

He shrugged. "Would he make her happy enough to compensate for what she would be giving up?"

Margaret shrugged. "How can one know?"

He smiled. "How indeed."

The breeze off the Thames had turned chill. Margaret pulled her shawl around her shoulders and tied the strings of her bonnet to keep it from blowing away. As they turned the corner by an abandoned wooden warehouse building, Margaret saw a woman huddled on a crate in the corner, nursing a child. An older child tugged at her skirts. None of the three were adequately clothed or fed much above the point of starvation.

The woman looked up at them as they passed by, her eyes flat and colorless with defeat. Margaret was touched by her hopelessness. Stopping abruptly, she asked the duke to wait for her for a moment, then rushed back and laid her shawl around the woman's shoulders and tucked a guinea into her pocket.

When she came back, the duke looked at her in surprise. "And what do you hope to accomplish by that? London is crawling with hundreds of women like her. It's reform they need, not handouts. At least you didn't give her money. I'm surprised you didn't also offer your bonnet."

His sarcasm irritated Margaret. "Had it occurred to me, I would have," she said. With that she snatched off her bonnet and, running back to the woman, put it on her head. By the time she got back to where the duke stood, mouth open in amazement, Margaret's hair was falling down around her shoulders in a dark cascade. The duke threw his head back and laughed.

"I keep thinking that I have seen the last of your unpredictable pranks, but you continue to surprise me. Perhaps we had better return before another waif appeals to you for an entire wardrobe. There are no sheets here to cover you this time."

Margaret's face burned. He had an uncanny way of bringing up past embarrassments while making certain to always have the last word.

By the time they arrived back at the shipyards, she was quite chilled but would rather have died than admit it when the duke queried her. Seeing the shocked expression on the duchess's face, Margaret almost regretted her generous impulse. Surprisingly the duke came to her aid.

"I'll grant you, Mother, it was an unusual gesture, but under the circumstances one could hardly do less. The woman was in dire need. We should have slipped her a coin."

"I did," Margaret admitted.

He laughed. "I know. After you turned away, I saw her bite it to test its authenticity."

Margaret sighed heavily. "Then why did you say what you did?"

He shrugged. "To see if you would admit it, I suppose."

"That was rather shabby of you."

"Yes, it was. I'm sorry."

Margaret nodded without responding. Oddly enough it seemed to her that some of the stiffness between them disappeared during the ride back to the mansion.

After seeing them safely home, the duke excused himself for the rest of the day.

"But you will return in time for dinner, won't you?" the duchess asked.

He nodded. "That is my plan. I have decided to remain at home this evening."

"Excellent." She patted his cheek. "I'll have cook prepare something special to celebrate the occasion."

Mr. Trembe stayed on for tea. Margaret, thinking they might enjoy some time alone, pleaded a headache and spent the rest of the day in her room.

When Corrine came up to help Margaret dress for dinner, she casually mentioned that the duchess planned to dine alone in her room. Margaret stood stock-still as the full meaning of the news dawned on her. The duke would be home for dinner, and she would be dining with him alone.

## CHAPTER TWELVE

Margaret rarely wore her hair down over her shoulders. It had seemed more businesslike to wear it in a coil on the top of her head while she was at the bookstore. Corrine had a penchant for sculptured curls and rebelled at the idea of letting it fall into its natural waves. But when she saw the effect, she grudgingly admitted her mistake.

"That's not to say, miss, that I admired the way it looked when you came home all windwhipped and wild from the docks this afternoon. Indade! I thought I would never get rid o' the rats nests short o' cuttin' it off." She stroked it with the brush until it crackled and glistened. "I'll wager hit will look right presentable when we've finished."

She handed the mirror to Margaret, who walked over to the pier glass and studied the back of her head.

"Does it truly look all right, Corrine? I'm not too old to wear it down over my shoulders like a schoolgirl?"

"Indade not! You aren't old. Stop fretting about it or you'll get lines. That's when you start thinkin' old."

Margaret was still smiling when she went downstairs to dinner. She had chosen the green dress, an unneccesary luxury for dinner at home, but she wanted to make it a special occasion. This was the first time that she and the duke had dined alone in the evening.

The dress was cut fuller than most. Its soft fabric was laid in overlapping tiers, which gave the effect of flower petals floating one on top of the other. The waist was pulled tight while the bodice blossomed out to emphasize the fullness of her bust. Designed to take maximum advantage of a woman's natural attributes, the dress was less conservative than Margaret would have wished.

Its design was not lost on the duke. He turned as she entered and lifted his glass. "I see you have fully recovered from your expedition to the docks. You look lovely, Lady Margaret." He offered a glass of sherry which she accepted.

"Thank you, your grace. I perceive that the afternoon bore no ill effects for you."

He smiled dryly. "At least nothing discernible." He motioned toward the dining room. "I was surprised to see but the two plates set for dinner. Can it be that the duchess is indisposed?"

"Not unduly so. According to Corrine, her grace simply prefers her own company tonight. Regrettable, since she made such a point of your being home."

He shrugged. "Not entirely. I had, at any rate, planned to remain at home this evening."

Margaret smiled. Their gaze met and held. It was an awkward moment which was saved when Thomas gave the signal that dinner was served. The duke bowed and offered his arm which, after a slight hesitation, Margaret took, allowing herself to be escorted to the table.

He seated her on his left. A silver candelabrum was placed at their end of the table, leaving the other end in semidarkness. It gave an intimate feeling to the room, as if they were isolated from the rest of the world in their own small bubble of light.

The table was laid with a pale pink damask cloth

embroidered at the hem with tiny flowers in a darker shade of pink. Green leaves stitched to create a garland effect were repeated in a garland of living leaves at the base of the candelabrum. Waxy camelias in shades of red and pink were set among the circle of leaves. A narrow silver edge on white porcelain plates matched the heavy silver water goblets.

Margaret was impressed. "If the food compares to the quality of the decor, I'm sure we will dine in style tonight." She picked a pink camelia and held it to her face. "One of the things I've missed most . . . fresh flowers from the hothouse. Pink is one of my favorite colors."

"I'm relieved to hear that."

"Indeed?"

She waited for his response, but he chose to ignore the question. There was little time to puzzle over it because the butler appeared with a steaming tureen of oxtail soup. The rest of the meal included such delicacies as pheasant baked in red wine, reindeer's tongue, truffles, ham from Portugal, and cheese from Parma.

While they waited for the table to be cleared between courses, the duke leaned back in his chair. "I see from the number of finished drawings that you have gone a long way toward completing the documentation of the collection. It never occurred to me that you would have done so much in such a short time."

Margaret was amused by his comment. So much had happened to her since she had come to Walden House that it seemed as if she had been there forever.

She folded her hands in her lap. "Learning a new hand script is sometimes rather arduous, but once one becomes familiar with the style, using it is not difficult." She smiled. "Of course this is dependent upon early training in the basic calligraphy skills. I was fortunate enough to learn from a master."

"You are better educated than any woman I know."

"Apparently that distresses you."

"Not in the least." He cleared his throat and attempted to change the conversation. "The season will be over soon. At that time I will be in residence at my country house in Waldenspire. The duchess, of course, will accompany me. It was my plan to take you with us, should you care to go."

Margaret tilted her head. "I am honored, your grace. But I find myself wondering to what end you wish to include me. As you say, the calligraphy for which you hired me is nearly complete."

He stroked his hand across his chin. "A small portion of the collection which still remains to be cataloged is housed at the farm in Waldenspire. It would be more expedient to take you there than to try to bring the pieces here. One of them is a large sundial mounted on a stone wall in the garden."

Margaret breathed a sigh of relief. She had not yet saved enough money to reopen the bookstore. Before she could obtain a loan from the lending bank, she would have to save a considerably larger amount.

She laughed. "Under those circumstances I would very much like to go to the country house." Surely it must have occurred to him that it was unnecessary for her to actually see the items she was cataloging. All she required were a few notes with a brief description and historical background for each item. She reached for the goblet and sipped her water.

"How soon do you plan to leave?"

"As soon as possible. A good deal depends upon how things go with the administration. With a little luck the four of us should be able to leave by this time next week."

"The four of us?" Her voice sounded thin and brittle to her own ears but she had to know. "Is Lady Jordice expected to join us in the country?"

He leaned back and drummed his fingers on the edge of the chair. "I was referring to Mr. Trembe. As to Jordice, I rather think we have seen the last of her." His fingers paused in midair. "The subterfuge which you used to hide her penchant for other people's possessions has finally surfaced, Lady Margaret. I do appreciate the fact that you tried to spare my feelings, but, in truth, there was little need."

He moved forward and leaned his elbows on the table, resting his chin in his hand. "While I do not deny that Lady Jordice has a tremendous physical attraction, and that our families went to great length to effect an alliance between the two of us, I have known for some time that a marriage between us would never work. Our betrothal was never official. You must have realized that since you knew that I had been seeing other women."

"Ah yes. Lady Alvira, for one. How could I forget the brooch you brought back from America?"

He gave her a look and continued as if he had not heard. "I must admit that at one time I seriously considered marrying Jordice simply for the good of our shipyard. However, she was attracted to another man who has since agreed to marry a German princess. At any rate, now that I know Jordice better, I find I could never live with some of her frailties, no matter what would be gained by uniting our two families."

"And yet you gave her that magnificent ring with the inscription which pledged your undying love."

He grinned. "Aha. You must have been snooping. The ring was given to her by the man I was telling you about. She went to great extremes to let me know he had given it to her."

Margaret looked appropriately embarrassed. In an effort to hide it, she hurriedly asked if he had told the duchess of his disassociation with Lady Jordice. He shook his head.

"No, but I doubt that she will be surprised. She is rather astute about such things. Mother will probably be somewhat disappointed since her one goal in life is to see me married to a woman who will provide her with a grandson."

Their conversation was interrupted when Thomas served the dessert—tall crystal goblets filled to the brim with fat, red strawberries dipped in sugar and surrounded by scoops of thick Devonshire cream. After they had finished, they went to the study, where Thomas served coffee in sprigged porcelain demitasse cups.

Later Margaret sat down at the pianoforte and let her fingers wander over the keys. The duke sat facing her and for a long time she felt rather than saw his gaze fastened on her. She was afraid to look up, afraid of what she might see in his eyes. Margaret knew beyond a doubt that the duke desired her. He could be forgiven that—he was human, after all. But she wanted more than that. When she gave herself to a man, it would be with everything that was hers to give . . . for as long as she lived.

Such thoughts reminded her of the night they had danced in this very room. For the first time in her life she would have thrown caution to the wind and gone with him to whatever length he desired. By the grace of God she had been spared such indiscretion. Given time to cool her fevered blood, she realized that for a brief moment of pleasure she might have sacrificed her own self-respect.

Drifting into a Mozart melody, she dared to look up. The duke's eyes were closed and, as he rested his head against the back of his chair, he looked so tender, so vulnerable that her heart went out to him. Dear heaven! Why did she have to love him? Seeing him now, like this, she wished for a moment that she *had* given herself to him. The thought that she might never again feel the touch of his hands against her skin was enough to break her heart.

Thinking him asleep, she allowed the song to dwindle off into silence. But he hadn't been sleeping. He lifted his head and considered her for a moment.

"Don't stop unless you are tired. You play well, Margaret."

"Thank you. I was afraid I might be disturbing you." He had called her by her first name, something he had avoided since that awful night. Was he beginning to believe that she was innocent of any wrongdoing or was he simply learning to forgive?

He got up then and came to stand behind her. She played as she had never played before, partly to keep her hands from shaking and partly because she wanted to please him. From time to time when he reached down to turn the page, Margaret breathed the faint odor of his skin, and it sent a surge of sweet pain through her body. She shivered despite herself.

He sat down on the bench next to her. "Are you chilled?"

She lied. "A little. I should have worn a shawl."

"You gave it away."

"I have another."

"One to match the blue dress you were wearing this afternoon?"

She laughed. "No. I'm afraid not. Are you still angry with me for that?"

"I never was angry." He got up quickly. "Stay right there until I return." When he came back into the room, he was carrying a parcel wrapped in silver paper with a wide silver ribbon tied around it. "Open it, Margaret. It's for you."

"I . . . but what's the occasion?"

"Must there be one? I simply wanted to give you a gift. Open it."

She slipped the ribbon from the end of the box, then broke the seal on the paper and lifted the lid. Inside, Margaret discovered the most incredibly soft and beautiful wool shawl she had ever seen. She looked at him unbelievingly.

"Go on, Margaret, take it out of the box. It came from Scotland, Paisley, to be exact. They have made something of a name for themselves with that particular design."

She lifted it from the box and touched it to her cheek. "It's so soft. And the colors—pink, blue, raspberry, white. How utterly perfect."

He laughed with unconcealed delight. "Now you know why I was relieved to learn that you are partial to pink." He took the shawl from her hands and draped it around her shoulders. "There's more. Look in the box."

"More? Surely not . . ." She turned the paper to reveal a bonnet of a matching fabric. "It is beautiful beyond words," she said, lifting her gaze to his face. "How can I ever thank you, your grace?"

"You called me Peter, once."

She straightened the cover and replaced it on the box before she answered. "I know. I was upset at the time and not at all responsible."

"Is that what it takes?"

She turned and faced him, her longing evident in her voice. "I don't know what you want from me. What is it you want me to say?"

He stared at her and shook his head. "God help me, I wish I knew. For the moment all I know is that I want desperately to hear you say my name."

Her gaze never left his face. Putting the bonnet down on the box, she placed her hands on either side of his face and pulled his head down to hers. She kissed him then gently on the mouth. It was a kiss of innocence, not intended to stir the blood but to seal a bond of friendship.

"Peter," she whispered. "Peter." More than anything she wanted him to take her into his arms. When she finally stepped back, she saw a muscle begin to twitch at the side of his jaw. His hands, which had remained at his side, were knotted into fists, and she wondered at his rigid control. Dear God, she thought, why is he doing this? I know he loves me. Why must he be so strong?

She lowered her gaze and turned away. Gathering the bonnet and the wrappings together, Margaret held them in her arms and turned to him. "If you will excuse me, your grace, I would like to retire. Thank you is so little to say in return for your generosity." She forced a smile, hoping that he was far enough away so as not to see the tears which glistened in her eyes. "I shall always treasure my paisley shawl and vow that I'll never, never give it away." With that she turned and fled. Without looking back, Margaret knew that he was still standing there long after she had quit the room.

Hours later she heard him come up the stairs past her bedroom to his own suite in the east wing. Whether or not it was her imagination she couldn't decide, but she could have sworn he stood for a full ten minutes outside her bedchamber door. She ached to open it and find out, but she knew that to do so would open doors that could never be reclosed. Instead she lay still among her silken sheets until the heat of her body dissipated with the night.

For the first time in many days the duke joined her at breakfast the next morning. Both of them experienced a certain shyness which, thanks to the presence of the servants, was slowly overcome. Neither Margaret nor the duke mentioned the previous night, but Margaret was secure in the knowledge that it was uppermost in both their thoughts. They spoke of casual things—the food, the weather, the house in the country. Margaret professed a curiosity she was not sure was genuine, but it filled the empty spaces between words.

"Is Waldenspire a working farm?" she asked.

"Yes indeed," he answered. "Of course I do not run the farm myself because I have neither the time nor the knowledge to do so. We have a very competent family who has looked after things for the past three generations."

"Is it large?"

He grinned. "Comparing it to this place is like comparing Hyde Park to the whole of London. We have acres of woodland, fields, streams, and even a small lake. The village of Waldenspire itself is part of the ducal grant from the king. The people who live there work our lands for a portion of the crop. Those who choose not to farm are involved in cottage industries, although the number is steadily decreasing because of the trend toward machine-made products."

She nodded. "As in the case of the Luddites. I perceive there is no way they can compete with the modernization of industry."

"Except that in the case of our people they can always return to the land. The Luddites found themselves without a way to survive. Their entire lives are dependent upon the factories."

Margaret raised an eyebrow. "You sound as if you are defending their cause. I thought you were against them."

"I am against violent rebellion. There is nothing to be gained by breaking machinery and murdering the bosses."

"Have you heard anything concerning the disposition of the cases of the men who were arrested at my bookstore?"

"Regretfully they are still being held. A solicitor whom I know tells me that he expects their release within the month. I certainly hope it is forthcoming. There are those in the House who seek to make it a capital offense to perpetrate a crime against industry."

They continued to discuss the political aspects of the proposed law until the duke consulted his timepiece and declared that he would be late for an appointment if he didn't leave at once.

Left alone, Margaret found herself in an unusually strange mood. She wandered into the study but found it impossible to get started on the collection. Instead she picked up the model of the *Mariposa* and stared at it for several minutes. Maybe, just maybe, she could find a way of lettering the name on paper, then, when it was dry, affixing it on the hull in such a manner that the background was unnoticeable.

For the next few hours she experimented with various weights of paper until she came up with a solution. Using a very thin, tissuelike paper, she lettered the name in waterproof ink. When it was dry, she went over it again until the name was raised slightly above the surface. It was tedious work since the letters were of necessity quite small. Afterward she went down to the workrooms belowstairs and consulted with the handyman who repaired all manner of household items. He gave her a small container of clear varnish which was used to finish furniture. After experimenting on a scrap of wood, Margaret decided to make the attempt.

The results were more than she could have hoped for. Having seen the real *Mariposa* as it sailed from the harbor on its way to Germany, she knew the style, color, and placement of the letters. When she had completed the job, the model was a replica of the mother ship in every sense of the word. She could hardly wait for the duke to see it.

When he failed to return home for the noon meal, it came as no surprise. He often worked through the day instead of making the carriage trip home and then having to return for the afternoon session. But when Thomas reported that he had sent his carriage on home, Margaret became concerned. She thought it wise not to question the servants but waited until the duchess appeared. When she finally did, her hair was swept into an attractive wave which began at her forehead and was confined in a jewelled pouf at the back of her head. Her eyes were clear and sparkling with anticipation.

"Have you heard the news, my dear Margaret? John Trembe has agreed to accompany us to the estate at Waldenspire. He had given a tentative 'yes,' but he sent word by messenger this morning that he has made definite arrangements."

"How wonderful for the two of you. Does this mean that you have given him the answer he is looking for?"

The duchess sighed. "No, not as yet. It is a decision not easily made. Nevertheless he is willing to put up with my uncertainty, at least for the present." She dabbed at an imaginary spot on her dress with the corner of a lace handkerchief, then tucked it into her bodice. "I've been wanting for years to show him the farm. John has a good eye for horses, and the farm has the best breeding stock for miles around."

Margaret studied her face to watch her reaction. "At breakfast this morning the duke invited me to accompany you to the farm when you go at the end of the season."

"My dear! How utterly divine. I was hoping he would. Of course had he not invited you, I would have taken it upon myself to do so. May I assume that you agreed?"

Margaret returned her smile. "How could I refuse? He made it very appealing."

The duchess looked at her curiously, and Margaret's face flamed. "Please, don't misunderstand. He told me that there was additional work to be done on the collection. Since I have as yet to accumulate enough funds to reopen the bookstore, I was grateful for the opportunity to continue on in his employ."

The duchess patted her hand. "We shall all be pleased to have your company. Speaking of the farm, I must talk to Peter when he comes in about sending some staff on ahead to ready the house for us."

"Thomas said that his grace sent the carriage on home today instead of coming home for tea."

"Indeed? How very odd. Did he give a reason?"

Margaret shook her head. "I don't know. I didn't question Thomas about it."

The duchess rose and gave a yank on the bellpull. "Well, we shall soon see!"

When Thomas came in response to the bell, he told them that the duke said he would not be coming home at all that night.

The duchess looked mystified. "Did he say where he would be?"

"Yes, mum. His grace said in event of an emergency

a messenger could reach him at the Simpson estate on Weymouth."

"Was that all he said?"

"Yes, your grace. The driver, Mr. Smithers, said his grace was in a fair rush to get away."

"Thank you, Thomas."

He bowed and left the room.

The duchess came back and sat down on the love seat, then began to flutter her fan as if in great agitation.

"Hmph. How peculiar. I've never known Peter to behave so strangely."

Afraid to speak lest she break into tears and betray herself, Margaret sat with her eyes averted. It was no mystery to her. The Simpson estate on Weymouth was a familiar name. She had been there many times during her coming out. It was the home of the Archibald Simpsons. Peter had gone to Alvira.

## CHAPTER THIRTEEN

It was worse than she could have imagined. Making a pretense of going to look out the window, Margaret used the much needed time to get her feelings under control. How could he turn to Lady Alvira at a time like this? He had made it plain that friendship was the only bond between the two of them. Could his falling out with Lady Jordice have forced him into Lady Alvira's arms? He had, after all, purchased the brooch for her on his trip to America. Margaret placed her hands against the cool windowpane, then touched them to her face in an effort to chill her heated skin.

Coming over to stand behind her, the duchess put her arm across Margaret's shoulder. "Now, Margaret. You must not jump to hasty conclusions. There could be any number of reasons why Peter is staying at the Simpson estate. It is not uncommon, you know, in this day of thugs and cutpurses, to want to avoid a carriage ride after dark."

Margaret turned and smiled with a confidence she didn't feel. "Of course. At any rate the duke is free to come and go as he pleases."

The duchess looked closely at her, then, as if satisfied, drifted to other subjects of conversation. Neither of them felt inclined to plan an interesting evening. With the duke out of the house, the main reason for existing seemed to have been removed. By mutual accord they finished their dinners and retired soon after to their separate rooms.

Satiated with sleep, Margaret rose early the next morning and, breakfasting alone, finished quickly in order to start work on the collection. Two hours later the duchess came bouncing into the room, her eyes sparkling with excitement as she held out the morning newspaper.

"Have you read the news? The Tory administration has resumed office with Liverpool at its head."

Margaret stood up in order to share the paper with her. "I wonder if it comes as a surprise. Surely they'll have to make a go of it this time."

"Peter gave me the impression that they expected a comeback even after the setdown on the vote of no confidence. But I don't think they expected it to happen this soon."

"I'm sure they must be relieved. When was it supposed to have been voted upon?"

"Yesterday."

Margaret laced her fingers together. "Perhaps they were celebrating the event last night."

"Perhaps, but if they were, it is nothing to the celebration we'll have in a few days. I'll wager there will be a party within two weeks in honor of the Tory victory."

The invitation came the following day, but even before that the duchess was in a fettle over what they would wear. She had ordered two new gowns from Madame Marie and finally settled on a violet-pink, shadow lace with a beaded bodice.

Her real indecision was over what to do if Mr. Trembe did not receive an invitation to the ball. It was highly unusual for a commoner to be included on such occasions, but his profession brought him close to people of importance. Also Mr. Trembe was quite an entertaining conversationalist. Even if he were not a special friend of the duchess, Margaret suspected he would not be overlooked on the guest list. His invitation was received by messenger, two days later.

The duchess was so excited about the party that she failed to query the duke about his overnight absence from the house. Margaret was aching to know why he had not come home but would never have dreamed of asking. And so nothing was said.

He seemed to be in good spirits. Whether this was because of the recent Tory victory or his own personal victories, Margaret could only guess. As a result she found herself remaining somewhat aloof whenever he was near. At times he appeared rather puzzled but made no comment.

One morning at breakfast he laid the paper aside as she took her place opposite him. "I have decided to set the date for our sojourn to the country for the day after the ball. It is later than usual, but because of political unrest the season was necessarily extended. I assume from what the duchess says that you are definitely planning to accompany us?"

"If that is your wish. I look forward to seeing Waldenspire, and I'm certain it will be an interesting change."

"I warn you, it is quiet compared to the life of London. Some people consider it dull."

She smiled. "I am not one who constantly needs to be entertained. Besides, there is my work to keep me busy."

"You will want to make sure that Thomas assigns one of the maids to pack your drawing tools. Things of that sort are hard to come by in the country." He drummed his fingers on the table. "Are you looking forward to the ball?"

"Yes, very much, but I confess, not as much as the duchess. She is thrilled beyond words."

"Yes, I know. Were it not for your presence in the house, she would probably have turned down the invitation. You've added another dimension to her life, and I thank you for that. It does her good to have someone young with whom to share things." He stroked a hand across his moustache. "In regard to that, I have a favor to ask of you."

"But of course. Anything; all you have to do is ask."

He looked at her speculatively, then cleared his throat. "Yes, well. The duchess seems to have discovered, as she puts it, 'a simply divine creation that is absolutely perfect for Margaret.' She wants it to be her gift to you for the ball, but she is concerned that you will not accept it. That is why she has enlisted my services to plead her cause."

Margaret knotted her fingers on her lap. "Surely she must know how I feel about accepting such gifts. Indeed, the salary which you are paying me is in itself almost a gift. It is much more than could be expected for services of this sort. You must be aware of that."

"I am entirely satisfied with our arrangement. As to the other, has it not occurred to you that there are times when it is more generous to receive than to give?" He reached down and took her hands, then held them between his palms. "You are a very difficult person to do things for, Margaret Battersby Spence. Can you not find it in your heart to forgo your blessed independence just this once and please a dear old lady?"

Margaret was surprised at the seriousness of his tone but, looking into his eyes, she saw the flicker of devilment. She smiled, dimpling the corners of her mouth.

"Stop playing the fool, your grace," she said as she gently removed her hands. "If providing me with a new gown will give your mother such satisfaction, her pleasure will surely not exceed mine. Indeed the real joy is sharing her companionship. We have become quite good friends during the past weeks."

"I can see the change in her, and it pleases me. It's settled then. I can tell her you will accept the gown?"

Margaret nodded.

He laughed. "That is certainly a relief. I believe she has taken the liberty, knowing my powers of persuasion, of purchasing the gown and having it sized to your particular measure."

Margaret raised an eyebrow. "Indeed? Knowing you, your grace, I'm sure it was *you* who told *her* to rely on your persuasive powers. Your charm is only exceeded by your self-confidence."

He grinned. "Would that it were true. You may have a point, though. I've been working hard and long to convince Parliament to settle with the Americans in order to avoid another war. I think we have just about reached an agreement."

Margaret moistened her lips. "How wonderful. Was that what you were doing the night you stayed at the Simpson estate?"

He looked up surprised. "Oh no, that was . . ."

Before he could finish his sentence, the duchess walked in, full of energy and bubbling with excitement.

"Good morning, you two. I decided the day was just too lovely to spend in my rooms."

The duke rose and bowed her to a chair. "It's a fine day, even for the early part of June. I thought the weather would be oppressively hot by now. May I serve you some strawberries?"

"Indeed, and some scones, too, if the candle burner

168

has kept them warm." She turned to Margaret. "My dear, has he had a chance to talk to you about my little surprise?"

The duke laughed. "It was a struggle, Mother, but I finally convinced her to accept your gift."

The duchess clasped her hands under her chin. "Splendid! Immediately after breakfast you must try on the gown." They talked for a while and then the duke excused himself and promised to be home in time for tea.

Margaret watched him go. She had held to the slim hope that his visit to the Simpson house could have been other than social, but even though he had not finished what he had begun to say when the duchess walked in, it was apparent he had not been concerned with the Regent's business. The knowledge dimmed considerably the happy glow which surrounded preparations for the ball and the move to the country estate.

During the next few days there was little time to think of anything save the work at hand. Because several members of the duke's staff had been sent on ahead to prepare the country house for the family's arrival, there remained much work to be done within a limited time. Margaret, having completed the calligraphy by working long after the best light had faded, did her part by putting the dust covers on the furniture in rarely used rooms. Afterward she saw to it that her own things were in readiness to be packed for the trip. The heavier, cold-weather clothing would be left to hang in the closet until her return.

Before anyone was ready for it, the day of the ball had arrived. Originally planned to take place in the palace, the decision was made to hold the ball at Carlton House, the residence of the Prince Regent. King George had improved considerably during the past weeks, but that particular week in June he drifted into another bout of uncontrollable frenzy, and his physicians found it necessary to confine him to a straight jacket.

Corrine had gone into ecstasy when she saw the ball gown the duchess had bought for Margaret. The fabric was watered silk of a kind unfamiliar to any of the women of the household. The pale, misty colors of pink, blue, green, and yellow gave the illusion of movement, like water drifting over the white background. The skirt was cut slim but was overlaid with loose panels of the same material. It was cinched tight at the waist and the bodice molded to the figure with uplifting reverence. While the current fashion dictated a rather generous display of the upper bosom, this dress was designed to titillate rather than shock.

Margaret loved it from the moment she saw it. By the time Corrine had worked her magic with the curling tongs, Margaret was convinced that never again would she look as presentable as she did that night.

When she and the duchess were met at the foot of the great staircase, the duke and Mr. Trembe regarded them with proper awe.

Mr. Trembe turned to the duke. "Your grace, I'm sure you will agree that we are favored by the gods to merit the privilege of escorting two such beautiful ladies."

The duke smiled and bowed in his most formal way. "Suffice it to say that if perfection is possible, the ladies have certainly attained it tonight."

The duchess laughed. "My dears, if courtliness were a crown, the two of you would surely be kings."

Margaret was suddenly very shy. Rather than trust her voice, she smiled and curtsied to each of the men in turn. She thought the four of them were a fine-looking group. Mr. Trembe wore a pale blue waistcoat and matching breeches with the traditional white stockings. A white ruffled neckcloth complemented his deep thatch of snowy white hair.

The duke was dressed more formally than she had seen before. His waistcoat and pants were the color of thick, heavy cream topped off with a matching cravat edged with tatted lace. He, too, wore the white stockings and diamond-buckled dancing shoes which were considered an absolute necessity for formal wear.

They were off to a good start. The conversation was pleasant during the carriage ride to Pall Mall. The streets were already jammed with carriages from the wealthier houses in London. Matched teams of horses decked out in gold and silver harness vied for attention with the satin and gold braided livery of the drivers. Gas lanterns lighted the avenue as they turned toward St. James's Park and drew to a halt in front of the colonnade of Ionic columns which screened Carlton House from the street. Carriages were directed by a sergeant-at-arms to enter through one of the imposing gateways and exit by the other after having deposited their passengers.

The duke handed them down and waited for Mr. Trembe to offer the duchess his arm, then offered his own to Margaret. The mere fact of his touch reminded her that there would be dancing tonight. Would he disappear this time, as he had when Jordice accompanied them to the party? Or would he remain to dance with her? The anticipation sent warmth flooding her skin. It was tempting fate. Things happened to them when they danced.

She found herself being greeted and making appropriate responses, but it was as if she were watching herself from a distance. Carlton House was packed with celebrants, but the Regent had yet to make his appearance. Perhaps this was fortunate because bits of conversation drifting about the room alluded to his extravagant tastes. They gossiped about everything from the impressive entranceway, which architect Henry Holland was supposed to have adapted from the Hotel de Salm in Paris, to the Regent himself, who wore false whiskers to fill the bare spots and tight corsets to restrain his ever-increasing girth.

Margaret asked the duke if what she had heard was true. He tilted his head and curled his lower lip over his moustache, as he was inclined to do when thinking.

"Yes, I suppose it is, but there are many things about the Regent which are quite admirable. To begin with, he is far more intelligent than people suspect. He has a fine eye for artistic merit and a great sense of humor. Unfortunately he is inclined to extravagance in whatever he does, and that is one thing people find hard to forgive."

From a distant room they could hear the musicians begin another song. The duchess motioned them to follow, and they made their way through the crowd to the ballroom. A few dancers were twirling to a Devonshire minuet, the ladies with their skirts held just high enough to afford the briefest glimpse of a white-clad ankle, while the men, keeping their distance, bowed and pointed their toes.

They had found a spot to gaze at the dancers when the duchess and Mr. Trembe became involved with a group of their cohorts and drifted to another side of the room. The duke ran his finger around his high starcher and looked at Margaret.

"Would you like to dance, Margaret?"

She ran a swift tongue across her lips. "I . . . I. Yes, if you would."

He bowed and handed her onto the dance floor. Margaret was grateful that the dance was another minuet and not a waltz. As much as she hated to believe it, she was beginning to wonder if Lord Byron was right when he said that the waltz encouraged wantonness.

They danced for a few moments until she was claimed by the lieutenant whom she had met when she first came to live at Walden House. He was a reasonable dancer but was so impressed with the sound of his own voice that it began to sound like a bee buzzing in her ear.

A sudden turn to the right gave her a brief glimpse of Count Dantoni, who appeared to be under the spell of a red-haired beauty. Margaret caught her breath and prayed that he wouldn't notice her as they danced too nearby for comfort. When the song ended, she managed to leave the floor in record time, with the bewildered lieutenant following after her. Before she had time to meld with the crowd, another man claimed her for the first waltz of the night.

She gritted her teeth, but oddly there was no sensation of intimacy with this young man, just the pleasant feeling of being guided expertly across the floor. Still she never felt safe. Her gaze constantly searched for Count Dantoni. At one point they passed dangerously near where he stood talking to a pretty debutante. Margaret decided she had danced enough for the moment and, when the dance was over, she dropped a curtsy to her partner but declined another round.

Luckily the duke had seen her leave the floor and came forward.

"Are you all right, Margaret? You look a little faint."

She unsnapped her fan and began to flutter it in front of her face. "I'm quite well, thank you. Just a little breathless. The air is rather close in here."

He offered his arm. "Shall we find a room that is less crowded?"

Margaret studied his face for an instant, then nodded. "I'd like that very much. Have you been here before, to Carlton House?"

"Yes, two years ago when the gala was held in June, and a few times since then to more intimate dinners for fifty or seventy-five."

"Where are we going?"

He looked amused. "Do I detect a note of alarm?"

She gave him a look intended to sear. He appeared hard put to keep from laughing.

"Save your panic, Lady Margaret. We are going through the small salon toward the conservatory. You told me once you are partial to hothouse flowers. I thought you might like to see a particularly nice collection."

She smiled, relaxing against his arm. As she did she felt him stiffen for an instant, then draw her closer against him. A thread of fire began in her feet and slowly spread upward through her legs. Both of them seemed afraid to break the spell with conversation. They paused once in the small salon to view a group of paintings by the old Dutch Masters. Another group of fugitives from the dance floor remarked that the Regent had bought a dozen priceless paintings from a French collector who was impoverished because of the war.

They moved on toward the conservatory. The strains of music were muted now with distance but were still loud enough to provide a pleasant background. Through the screened entrance to the hothouse one could already catch the aroma of damp earth blended with the scent of exotic flowers. The duke opened the door and motioned her to precede him.

Margaret stared in wonder. "But it's more than a

hothouse. One could almost hold a dance in here." She walked over to the wicker chairs and tables which were placed at intervals for maximum comfort.

Everywhere they looked, gigantic vines with purple flowers, strange foliage plants with multicolored leaves, and all manner of tropical flowers assailed their senses. Great palm trees stood in granite tubs with their fronds reaching for the roof, which was dark now save for the light inside from a dozen torches affixed to standards near the outside wall.

As they strolled beneath a thick-trunked vine which arched overhead, Margaret let out a shriek and brushed at her shoulder.

The duke was instantly alert. "What is it? Are you hurt?"

"I . . . No, I don't think so. Something touched my shoulder."

He brushed at the corner of her skirt and turned her around. A leaf dropped to the ground and he picked it up, rubbing it between his fingers.

"See. It was nothing but a leaf from the olive tree."

"I . . . I'm sorry to have been so giddy. I thought it was a spider." She lifted her face to his. "What you must think of me."

His voice was deep and husky when he finally spoke. "Suffice it to say that I think of you, Margaret. I think of you."

As they stood looking at each other, the music began again, this time in the strains of a waltz. After what seemed like an eternity, the duke bowed. "May I have the honor of this dance, Lady Margaret?"

She curtsied long and low. "The honor is mine, your grace."

She went into his arms as if she belonged there. This time there was no question of him holding her at a distance. They came together as if their bodies were cut from the same mold, hollow meeting curve, curve meeting hollow. Margaret gloried in the strength of his body and prayed that the moment would go on forever.

# CHAPTER FOURTEEN

His lips were against her temple as they circled the room in time to the music. She caught the scent of his body, a blending of musk and bay leaves from the clothespress where his clothing had been stored. She inhaled deeply, treasuring the aroma against the inevitable times of loneliness and despair.

She was like a dandelion seedling in his arms, light and airy, made weightless by a thousand sensations of joy as they floated through the haunting melody.

He breathed her name against her hair. "Margaret, Margaret, my miracle of miracles."

She lifted her face. His mouth was inches away. His eyes, dark with desire, memorized her face. Their footsteps slowed as if some great weight pulled against them, dragging them to a halt in the circle of light beneath the torch. He bent lower, drawing her closer still, until his mouth found hers in an agony of bliss.

Margaret responded with an eagerness born of a need too long denied. As he drew back for a moment, she reached for his hand. Cupping his palm against her mouth, she drew circles of fire with her lips. He pulled her head against his chest and buried his face in her hair.

The music had ended, but they clung to each other, swaying in time to a rhythm older than song, punctuated by the pounding of their hearts.

The sound of voices brought them back to their senses, voices of women laughing and chatting as they came down the corridor which led to the conservatory. Margaret pulled away and smoothed her gown into place as they pretended to inspect the foliage of a banana tree.

The door burst open and a half-dozen women converged around them. Lady Alvira, in the foreground with her mother, pulled the duke to one side and spoke to him in a low voice. He nodded once or twice, looked over at Margaret who was surrounded by the group of women, then nodded in her direction and proceeded to leave abruptly with Lady Alvira on his arm. The Marchioness Simpson remained behind and turned to Margaret.

"My dear Margaret, I hope you will forgive our stealing Peter away from you for the moment. But really, dear, you have had him to yourself for an unconscionably long time."

Margaret fought grimly to control her temper. "Indeed, Lady Simpson, the duke is free to come and go as he pleases. I profess no claim to his time."

"Of course, my dear. I simply didn't want you to get your hopes up. We do, after all, feel responsibility to you since the tragic death of your parents . . . a year ago, wasn't it?"

"Nearly four years ago, your ladyship."

The marchioness fanned herself rapidly. "Indeed? Well, time does have a way of passing. Alvira tells me that you are living under the protection of the duke. Just what is it you do for him?"

Before Margaret could answer, there was a titter of laughter among the girls who were listening to the conversation with undisguised curiosity. At that moment Count Dantoni walked in with a woman on each arm. He looked quickly from Margaret to the marchioness, taking stock of the unpleasant situation.

The marchioness continued to prod. "Well, tell us, dear. One can't help but be curious just what it is you have to offer to a man of his stature. My solicitor, who happens to be a friend of your Mr. Darchester, said that the duke paid off your debts from the bookstore to save you from prison."

Margaret felt trapped. They were all looking at her, save the count who seemed to be doing something to a bed of vines. She started to reply to the marchioness, when he let out a yell.

"I say there . . . look sharp." He dropped to his knees and scrambled around on the floor as if looking for something.

"What is it, Adolfo?" the marchioness demanded.

"Nothing, my lady. Only a small green snake. I simply didn't wish you to step on it."

The room erupted in a chorus of shrieks as the women scrambled to be the first one through the door. Too stunned to move, Margaret remained where she was. Then, seeing the grin on the count's face, she leaned against the planting bench and shook her head.

"I might have known it was a ruse. There isn't an honest bone in your body, Count Dantoni."

He stood and dusted his hands together. "What an unkind thing to say when I have just saved you from being torn to shreds by a flock of harpies."

She inclined her head. "I suppose I do owe you an apology. I'm afraid I had allowed the conversation to get out of hand. Thank you for intervening."

He clicked his heels together and bowed. "The pleasure was mine." He grinned. "How else was I to manage to get you all to myself?"

"Don't think you've gained an advantage. One experience of being alone with you is quite enough for me. If you'll excuse me . . ."

He put his hand on her arm. "Don't go, Margaret. I want to talk to you. I've wanted to talk to you ever since that night." He rubbed his chin and moved it from side to side. "But it took me half a month to be able to talk at all. Your knight in shining armor fights like a pugilist."

"Whatever you got, you deserved. The damage done to my reputation will not soon be forgotten."

"God's truth! I tried to tell him you were untouched, and yet he bears me this deep enmity. I cannot for the life of me understand it. Did you tell him I dragged you to my room?"

She lowered her gaze and shook her head. "I told him I went willingly."

He groaned. "So that's it. By all the saints. Had you sense enough to lie, he would have struck me and that would have been the end of it. The way it is, he will carry his hatred of me until I rot in the grave."

"Indeed. But that is better than having him hang for sending you to the grave, for that is surely what would have happened had he known the truth."

He shrugged. "You may be right." Reaching for a tendril of her hair, he curled it around his finger. "And what of the torch you carry for him, little one? Has he come to realize what treasure awaits on his doorstep?"

Margaret hesitated. How could she answer such a question? The duke must surely know the desire that burned within her when they touched. Indeed, had she tried, she would not have long succeeded in hiding her feelings. Before she could frame an answer, the count grew serious.

"In heaven's name, Margaret. He hasn't taken advantage of you, has he?"

Margaret's face turned bright pink. "Indeed not! It is impertinent of you to suggest such a thing, Count Dantoni. The duke is always a gentleman."

"My apologies, my lady. I didn't mean to tread on a sore spot. How is it that such a gentleman can desert a lady to twirl another lady on the dance floor? I'll wager he is this very minute waltzing the Lady Alvira around the ballroom."

She tried to keep the hurt from showing in her face but was apparently unsuccessful. He picked up her hand and touched it to his lips.

"Forgive me, Margaret, but isn't it best to be prepared? Come, dance with me and show him how little it matters what he does."

She bit her lip to fight back the tears as he continued.

"You look stricken. Don't let him see it, my lovely. The lion only pursues the prey which flees. Waiting alone in the dark will gain you nothing." He took her hand and led her unprotestingly back to the ballroom.

The music had been going on for hours and the dancers, beginning to tire now, had drifted to the refreshment table to fill their glasses with syllabub punch laced with wine. Only a few determined couples remained. The duke was not among them. Margaret searched the count's face for a clue. He blanched.

"On my word, your ladyship, I swear I saw him dancing with Alvira just before I came to find you."

She spied him at last, talking to a group of distinguished-looking men. Lady Alvira, a cat-in-the-cream smirk tattooed on her face, clung to his arm like a leech on a boil.

Margaret pulled herself up straight. Would she never learn? The extent of her stupidity appalled her. Whenever they were alone, the duke practically groveled at her feet, but when Lady Alvira crooked her little finger, he went running without so much as a by-your-leave. She forced a smile on her face and curtsied to the count.

"I believe you invited me to dance, Count Dantoni?"

He offered his arm. "Your wish is my command, Lady Margaret."

Save for two other couples of vintage age, Margaret and the count were the only dancers on the floor. As the music swelled into the strains of a double-time waltz, the count swept her into his arms and whirled her around the floor. He was an expert dancer and he threw all caution to the wind as he dipped and swooped, lifting her and twirling her with incredible grace. Their performance was not lost on the bystanders. All conversation stopped as group by group the people in the ballroom paused to watch them. The two couples moving sedately through the paces of the dance left the floor to join the watchers.

Margaret knew they were creating a sensation, but she didn't care. What was there left to lose? The duke had lost Jordice and her shipyards, but he had Alvira with her great expectations. How could Margaret compete with that? Better to cut her losses and run before it was too late. She closed her eyes and let the music wash over her. By the time the music was over, she had made up her mind.

To her surprise and embarrassment, the watchers applauded as they left the floor. Count Dantoni, rarely taken by surprise, bowed deeply, then nudged Margaret into making a curtsy. She pasted a smile on her face in the hope that it would cover the turmoil in her heart.

The duchess looked more than a little puzzled by Margaret's action as the crowd parted to let them through. She greeted Count Dantoni with a frozen smile, then proceeded to cut him dead by turning her back to him as she spoke to Margaret.

"Wherever have you been all evening, Lady Margaret? John and I have been looking everywhere for you. First the duke disappears for an unconscionably long time, only to reappear with Lady Alvira on his arm. When you finally return from wherever you were, you make a public display of yourself. I find it most distressing."

Margaret laid her hand on the duchess's arm. "I most humbly apologize for any concern I have caused, your ladyship. Suffice it to say, after today it will never happen again."

"Indeed? Just what . . . ?"

She didn't have time to finish. The duke, obviously caught up in a towering rage, converged on them like an army of one.

"I've summoned the carriage. It's waiting for us now, and I would like to depart at once."

"Really, Peter. I can't countenance such a rude departure. The Prince Regent has yet to make his entrance."

"The devil take protocol. I'm leaving. Unless you wish to make a scene which defies description, I suggest you do the same." He turned to the count. "As for you, Dantoni, keep away from my family. Another such display as we saw tonight, and I shall have you answer to my seconds." With that he strode from the room.

The count hovered over Margaret. "It's finished, Margaret. Let it die a decent death." He reached for her hands. "Come with me, my lovely, and I will treat you like a queen. Nothing you want will be denied."

She shook her head. "No, Adolfo. I can't. Please, don't follow me. It could only mean more trouble."

Mr. Trembe put his arm around her shoulder. "She

is right, Dantoni," he said gently. "You would be well advised to stay out of it while tempers are so flammable."

Dantoni started to protest, but the solicitor raised his hand. "Please, not now. There is nothing to be gained by a public display."

The count nodded and stepped back. Through the blur of her tears, Margaret saw his face. He wore an expression unlike any she had seen before. It spoke of anger, pain, frustration, but above all, loss. Numbly she accepted Mr. Trembe's arm. With the duchess on his other side, they proceeded to the grand entrance where the duke was waiting for them in the state carriage. The duke made no move to get out but allowed the coachman to assist them inside.

For the first quarter of a mile no one broke the awful tension inside the carriage. The silence was punctuated by the grate of iron-rimmed wheels against cobblestone, coupled with the noise of carriages pulled by temperamental horses jockeying for position on the crowded streets. Margaret tried to make herself as small as possible against the side of the coach in the hope that she could escape further censure.

But it was not to happen. Still obviously fuming, the duke impaled her with his dark gaze. She would have felt his gaze even without the flicker of the lantern to light the inside of the coach.

"I trust you were proud of yourself tonight, Lady Margaret. You made certain no one missed your impressive display."

The duchess reached out to touch his arm, only to have her hand flung aside. "Please, Peter. Can't we refrain from a discussion tonight while our tempers are still high? The morrow will give us better insight into the problem."

"Keep out of this, Mother. It has nothing to do with you."

Mr. Trembe's voice broke calmly into the center of the storm. "You will forgive my interference, but my very presence gives me a small right to have my say. Her grace is right. The coach is no place to begin a discussion. Indeed it is my humble opinion that the less said, the better."

Margaret cleared her throat and spoke in carefully measured tones. "You are right, of course. I will under no circumstances discuss what has happened now. But the plans for our departure tomorrow preclude waiting until then to say what I have to say." She took a deep breath. "If you will, your grace," she said, turning to the duke. "I would like to see you in the study immediately after we arrive . . . home." She faltered on the last word but was grateful to have gotten through it. The duke stared at her for a moment, then nodded his head. Not another word was spoken until they arrived at the mansion.

The duke managed to stride ahead of them all, not pausing to assist them to the ground or greet the startled butler, such was the measure of his anger. The knowledge chilled Margaret, but she had determined her course of action and was committed to it.

The duchess took her arm. "My dear, let me come with you."

Margaret shook her head. "This is something I have to do alone, your grace."

"Then be careful. Be very careful not to further antagonize him. I have never seen him in such straits." She pulled Margaret to her and kissed her on the cheek.

Mr. Trembe's voice was gruff as he took her aside and whispered, "I'll be right here, my lady. If you should need me, all you have to do is call."

She squeezed his hand and turned to walk the lonely corridor which led to the study.

The duke was waiting at the window, his back to the room, his hands placed high on each side of the window frame. His stance resembled a crucifix and the thought struck her that they each in their own way were undergoing infinite pain. But it would be over soon, the wracking, tearing agony of verbal combat. Soon all that would remain would be years of aching loneliness. Count Dantoni was right. It was over.

She closed the door with enough sound to let him know she was there. He turned. His face was flushed and hard like chiseled granite. He motioned her to a chair, but she shook her head.

"Thank you. I prefer to stand. What I have to say will detain you for but a moment, your grace. I have come to submit my resignation from your service. It would be a senseless expenditure on your part to have me accompany you . . . your household to the farm. From what I can deduce, there remains very little of importance to be tabulated in the collection. It is time—indeed, past time—that I returned to my own world."

His face became livid. "Your own world, Lady Margaret? And just where is that?"

She took a deep breath. "In truth, that is no concern of yours."

"I'll warrant Dantoni has convinced you it is his concern."

She felt her temper flare. "Count Dantoni is a friend, nothing more. While I confess to having strongly disliked him at one time, he has behaved in such a manner to change my opinion."

"Indeed? And just how has he demonstrated his concern? By offering to be your protector?"

He had hit too close to home for comfort. She lifted her chin. "Tonight when you left my side on the arm of Lady Alvira, her mother and friends remained behind to verbally tar and feather me. Had it not been for Count Dantoni, I would have been reduced to complete humiliation."

He had the courtesy to blush. "I had no choice in the matter. I had to leave. That does not excuse your unseemly exhibition on the dance floor."

"It was not intended as such. However, I will not apologize for something of such relative unimportance. The matter is no longer worthy of discussion." She set her feet at a determined angle and folded her arms across her chest.

He came toward her, a look of pure rage distorting his features. "You plan to go to him, don't you? I won't let you do it, Margaret. God help me, if I have to kill him, I won't let him have you again."

Her temper broke, and she pounded on his chest with her fists. "You unspeakable fool. Are you so granite-headed as to listen to nothing except what you believe to be true? I have told you before that I have allowed no man to bed me." She watched his eyes narrow and, to save herself, she couldn't stay the taunt that cried to be said. "And if I had, what concern is it of yours? You sleep where you will and with whom. I belong to no man, Peter James Carrington, Duke of Waldenspire, master of all you survey . . . save one. I bend to no will but my own and that of God Almighty."

With that she turned and strode from the room.

"Margaret." His voice was soft and heartbreakingly gentle. "Margaret, come back."

Surprised, she hesitated, then turned and retraced her steps until she came face-to-face with him. He put his hands on her shoulders and in that instant she knew that she had misjudged his quiet tone. There was a look of pure animal hunger in his eyes.

"Damn you and your independence, Margaret Spence. As God is my witness, I swear you will do as I say."

"Never. If there is nothing left in this world for me but my pride, no man, not even you, your grace, will take it from me."

His fingers gripped her shoulders until it was all she could do to keep from crying out. He pulled her toward him.

"Can you deny that your body burns with fire from wanting me?"

"Why should I affirm or deny what you have no right to ask?"

"Keep silent then, if you insist. I am no fool, Margaret. Take care not to make that mistake. I judge your hunger to equal that of mine. How is it that you give to him so freely, yet you also seek satisfaction from me? Are you then a wanton?" He reached for the neck of her bodice in an effort to pull her up to his level. As he did so, the fabric gave way, leaving a long tear down the front.

She reached up and swung her hand, bringing it full force against his face. The impact stung her fingers, but she savored the pain as release from the greater hurt inside.

Instinctively he clutched his cheek, not so much from pain as from surprise. Before she knew what was happening, he had picked her up and carried her to the love seat.

"My God, I've been patient too long. You have tempted me, baited me, and defied me. Now I will do what I should have done a long time ago."

She was beyond fear. She knew that if she goaded him now, there would be no stopping him, and the knowledge was tempting beyond belief. To know the power of this man driven to the very edge . . . to have him possess her . . . She groaned at the thought of it. But something held her back. She blinked twice to clear the madness from her brain.

Pulling herself to a sitting position, she spoke quietly. "You have torn my gown, your grace. You have the strength to defile me, to kill me if you wish. But you will never humble me. Nor do I think it is in you to do such a thing. What manner of man could find satisfaction in forcing a woman to submit? Such an act would place you at the level of pigs rutting in a sty."

He had stripped away his shirt and thrown it on the floor. Margaret was so entranced with the dark thatch of hair on his chest that it took all her will to drag her eyes away. He stood over her, waiting.

She moistened her lips. Keep talking, she thought. It's the only thing to save you now. She pressed her palms together.

"I beg of you, Peter. Don't take from me the one gift I have left to bestow upon the man I love. I'll never forgive you, never!"

With a cry that came from deep inside him, he turned and strode to the window. "Go then! Be gone before I change my mind."

She clasped her gown around her and ran from the room. At the doorway she turned. He was standing once more with his arms braced against the window frame on either side of him. The flicker of the candles outlined in detail the tense hard muscles of his naked back.

You fool, Margaret, she thought. You absolute fool. You could have known the splendor of that man, but you've lost him.

# CHAPTER FIFTEEN

The night was an endless tunnel of despair stretching toward dawn. Even the sunrise brought no relief from her misery, but at least the need to be up and about gave her hands something to do. Margaret forced herself to think about breakfast. She had to eat to keep up her strength. More than anything, she dreaded facing the duke. But she needn't have worried.

Surprisingly the dowager duchess was ensconced in a chair, daintily sipping chocolate as she nibbled a piece of toast. Her gaze was guarded as she greeted Margaret.

"No, my dear, he isn't here. He's left a message for you, however."

Margaret sank down in the chair and, placing her elbows on the table, rested her face in her hands. "I've made a botch of it, your grace. I wanted so dreadfully to make a go of it on my own. Now I've lost everything in the world that mattered to me."

The duchess patted her shoulder. "A passing thing. Hasn't it been said that the sky is always darkest before the dawn?"

Margaret shrugged. "I sincerely regret that I have brought any manner of discontent on this house. It was not my intention to do so. As I told his grace, I will be leaving today. I still hold to the hope of opening my bookstore again. To that end I shall work until I have enough money to procure my loan from the lending bank."

The duchess wrung her hands together as if for once she was left speechless.

Margaret sat up. "You said that Peter had left a message for me?"

"I don't know how to tell you this. I know it's going to upset you." Her forehead creased in a web of intricate lines. "The fact is, Peter has refused to allow the comptroller, Mr. Dobson, to give you your money until the entire collection has been recorded."

"But that is absurd. He has admitted that the few pieces which are stored at the country place are of little value."

The duchess bobbed her head. "I don't know, Margaret. I just can't understand what's happening."

"But, your grace, don't you see? If the money isn't forthcoming, then I have nowhere to turn. I was depending on it to see me through until I could get myself established. What on earth am I going to do?"

"There is only one choice, Margaret. To do as he says."

"And that is . . . ?"

"Why, to go with us to the farm as planned."

"Never! I'd rather die than accompany him to the country."

"That's just it, Margaret. Peter has decided to remain here."

Margaret was taken aback. "But I don't understand. He so looked forward to a sojourn at the farm."

"Nor do I understand. As for that, I perceive that the less said, the better. Peter seems disinclined to talk about it. He has relegated to John Trembe the task of seeing that we are safely delivered to Waldenspire. Since John already planned to make the trip, it comes as no hardship."

Margaret folded her arms across her chest. "You surely must realize, your grace, that this trip is not in my best interests."

"How can you possibly know that? You have no place to go, no one to turn to . . ." She looked askance, "as far as I know. Wouldn't this be the best thing for you to do until tempers settle down a bit?"

Margaret ignored the question. She pounded her fist on the table. "He is so utterly determined to have his own way! I have never met a person so set on being in control."

The duchess raised an eyebrow. "Indeed? If you will forgive my saying so, Lady Margaret, the duke has met his match."

Margaret's face flamed. "But it is my life, your grace. Why should he choose to interfere?"

The duchess took Margaret's hands between hers in a fine, gentle gesture. "My dear child. We all affect one another's lives, whether by accident or design. No one can live unto himself, isolated and insulated from the world. We are each a part of the whole. You came into our lives quite by chance, but neither our lives nor yours will ever be the same. We have to accept it and be grateful for the good things that have happened."

Margaret nodded. "Please, your grace. You must understand that I am not lacking in gratitude. In truth, these days spent under your roof have been the nearest to having a family that I have known in four long years. I shall always treasure your friendship and thank God for having known you."

"Then grant me one last favor and come with me to the country. I was counting on it, Margaret. It would mean a great deal to me."

"Surely Mr. Trembe will be company enough."

The duchess dimpled. "In truth, I am quite pleased

to have him along, but that in no way alters my request."

"Very well. Since it is your wish. I want your word, though, that the duke does not plan to follow along afterward."

"You have it, my dear. The duke has no plans to go to the country but will remain here at the London house."

Margaret nodded. "If you will excuse me, your grace, I have a great deal to do before we leave. The calligraphy supplies will have to be repacked."

Margaret watched ahead of her as she moved about the house. She had no desire to see the duke, now or ever again. But she could have spared herself the trouble. He didn't return to the mansion until long after they had departed for the country.

Once they had left the clatter of wheels on cobblestones behind them, the rumble of the high-sprung carriage along the country roads would have lulled Margaret to sleep had it not been for the duchess's concerted attempt at conversation. She seemed obliged to entertain Margaret in the hope of lifting the cloak of gloom.

Mr. Trembe reached over once and patted the duchess's hand, a simple gesture of affection, but one which warmed Margaret's heart. She smiled and the duchess mistook it for a lifting of spirits.

"Now then, Margaret. It's good to see you looking more cheerful. I promise you'll enjoy the country. I nearly forgot. You do ride, don't you?"

"Yes, although I haven't for years. And unfortunately I do not have a riding costume." .

"Oh, I'm sure we can outfit you suitably. We keep a supply of such things for our houseguests. Mr. Trembe has promised to take me riding in the morning. We'd be pleased to have you join us."

Margaret demurred. "Another time, if I may. I would like to begin work on the collection as soon as possible."

The road meandered through woodlands, fields, and small villages, with the inevitable white steepled church set in the middle of the square, the blacksmith shop off to one edge of town, and a chandlery with a green roof and cattle grazing in the field nearby. At tea time they halted at the Horn of Plenty posting inn. An hostler took charge of the team of matched blacks, rubbing them down and giving them food and water while the travelers went inside.

The pleasant daub and wattle room was rustic in appearance, but clean and inviting. Mr. Trembe commented on the collection of beer steins which filled the shelves around the perimeter of the room, and the duchess told him that some of them belonged to famous people who had visited the inn. One particularly large mug was said to have been a gift of George the Third when he stopped there on his way to Balmoral Castle. The duchess looked around in satisfaction.

"This place never changes. We've been coming here since Peter was a boy."

Margaret wrinkled her nose. "Somehow I can't imagine him as a boy."

The duchess laughed. "He was a smaller version of what he is now, always set on doing things a certain way, what he considered the right way—his way, of course. He loved to ride in the woodlands, but he didn't care much about riding to the hounds. He thought it was too cruel. His real passion was for the sea and anything that he could make float on it." She drew a line on the tablecloth with the handle of a pewter spoon. "Had it not been for the demands of the estate, he would have bought a commission in the Royal Navy. As it was, the duke, his father, worked him harder than anyone else. He maintained that rank had its responsibilities. To deny them was to court indolence."

Mr. Trembe paused, his fork suspended over his mutton stew. "I'll say this for his grace. It is a rare thing to see a nobleman of rank attend so faithfully to duties. More often than not they prefer the gaming tables at Whites or Watier's Club to the call for the opening of Parliament."

Margaret stirred uncomfortably. She had the feeling that they were trying to tout his cause. "I'm sure the duke has many good qualities. Of late, however, I seem to have discovered a chink in his armor."

Mr. Trembe reached over and touched her arm. "One rarely finds perfection, my dear. Indeed an argument or misunderstanding now and then can add spice to a friendship."

"Indeed?" The duchess raised her eyebrows in mock astonishment. "How is it then that we have yet to disagree?"

He laughed. "My dear Eleanor, if we agreed about everything, you would now be Mrs. Trembe instead of the Dowager Duchess of Waldenspire."

She blushed prettily and lowered her eyes. "Touché, John. That should teach me not to fence with a solicitor."

The mail coach had just arrived with its load of passengers and mail from London. They finished quickly to avoid the hustle and bustle of travelers on the public transportation and were soon on their way.

Less than three hours later the duchess told them they were entering within the bounds of the Carrington grant. The farm was far from the rustic, countrified setting Margaret had expected. The house, constructed of gray weathered stone, rose like a castle above the ancient oaks, pines, and elms. Ivy vines, some with trunks as thick as a man's arm, grew against the stone with such diligence that they had become a living part of the house. They had been trimmed away from the leaded casement windows to permit the sunlight to enter, but overall they gave a softening effect to the otherwise cold, cheerless walls.

Crossing a short, wide bridge over a small stream, they entered the wide drive leading to the house itself. As the coach ground to a stop, the great oak doors of the house opened, and Thomas, shining and spotless as usual in his black butler's garb, bowed to receive them.

The house servants were lined up inside the front entrance like soldiers on review, but it occurred to Margaret that they were more like soldiers on holiday. Despite the extra work involved, the change of scene evidently appealed to them because each face displayed a bright smile.

Corrine bobbed a curtsy when Margaret came in and surveyed her hair with obvious concern. "Aye, miss, hit's a good brushin' you'll be needin' to bring the shine back to yer 'air."

Margaret laughed. "I'm sure you are right, Corrine. One night without you and I'm already in dire straits."

"Go along wi' you now, miss. I knows when yer funnin' me, but 'tis glad I am to see you safely in."

The house was large, although its low-beamed ceilings gave less feeling of spaciousness than the house in London with its high, vaulted ceilings. Ancient pieces of furniture with ornate parquetry designs lined the halls and corridors. Tapestries and portraits of Carringtons long dead covered the walls above them.

Their footsteps echoed hollowly on the polished oak floors, but it was not an eerie sound. Instead Margaret felt the house reaching out to welcome her.

"You've put Lady Margaret in the blue suite?" the duchess asked as Thomas directed their luggage to be brought in.

"Yes, mum," Thomas answered. "Miss Corrine has already unpacked her gowns and hung them in the armoire. I think everything is satisfactory."

"Thank you, Thomas." The duchess took Margaret's arm. "Come, we have to climb the stairs. Then I'll show you to your room."

The first thing Margaret noticed when she opened the door was the scent of lavender. It blended with the odor of beeswax from hand-rubbed furniture which glowed richly in the light of the candles. The floor was covered by a pale blue rug which softened the wood floors. White velvet chairs topped with blue-flowered pillows afforded places to sit or recline near the fireplace, which boasted a small fire that had been lit to take the slight chill from the room.

The bedchamber was decorated in ivory with accents of midnight blue in the design of the rug and the heavy draperies. White shadow curtains next to the draperies would filter out the morning sunlight from the east. A polished mahogany secretary stood near the bay window, where a cushioned window seat held a large vase of lavender.

"I trust you will find this comfortable, Margaret," the duchess said. "You will not find all the modern facilities of the London house, but the air is fresher and the pace is considerably slower."

"I shan't object to that, your grace. For myself, I've had enough of balls and assemblies to last the rest of my life."

"I perceive we all could benefit from a strong dose

of the simple, uncomplicated life." She turned to leave and stopped at the door. "Thomas tells me there is a cold supper laid in the dining room, if you would like to go down and help yourself when you are ready. For my own part, my disgestion is somewhat unsettled. I plan to retire earlier than normal, so I'll say my good nights."

Margaret bid her good night, then closed the door to her room so that she could freshen up before going in search of the dining room.

She was weary from the trip, but her mind was far too active to allow her to contemplate sleep. Instead, after a simple supper of chilled beet soup, thin slices of dark, buttery bread, and an assortment of cheeses, Margaret decided to go on a tour of the house. Thomas assured her that there could be no possible objection. Although it was not yet dark outside, the rooms were growing dim, and he gave her a fat beeswax candle in a wide-handled holder.

"The servants' quarters are on the top floor, your ladyship," he said. "Mr. Trembe will be in his room in the east wing, and you will probably also find the door closed to her ladyship's suite, which is across the hall from your quarters in the west wing."

"Thank you, Thomas." He had tactfully saved her possible embarrassment should she be tempted to open closed doors. Also the Carringtons were known for the great degree of privacy allotted to their servants. It was a tacit understanding that, except in the case of extreme emergency, the family would not infringe on the area occupied by the staff. Mr. Thomas was soley responsible for the behavior of the servants, as well as the neatness of their person and living quarters. He ruled inflexibly but with fairness.

Margaret thanked him, then pulled the paisley shawl around her shoulders and set off to explore the downstairs rooms. It was growing late. Most of the servants had finished their duties and had gone to their own floor. The country quiet sat strangely on Margaret's ears. She was used to the scrape of carriage wheels, the chants of scrap mongers and flower sellers, the shouts and cries of unidentified people in the night, all the familiar sounds of the city which one grew accustomed to over the years. Country evenings had a velvet sound, as if each cricket's chirr, each dog's bark was muted against the cloak of darkness.

She began with the ground floor, leaving the below-stairs kitchen and scullery for another day. It was a solid house, build like a fortress, not just to endure the passage of time but to become enriched by it. A great stone fireplace dominated the salon where braided rugs, a product of the farm's cottage industry, Margaret suspected, were scattered liberally around the room. Deep, comfortable-looking chairs were placed to permit easy conversation. She found the jade green, tan, and rust color combination pleasing to her mood. Heavy draperies of a tan, plushlike material hung at the bank of narrow windows which, stretching from floor to ceiling, punctuated most of the outside wall of the room.

Moving past the dining room, which she had seen earlier, she looked into several sparsely furnished rooms which seemed to have no particular function. She supposed that had the family been in residence during a greater portion of the year, the rooms would be used to greet visitors or for extra work space. Following the corridor to the end, she discovered the study or library, as it might have been called, since there seemed to be no separate library. Two walls were lined from floor to ceiling with expensive-looking leather-bound tomes. A quick glance confirmed her suspicion that many of the books were extremely rare.

She vowed that she would come to know them better before it came time for her to return to London.

Dark leather covered the chairs which were placed next to tables for convenience in reading. Polished brass and wood shone with the brilliance of reflected light. She put the candle down on the table and, reaching for a taper, touched it to the flame and lighted another candle. The other half of the room merged from the shadows to reveal the portrait of a young man standing on a wharf, the tall masts of a ship visible in the distance.

Margaret stepped closer and held the light at shoulder height. It was Peter, beyond all doubt, but a younger Peter, vulnerable and untested. Slowly she started to breathe again with an effort almost too great to bear. The need for him was like an ache deep inside of her, made worse by the knowledge that there was no cure for her pain.

She studied the portrait: the mouth, generous and soft, a boy's mouth still, without the moustache she so dearly loved; the eyes the same, straightforward, honest, unflinching. Did he know then what havoc he would wage on women's hearts? She listened. In truth, she seemed to hear him breathing. Turning suddenly, she saw someone standing in the dim light near the door. For a moment she thought . . . She shook her head, chiding herself for such foolishness. It was Mr. Trembe.

He bowed. "I beg your pardon, Lady Margaret. I didn't mean to disturb you. May I come in?"

"Indeed. I would be pleased for the company. I had assumed I was the only one unable to sleep."

He came over to stand beside her. "When one reaches my age, one requires very little sleep," he said. He motioned to the portrait. "I see you've discovered Eleanor's treasure. That was painted when Peter was sixteen. She has always loved that portrait. There's one of his father at the same age in the upstairs sitting room, or so I'm told. They were much alike, Peter and his father."

"I would like to have known the duke at that age."

He gazed at her for a moment. "You're in love with him, aren't you?"

She thought about protesting but knew it was hopeless. "Yes, I'm afraid I am."

"Then why don't you fight for him?"

"I can't, Mr. Trembe. He must come to me."

"I thought he had."

She looked surprised. "I don't understand."

"It is obvious that Peter is in love with you. I've seen the way he looks at you. Surely he must have said something."

Margaret shook her head. "There is a . . . a physical attraction, but beyond that . . ." She shrugged. "There are so many women with much more to offer than I could possibly give. Besides there are other factors preventing a complete understanding."

"Indeed?" He moved into the shadows and leaned back with his hands supporting his weight on the edge of the table. "Would it help to talk about it?"

"It would if I could bring myself to do it, but I fear I cannot. It concerns another man . . . whom he thinks . . ." She shook her head. "It's useless to discuss it. It can only serve to open old wounds. Better that I try to forget him."

"Can you, Lady Margaret?"

"Never . . ."

He came close and took her hand in his. "If I can ever be of service, my dear, all you have to do is ask."

"You are more kind than you know, Mr. Trembe. Her grace would be well advised to marry you while she has the chance."

He smiled. "I keep telling her that. I think she is

waiting for the duke to marry before she steps down. So you see, my motives in settling things between you and the duke are not as generous as I pretend."

Margaret squeezed his hand. "Thank you for talking to me tonight. I needed to be with someone. I'm glad it was you."

He excused himself then and went off in the direction of the east wing. Margaret turned once again to the portrait. Lifting her paisley shawl in each hand, she fluttered it about her shoulders. It was soft and silky against her chin . . . and it reminded her of Peter. Peter . . . he was never far from her thoughts. Here, in his house where he had lived as a boy, filled with his things . . . filled with him, she longed for him with a yearning far beyond the passion she had known in his arms, far beyond distance, far beyond time.

# CHAPTER SIXTEEN

Well after midnight Margaret finally slept. She woke heavyhearted, reluctant to begin the new day. The lack of enthusiasm was unlike her, and she struggled to overcome it. A tug on the bell cord brought Corrine, who was dressed in a comfortable-looking blue-gray uniform. She looked happy and relaxed.

"Aye and 'tis glad I am to get out o' me blacks. The blue shows the dirt sooner, but hit's a mite more cheerful than wearin' black day in and day out." She pulled open the drawer of the clothespress. "And wot will you be wearin' today, miss?"

Margaret didn't care enough to make the decision. "One of the old dresses will do very well. Perhaps the sprigged muslin with the red piping on the bodice. I expect to be working on my calligraphy today."

"Yes, miss. I'll lay it out for you. As to your other gown, the new ball gown 'er grace bought for you, it will 'ave to go to the dressmaker. I can mend a torn seam and fix most anything, but this one's ripped down the front." Her face looked gray with disapproval. "Men . . . such animals. They've no proper respect for beautiful things."

Margaret felt her face go red. "Yes, very well. I'll see that the dressmaker has a look at it." She stood still while Corrine helped her into the muslin, then waited to have her hair combed and brushed for the day. A short time later she finished her breakfast and went in search of Thomas, whom she hoped to persuade to arrange for a worktable to be set up in the study.

Thomas pressed his fingertips together as he puzzled over the question. "The only table I can think of at the moment, your ladyship, is the one his grace used to work on models of ships. He worked in his rooms, and I think it is still there. I'm not certain that it would be the right height for you." A frown creased his brow. "If your ladyship wouldn't mind looking at it before we move it downstairs, it might save us the extra work."

"Indeed. You say it is in the duke's suite?"

"Yes, miss. In the east wing. The third door on the left."

Until Margaret approached the door, which was slightly ajar, the thought that she was going into the duke's private rooms never entered her mind. Suddenly she felt a reluctance to invade his privacy but, as she hesitated at the door, curiosity overcame her innate modesty.

There were three rooms in all. The sitting room was comfortably decorated with tones of buff and rust brown in the carpet and draperies, while the large chairs placed in front of the fireplace were a rich midnight blue. A low table standing between the chairs held an oil lamp for reading. A book marked with a thick, gold-colored silk ribbon was placed next to the lamp, as if he had laid it there just moments ago. She looked at the title: *The Way of the Sea* by Thurgood Meacham. Other books lined a narrow wall at one side of the fireplace. The titles also reflected his love for the sea.

One corner of the bookshelves held a piece of driftwood, polished to a dull gray sheen by the action of the waves, some shells, and a dull orange shape resembling an intricately carved fan, which Margaret assumed to be dried seaweed. She picked it up and held it to her nose. She thought she could smell the sweet tang of the sea.

Another door led to the bedchamber. After a brief hesitation she walked into the room and opened the armoire. For the most part it was empty, save for a few things which were hung at one end on the wooden rod. She lifted the cloth dust cover and saw that there were riding breeches and tweed jackets which he no doubt saved to wear in the country. A worn, bedraggled-looking riding cap lay on the top shelf. She took it down and held it to her cheek. It was old enough to have retained the scent of his hair, and she inhaled deeply, touching it to her lips. Suddenly it was as if he were in the room with her, and she felt drained of strength. It was foolish to go on like this, but she was loath to move.

Finally, with a sigh of despair, she replaced the cap and closed the door to the armoire. She was out into the hallway before she remembered to look at the table. A hasty glance into the room assured her it would be satisfactory, and she hurried downstairs.

The days passed slowly, despite the fact that Margaret managed to keep busy. She found the items of the collection to be comparatively unimportant in monetary worth, but there could be no doubt of their great sentimental value. A set of pewter mugs was especially interesting. A morning-glory vine, on whose blossoms were poised dozens of tiny butterflies, wound around each mug to form the handle. The mugs were said to have been a gift to the duke's grandmother by the grandmother of the Duke of Wellington.

Margaret fell in love with a marble sculpture in the cemetery where the infant children of the duchess were buried. It was the statue of a tiny infant being borne heavenward by a multitude of pristine white butter-flies. The infant itself was carved of pink marble, faded by the years to the soft pink of a winter sunrise. She spent more time in the burying ground than she should have, but the Carrington family intrigued her as her own family never had, and she wanted to know more about them.

As the days blended one into the other with the simi-larity of routine, the duchess and Mr. Trembe ap-peared to have plumbed the depth of happiness. They were rarely apart during the daytime. Margaret felt warmed by their obvious love for each other, and en-vious, too, although she tried hard not to let it show. The duchess fussed over her, saying that she was work-ing too hard and needed to take time to enjoy the countryside.

One such afternoon Margaret had walked into the garden, which extended from the back around one side of the house. As she let her gaze drift over the hedges to the distant farm, she saw a column of dust rising from the road behind a team of swift horses. She stared at it, trying to identify the carriage. There was no doubt in her mind that it belonged to nobility. It was a state carriage, gold trim on black or dark blue, with the unmistakable sign of a crest emblazoned on the side.

A lump settled in her chest, and she found it diffi-cult to breathe. "No," she whispered. "He couldn't be coming here. The duchess promised." It seemed to take an eternity for the carriage to round the curves, pass through the lane of trees which bordered the creek, and make the final turn into the lane leading to the farm.

She squinted against the sun. A closer look revealed the crest to be twin griffons holding a sheaf of arrows in their mouths. Mixed emotions flooded her veins.

This was no Carrington coach. But if not the duke, who was it? She turned and made her way quickly to the house.

"Are we expecting visitors, Thomas?" she asked.

"No, miss. No one has left a card in the last two days."

"There's a state carriage entering the drive."

"Indeed? Most unusual." The sound of the knocker echoed hollowly through the corridor. He bowed. "If you'll excuse me, miss, I'll see who it is."

The duchess was riding through the countryside with Mr. Trembe, leaving Margaret as unofficial hostess in the eyes of the servants. She took a quick glance in the mirror and smoothed her hair into place. Her rose gingham was clean and well pressed, if not stylish. A minute passed then Thomas returned with the calling card on a silver salver.

"The Count Adolfo Dantoni begs the privilege of an audience with you, Lady Margaret."

"Dantoni!" She had to repeat the name to believe it. Her feelings changed from irritation to curiosity and back to irritation. Thomas waited patiently, then cleared his throat. "Shall I tell him you will see him, your ladyship?"

Margaret touched her fingers to her lips. "No . . . I . . . Tell him that I am indisposed."

"Very well, your ladyship," he said, but before Thomas could return to the entrance, the count appeared in the doorway.

He held up his hand as if to ward off an attack. "Now, now, Margaret. Don't be churlish." He handed his walking stick to the butler and dismissed him with a look.

Not so easily set down, Thomas raised an eyebrow toward Margaret in an unspoken question. She nodded, and he left the room, closing the door behind him. Margaret guessed that he was within easy calling distance should she require assistance. She turned toward the count.

"I cannot conceive of any plausible reason for your being here, Count Dantoni. Indeed you are courting danger, as you well know."

He smiled, not in the least deterred by her cool reception. "I've been told that it's quite fashionable to act the rogue these days. Aren't you going to offer me a glass of brandy after I traveled this distance to see you?"

"Indeed not. I suspect, were I to smell your breath, that I would find you already far gone under the influence of your last bottle."

He stepped closer and put his hands on her shoulders. "Better yet, my lovely Margaret, taste my lips and know that I have forsworn food and drink to speed to your side."

She moved away and laughed. "You certainly haven't lost your way with words, Count Dantoni, but I fear I'm immune to your flattery. Just why are you here?"

"To see you, of course." This time there was genuine surprise in his voice. "What other reason could there possibly be?"

"To what end? We have nothing left to say to each other."

"Did you think I would give up that easily? You've gotten into my head, Margaret, and I can't seem to rid myself of you."

She laughed and shook her head. "How very crowded it must be up there," she said. "You have such a variety of young ladies following you in hot pursuit."

"Ah, but therein lies the problem. They follow me, not I them."

She raised an eyebrow. "So it is not the capture you enjoy, but the chase?"

He slowly shook his head from side to side. "With you it is different, my lady. True, at first all I wanted to do was possess you for a time . . . until I tired of you. Now, suffice it to say that each hour we are apart is for me an eternity."

Margaret sank down into a chair. "I am almost beginning to believe you, Adolfo." She smiled. "Such is the state of my temperament these days. But I am not desperate enough to seek a protector."

He took a chair opposite her and leaned forward until his knee grazed hers. "I am told that your work is nearly finished. What then, Margaret? How will you live?"

She sighed. "My plan is to open another bookstore as soon as I have sufficient funds to obtain a loan."

"That might be difficult. The talk is that no lending bank will grant you a loan because of your rumored connection with the Luddites. Feelings run high against the rioters these days, Margaret. It is likely that it will become a capital offense to run with them."

Tears of frustration burned behind her eyelids. "The duchess has asked me to remain here for as long as I want, but it is more expedient for me to leave as soon as I have completed my work. I'll manage, Adolfo. I have before and I will again."

He spread his hands wide. "But how can you go back to your poverty after living like this?" His eyes narrowed. "Oh, I see. The handsome duke rears his head. I wasn't going to tell you, Margaret, but he has been seen at Almacks, the Italian Opera House, Vauxhall Gardens, and all the important places in London with one debutante after another. You would be a fool to devote your life to his memory. I can give you a hundred times what this English duke has to offer you, and I lay it all at your feet."

He reached for her hands and held them against his mouth. "Margaret, don't cast me out of your life. I couldn't bear never to see you again."

"Please, you mustn't say such things. Our lives are too different, Adolfo. The things I value, you scoff at. Even our faiths are at war with one another. I could not give you what you want of me."

For a moment his eyes burned with remembered fire. "Absurd! I cannot forget the night when I held you in my arms and you responded with the true heat of passion."

Her face flamed bright red, and she turned to hide it. "I beg you, don't speak of that again. I was under the spell of your gypsy powder, as you well know. It was not you, Count Dantoni, who warmed my blood."

He blanched beneath his dark skin. "You strike for the jugular, Margaret. The gypsy powder does not create new feelings but only enhances what is already there. You ache for a man, Margaret; this I know. Your body yearns to be conquered. Why not let it be worth your while? Name your price. A castle in Spain? A king's treasure in jewels? Tell me what you want from me."

She slid her hands beneath his. "Your friendship, Adolfo. There is nothing else I want, or will accept, from you."

His upper lip was beaded with perspiration. "Your strategy overwhelms me, my lovely one. Have you not been told of the joys a woman knows from absolute submission to a man?"

She smiled. "I fear it is too late for me to pretend as other women do. Through a stroke of fate, I've learned pride in my own life. Few slaves love their masters, Adolfo. The man I love will find his strength in goodness, not through the power of domination."

His hands were shaking as he got up and came to stand behind her chair. He reached for a curl and twined it around his fingers. Margaret leaned back and looked up at him. At that moment the duchess, pink-faced and obviously out of breath, strode into the room, followed by Mr. Trembe.

"So it is true, Count Dantoni," she said. "You did indeed have the temerity to force your company upon us even here at the country estate."

He bowed. "I fear I must plead guilty, your grace, and beg your indulgence."

"You surely must be aware that you are not welcome here."

"Isn't that for Lady Margaret to decide?"

The duchess drew herself up to her full height and moved a little closer to Mr. Trembe. "Lady Margaret has a right to her own friends; however at this time she is under the protection of the duke and a member of his household. As such she must necessarily abide by his wishes. I think my solicitor will concur?" She looked toward Mr. Trembe for affirmation.

He put his hands on the back of a chair and cleared his throat. "It would behoove you, Count Dantoni, to take your departure at once. There is nought to be gained here but trouble."

The count came around the side of the chair to stand directly in front of the duchess. Margaret watched from the side, more amused than perturbed. It was interesting to see two strong people, whom she knew liked and bore grudging respect for each other, cross swords.

Surprisingly the count appeared at odds with himself. He drew his shoulders back to a rigid position and clicked his heels. "Your grace, I have come to your

211

house today to beg the hand of Lady Margaret in marriage."

Both Margaret and the duchess gasped. Margaret rose quickly and went toward them. "Adolfo, this is no time to jest. I really think you would be well advised to leave now before you create a scene."

He took her hand and, turning it so the palm faced upward, dropped something into it. "I have never been more serious in my life, Margaret. The ring is yours, whether or not you choose to honor me by becoming my wife. I offer it merely as a token of my sincerity."

Margaret held it up to the window. It was the most enormous, most beautifully cut ruby she had ever seen. "Why it's . . . magnificent. I can't accept a gift like this. It would be most unseemly."

He closed her hand over it. "It would not be unseemly for my betrothed to accept it."

The duchess looked from one to the other, her face a kaleidoscope of emotions. "Margaret, I had no idea that you and he were . . . That is, I thought he wanted merely to be your protector." She looked decently embarrassed after having said it, but the count was unperturbed.

"I assure you that my intentions are beyond reproach. If her ladyship agrees to the marriage, it will take place as soon as she wishes."

They all looked at Margaret, who felt her face turn pink under their scrutiny. "Please. I can't . . ." She handed him the ring, but he refused to take it.

"It's yours, Margaret. Yours to keep."

The duchess looked flushed and uncomfortable for the first time since Margaret had known her. She nervously fluffed her hair, then waved her fan repeatedly in front of her face.

"I think it might be wise if we all sat down, don't you agree, John?"

Mr. Trembe seated her in a wing-backed chair, then waited for the count to seat Margaret before sitting down near the duchess. Propping up his elbow with his other arm, he tapped his fingers against his face.

"It is my understanding, Lady Margaret, that although you are without family, you have in fact reached your majority?"

"Yes, that is true, Mr. Trembe."

"Legally, then, you are responsible to no one save yourself, but I would hasten to assure you that, should you seek advice, there are many who have your interests at heart."

The duchess wrung her hands. "Oh dear, I do wish Peter were here. John, do be an angel and ring for Thomas to serve some brandy. I think we all need something to calm our nerves."

The count shifted his legs to a more comfortable position. "It was not my intention to bring such distress upon your household, your grace." He turned to Margaret. "And indeed, I would not dream of trying to force you to make an instant decision. In truth, Margaret, I would urge you to take your time in the hope that, upon consideration, you will see my offer in a more favorable light."

Thomas arrived at that moment with the brandy. The duchess gulped hers down with uncustomary haste. Margaret sipped at hers, letting the warm glow spread through her body which had begun to feel numb from shock. She tried desperately to control her raging emotions. The count's proposal was unbelievably astounding. She was positive that he had had no intention of asking her hand in marriage save as a last resort. Her refusal of his offer to be her protector had apparently been the proverbial last straw.

From a practical standpoint it would he hard for her to better herself than as the Countess Dantoni. True, his title was not of English decree, but his name belonged to a centuries-old family of whom he was one of the last descendants. His wealth was astronomical, and he wanted her badly enough to follow after her. Wanted . . . that was the important word. He had yet to profess his love for her. Indeed, although he fascinated her, she could never come to feel about him the way she felt toward the duke. She rotated her glass between her fingers, watching the amber liquid twist into a self-contained whirlpool. That was the way she felt—as if she were being sucked into the center of a maelstrom, caught up in a current too strong to resist. She needed time to think, time to weigh her options before committing herself to a course from which there was no return.

Slowly she put her glass down on the table. "Thank you, Adolfo, for the great honor of asking for my hand in marriage. You know my feelings. I have never tried to hide them from you. If you were to insist on an answer tonight, I think you know that I would have to refuse you." He nodded, but refrained from answering, apparently for fear of interrupting her. She continued.

"We are from different worlds, you and I, and I find myself doubting that there is a common meeting ground somewhere in between. I think it would be most unfair to you to even consider your offer when I do not love you in the way a woman should love her betrothed."

"My dear Margaret, are you such an innocent as to believe that love must come before marriage? I'll wager that most marriages are contracted out of convenience for one reason or another But love can grow from mutual need. I will teach you to love me, that I promise you."

214

His face took on a gray look. "Can it be that you are afraid of me still? I would give a year of my life if I could remove the memory of that dreadful night of the party at Hampshire House." He reached out to her with his hands, and his voice faltered in its pleading.

"I didn't mean to hurt you, Margaret. I tried to tell the duke how it happened, but all he could see was you lying on the bed, your dress torn and . . ."

The duchess jumped up, her face a mask of horror.

"What are you saying? Great Lord in heaven, Margaret. Just what is he talking about?"

Margaret felt as if the roof had crashed down around her head. The last thing she wanted was the duchess to know what had happened that night.

# CHAPTER SEVENTEEN

The count's face flushed a deep crimson. "It appears that I have overspoken myself." He glanced at Margaret as the flush faded to a gray around his mouth. "Forgive me. I assumed you had told them everything."

She shook her head wearily. "It doesn't matter, Adolfo. Nothing matters now."

The duchess looked utterly distraught. Apparently realizing that the duchess was at a complete loss to know what to do, Mr. Trembe took charge of the situation. He stood up and put his hand on her shoulder.

"My dear, what we need now is a chance to regroup before we belabor the situation beyond repair. Count Dantoni, I assume you have taken lodgings at the inn?"

He nodded as Mr. Trembe continued. "May I suggest that you return there until tomorrow and allow us some time to digest and weigh what has transpired?"

Dantoni bowed and clicked his heels. "A wise suggestion." He turned to Margaret. "It grieves me to leave you like this, but I see no alternative. Consider my offer, Margaret. Take what you want from me. I'll accept you on your terms, no matter what they are."

He left quickly, without ceremony. Margaret wanted nothing more than to escape to the privacy of her own room. The duchess, too, wanted quiet. She begged their forgiveness and went directly upstairs.

Afternoon had faded into early evening before anyone stirred from their rooms. Finally Margaret pulled the bell cord to summon Corrine to help her dress for dinner. Predictably Corrine knew about the offer for Margaret's hand.

"Indade, Lady Margaret, you are a fine one for surprises. You, wi' your limited prospects for a dowry, landin' such a one as 'im!" She had the grace to blush. "Oh that's not meant to sound like a setdown, but 'im bein' so rich and 'andsome, 'e coulda' 'ad 'is choice o' 'alf the ladies of the *ton.*" She saw the ruby ring tossed carelessly on the dresser. "Would ya look at that! I never seen anythin' like hit."

"Put it in the drawer, will you, Corrine? I plan to return it to him tomorrow."

The girl looked at Margaret with an expression of incredulity. "Does that mean you plan to give 'im the boot?"

"I'd really rather not talk about it. There are a great many things to consider before I make a decision." She began unbuttoning her dress. "Bring out the blue cotton tonight and the paisley shawl." She had tried to save the shawl for special occasions, but tonight she felt the need for the comfort of Peter's gift around her shoulders.

Corrine went to the clothespress and lifted the shawl with loving hands. "Aye, 'tis a fine and delicate piece of goods, this. Much better than the one you 'ad before. You oughtn't to wear hit save for company." A sly, pensive look came over her face. " 'Tis a funny thing about the other shawl you used to wear with this dress. I'll wager you niver guessed wot 'appened to hit!"

"It was ruined when . . . when some ink was spilled on it. I assume it was disposed of."

Corrine shrugged. "That were all hit was good for,

but hit didn't get thrown away. Maggie found hit, and you'll never guess where."

Margaret frowned with impatience. "I really don't feel like discussing it, Corrine."

But Corrine was not the least abashed by Margaret's lack of interest. She waited for the dress to slip over Margaret's head and then grinned.

"She found hit in 'is grace's clothespress, that's where. Hit and a circlet o' flowers like you wear around the back o' your hair."

Margaret stared at her. "Surely you must be mistaken."

"Indade? And how many shawls do you know of wot's got ink spilled all over 'em? It was the same identical one all right. Maggie was firm about that."

Margaret fought to cover her emotions. "It . . . it was probably just an oversight. He probably meant to throw it away."

"Yes, miss. Whatever you say. If there's nothin' else you'll be needin', there's a Mr. Grover down in the stable who'd be right proud of my company."

Margaret had just told her she could go when a knock sounded on the door, and the duchess put her head into the room. "I wonder if I might come in, Lady Margaret. I would like to speak to you alone."

It had been weeks since the duchess had addressed her in such formal tones. Margaret felt a sick feeling begin in the pit of her stomach as she hurriedly finished her buttons and nodded to Corrine to leave. When the duchess was seated, Margaret took a chair facing her.

"Would you like me to send for tea, your grace?"

The duchess gave a wry twist to her mouth. "I daresay if I were to indulge at all, it would be something stronger than tea. I'm sure you know why I'm here, Margaret. Much as I dislike interfering with your life,

218

I really must question you about what happened that night during the party at Hampshire House."

"Yes, I can understand that. I hope you will forgive me for trying to hide it from you. I wanted so much for you to think highly of me as a person."

The duchess nodded, then waited for her to continue. Margaret pleated the fold of the blue cotton dress between her fingers, then for a moment rested her cheek against the paisley shawl.

"I hardly know where to begin. I was upset that night for a number of reasons." Her thoughts flew back to the study to the abortive attempt to draw the letters while Peter held the ship. No, she couldn't let the duchess know that the duke had made advances. She closed her mind against it as she continued. "Lady Jordice had, as you recall, accompanied us to the party. I confess to having been overcome with jealousy. When you invited me to be among those received by the Prince Regent, Adolfo pretended that he had invited me to view an ivory collection." She lowered her gaze in shame. "I went along with the deception."

There was a moment's pause, during which the duchess watched without moving. It was impossible to read the woman's expression. Margaret sighed and continued. "He led me to the garden . . . where he kissed me. In my haste to get away, the neck of my dress was torn badly enough so that I could not return to the party. The count assured me that one of the maids would repair it for me in the privacy of his room."

The duchess gave her a disdainful look, and Margaret held up her hand. "I know. The same thought entered my mind, but I had little choice. Besides, as we entered the house, we met one of the maids who took me alone to his bedchamber. Divested of my gown, I sat down to drink a cup of tea while the girl was supposedly repairing my dress. The next thing I knew, I awakened to find the count sitting in a chair at the side of the room. I was lying on the bed, still partially disrobed."

Fury was written on the duchess's face. "Dear Father in heaven. Had he . . . were you . . . ?"

Margaret shook her head. "I was under the influence of a strange potion which he called gypsy magic." She closed her eyes as the shame of her actions washed over her. "I confess to a moment of weakness, but the instant I realized who he was, I pushed him away." She reached for the duchess's hands and held them tightly. "He didn't try to force me, your grace. Once I convinced him that I was still untouched, he turned away. He could have taken me with none having been the wiser, but he chose to let me go. For this he has my gratitude, if not my respect."

The duchess paused, then shook her head. "Still there was the business of the potion. I'll grant him a measure of decency, but he is hardly free of blame."

"True, but he is a foreigner. Their ways are different from ours. Apparently the aphrodisiac is in common usage in some places." Margaret laced her fingers together. "I find myself defending the man, and I am hard put to understand why. Suffice it to say that he spared me when I had no recourse but to submit to his demands. For that I am grateful."

"Either he is a fool or amazingly astute. Gratitude is a powerful weapon to hold over one's head. Tell me, Margaret. Are you in love with him?"

"In love? Certainly not. But in no way can I bring myself to hate him."

The duchess considered this for a moment. "But there is more, isn't there? Obviously Peter had to learn of this. It was he who brought you home, or so he told me."

"The duke returned to Hampshire House just moments after I awakened. Count Dantoni had already left my room, but the duke had apparently questioned a servant girl who told him that the count had taken me to his suite. When the duke found me, I was still in a state of undress. He had already fought with the count and left him lying on the floor in a downstairs room."

"And then?"

"I assured the duke that I had not been violated, and fortunately he believed me. But he was extremely angry with Count Dantoni and swore to avenge my shame." Margaret lowered her face to her hands. "The only way I could make certain the duke would not seek retribution was to tell him that I had gone willingly to the count's bedchamber. In one sense of the word it was true, but as a result he is left with the conviction that I am a woman of small virtue. It grieves me, but there is nought I can do to rectify it without endangering both their lives."

The duchess studied her face as if seeing her for the first time. "You do love my son, don't you, Margaret?"

"Yes, your grace, although I have tried hard not to let it show. There were brief moments when I thought that he loved me, but I was apparently wrong. Adolfo tells me that the duke has been squiring any number of debutantes around town. Peter did, in fact, make no secret of his having been an overnight guest at the Simpson estate. But that comes as no surprise. He and Lady Alvira have been friends for a long time."

"Do not underestimate your own appeal, Margaret. However, I must tell you that your attachment to Count Dantoni had been something of a concern to us. Admittedly the man has charm, but with him charm is a profession. Wealthy as he is, he can afford to spend his time courting the ladies." She leaned back in her chair and chuckled softly.

"But this time our friend, Dantoni, has met his match. This is the first time he is reported to have offered for a woman's hand in marriage. He must be terribly smitten with you, or he would never have gone so far."

"I assure you, your grace, that I have done nothing to encourage him. I find him to be good company, and I enjoy dancing with him, but I could not countenance anything of a more personal nature. For a while last night I considered my limited assets and the constant struggle which lies ahead of me, but it would be better to live in poverty than with a man I could never love."

The duchess gazed at her in speculation. "I believe you really mean that. Have you truly considered what you are giving up? I hesitate to say this and trust that it will go no further, but I was once faced with a similar dilemma. I was terribly in love with a gardener employed on my father's estate, and he returned my love. But it was not meant to be. My family saw to it that the gardener was transported, and I was immediately betrothed to the man who was to become Peter's father. He wasn't the duke then but succeeded three years later. At first I was furious at having been denied my one true passion, but as soon as the first baby was on its way, I came to respect and eventually love James. Although I hate to admit it, my father was right. Being a duchess is better than wallowing in poverty as the wife of a gardener."

The duchess leaned back and tapped her fingers on the arm of the chair. "The man is incredibly wealthy, Margaret. As a countess you would be in an enviable position of prestige and power. Think what you could do for your children."

"I've weighed his offer from all sides, but it returns to one fact and that is that I do not love him, and I never will."

"I see." Grasping the arms of her chair, the duchess moved forward as if to emphasize her point. "Then there is only one thing for you to do; you will have to go to the duke and tell him everything about your association with Dantoni."

"I love him too much to do that."

"Nonsense. It's a chance you must take. The fact that you were unharmed should be a point in the count's favor."

"Surely you know your son. He has a granite-ribbed sense of right and wrong. He would insist that the count be paid in kind for what he did."

"Then would he not also insist on his right to know the truth?"

"Please, your grace, don't confuse me." Margaret was on the verge of tears. "I have thought about nothing else since that dreadful night, and nothing has happened to change my mind. I simply can't risk the duke's life . . . nor indeed would I choose to endanger Count Dantoni. For all his weaknesses, I deem him a good man."

The duchess rose. "Your strength of character amazes me, Margaret. I'm not sure whether this independence you've discovered makes for a happier life or simply multiplies your problems. Suffice it to say that I envy you more than you can imagine. With your courage I would not hesitate to accept John's proposal of marriage."

Margaret walked to the door with her. "Your courage is greater than even you realize, your grace. A faint heart would never have survived the difficulties you have been through. When you want him badly enough, you will open your arms to Mr. Trembe, and the title will lose its importance. As it is now, you have the duke to ease the lonely hours; for the moment perhaps that is enough."

The duchess looked at her for several seconds, then nodded. "Yes, I hadn't thought of it that way, but I can see the logic in what you say."

They went downstairs to join Mr. Trembe in the salon for a glass of sherry before dinner. Although Count Dantoni was the major topic of conversation, nothing changed beyond the fact that Margaret had made up her mind to send him away.

She slept in fits and starts that night, plagued by worries and uncertainties, and by ever-recurring dreams of the duke. Late the next morning Count Dantoni reappeared at the house. He looked nervous and somewhat glassy-eyed as Margaret motioned him to a wicker chair on the side veranda which overlooked the garden at the rear.

"You will have to forgive my appearance, Margaret. I brought my valet with me, but these country inns have little to offer in the way of conveniences. The bed must have been stuffed with corn husks."

She smiled. "You look well groomed to a fault, Adolfo, as you surely must be aware. May I offer you some refreshments?"

He studied her face, trying to read it. "Thank you, no. I don't want to do anything to prolong my agony." He sighed. "Neither do I want to rush you, my lovely, but I must know your decision."

She reached for her reticule, loosened the draw string, and extracted the ruby ring. Taking his hand, she laid the ring in his palm. "No, please don't try to insist that I keep it. It is lovely beyond words, and I am well aware of its value, but I cannot accept it. I cannot marry you, Adolfo. I have considered carefully, and while I am deeply honored, I fear the answer must be no."

He gazed deeply into her eyes. "Are you so terribly certain?"

"Beyond doubt."

"You have dealt a mortal blow to my pride, lovely one."

She reached for his hands and held them briefly. "Your pride, yes, Adolfo, but not your heart. Therein lies the difference between us."

"You are so sure of your love for the duke? This duke who sends you away while he cavorts like a ram among a flock of ewes?"

Margaret lowered her gaze and turned away. "I cannot deny my love for Peter. It is something that will never change as long as I live. But even the sure knowledge that I would never see him again would not change my mind, Adolfo. I could never consent to marry you. Our worlds are too far apart. Friendship is all I have to offer."

He walked across the porch, stood for a moment, then came back to her. "I would like to concede defeat gracefully, but I find my pain is too great. Forgive me, Margaret, if I do not wish you success where the duke is concerned. What are your plans should the duke be fool enough to let you out of his grasp? When your work is finished here, will you reopen your bookstore?"

"That is my intention, but first I must secure a loan from the lending bank to add to my own savings. I would like to reopen in a new location to avoid any possible association with the Luddite groups."

"Would you permit me to help you?"

"I think not, although it is dear of you to offer. I shall manage, Adolfo. Truly I will."

He came close and took her face in his hands. "There has never been anyone like you, Lady Margaret. It saddens me to have to say good-bye. If you ever change your mind, consider my offer open." He grinned. "It isn't likely that I will ever find the courage or the need to propose to another woman." He bent and kissed her on the forehead. "Take care, my lovely one."

Tears burned Margaret's eyelids. "Good-bye, Adolfo. Go with God."

Margaret stayed on the veranda for a long time after he left. She was hard put to know where to begin, now that some of the questions were settled in her mind. The air was turning warm with the stickiness peculiar to the middle of June. A storm would freshen the earth and lighten her mood. She felt as if she were waiting for something to happen, poised on the brink of some dark precipice.

Her only respite from her problems was to immerse herself in her work. She went into the house and walked down the hall to the study. Her pens were cleaned and waiting for her to begin writing up the history of a pair of ivory bookends which had been carved in a cluster of butterflies alight on a water lily. They had been purchased in India by one of the more recent duchesses, Peter's great-grandmother to be precise. The work was intricately fashioned in purest ivory and mounted on a brown marble base to give it the necessary weight. She held it in her hands and wondered about the Carringtons who had admired it before her.

Her gaze was drawn to Peter's portrait. "Oh, Peter, if I could see you now and tell you all that you need to know," she whispered. His schoolboy eyes smiled back at her, but she was not reassured. How simple it would have been if she had never met him. The Luddites' meeting place might never have been discovered, and she might still be running the bookstore. The thought shook her to the core. Was that her plan for the rest of her life? Would she be working so hard to keep bread on the table that she would never have time to marry and have children? She blinked back tears. There had to be something else to look forward to. She couldn't let these best years of her life just slip away.

Was the duchess right? Should she go to the duke and tell him everything? Would it be taking too great a risk? The questions nagged at her but always led to the same conclusion. No matter how much she wanted him to know the truth, she had to protect him from himself.

The duchess came in a short time later on the arm of Mr. Trembe. She was dressed in a buttery-yellow muslin with a matching sunshade and gloves. Margaret thought she had never looked so well, but there was an underlying expression of concern.

"Maudie tells me that Count Dantoni has come and gone. From the look of dejection written on your face, I assume that you told him your answer is no?"

"That is correct. I had no other choice, your grace."

"Will he be back?"

"I think not. It was my impression that he will return to London immediately." Margaret forced a smile. "He has no great love for the local accommodations."

"I thought about it much of the night, my dear, and I think you have made the right decision. Life is too long to live with make-do. You have the courage to find your happiness without having to buy it."

Margaret smiled. "Hearing you say that is just what I needed. Sometimes I seriously question my ability to make decisions."

Mr. Trembe shook his head. "I find that difficult to believe, my dear Lady Margaret. You seem to have an extraordinary head on your shoulders for one so young."

She smiled. "I hope you are right, but only time will tell."

The duchess slanted a look at her. "Then what about the duke? Have you made any plans to tell him the truth? With Dantoni out of your life, it should alleviate your concern on that score."

Margaret shrugged. "My only plan is to complete my work as soon as possible, take my money, and look for another location in which to open a bookstore."

"I see." There was disappointment in the duchess's voice and something more which Margaret could not identify. The duchess fluttered her fan as if she were preoccupied and a short time later said that she and Mr. Trembe were off for a carriage ride through the village.

Late that afternoon Mr. Trembe approached Margaret in the study.

"I'm afraid I have some very bad news, Lady Margaret."

She looked at his pale face as the sick taste of dread began to build in her throat.

# CHAPTER EIGHTEEN

Margaret was nearly paralyzed. Her first thought was that something had happened to Peter. Seeing her distraught expression, Mr. Trembe took her by the arm.

"I say now, it's not that serious. The duchess suddenly became ill while we were riding. I brought her home, and her abigail is seeing that she is put to bed."

"But I don't understand. She seemed perfectly fit when you left here. In fact I thought she looked remarkably well."

He patted her hand in a fatherly gesture. "Yes, I thought the same thing. I suppose it could have been something she ate which disagreed with her. It happened so quickly I find it difficult to believe that it is anything serious."

"I must go to her and see if she needs a physician."

"I suggested that we send for one, but she adamantly refused. Perhaps you can convince her not to take any chances."

Margaret took one look at the worried expression which he had tried so hard to hide and started for the stairs. When they approached the door to the duchess's bedchamber, Margaret touched his arm. "Perhaps you had best wait here until I see whether she is ready to receive you." He nodded and Margaret tapped on the door, then entered without waiting for an invitation.

The duchess was lying in bed in a gray dressing

gown, her head propped on a pillow, her hands lying limp at her sides. She looked wan and terribly fragile, completely changed from the buttercup-yellow vision of sunlight she had been when she had left for the carriage ride with Mr. Trembe.

Margaret approached the bed with considerable trepidation, then stood looking at her until her eyelids slowly fluttered open.

"Mar . . . Margaret, my dear. I . . . I am so dreadfully sorry to be such a bore. It happened so quickly. I . . . I . . . poor John. I hate to see what this will do to him."

Margaret felt more alarm than she dared show. The duchess was talking as if she were going to die. Margaret put her hand on the duchess's forehead, murmuring soft words of encouragement.

"You don't seem to be running a fever. Are you in pain, your grace?"

"Pain? Not at the moment. Weak . . . terribly weak . . . and faint." She fluttered her eyelids and rolled her eyes back into her head.

Margaret felt the woman's hands, and they were rather cool but nothing to be alarmed about. But the faintness worried her. "I'm going to have Thomas send for the doctor, your grace."

"No . . . no." For the first time Margaret saw animation in the pale face. "Promise me you won't send for him. This local witch doctor with his leeches and bitter draughts will only do more harm than good. If necessary, I'll make the trip to London."

"All right, your grace. I'll not send for him yet, but I can't promise for later on. Are you cold? Perhaps a cup of spiced tea would be of benefit."

Her eyes fluttered again. "A touch of brandy might be even better for me. Maybe John would be good enough to sit beside me for a while."

"He's waiting outside your door, your grace. I'll ask him to come in." She positioned a chair next to the bed, then invited him to come in while she summoned a maid to fetch the brandy.

An hour later the duchess complained of a blurriness of vision and a sensitivity to light. When Mr. Trembe left the room for a few minutes, Margaret took him aside.

"I'm dreadfully concerned about the duchess, Mr. Trembe. Thomas says that it is unlike her to complain of illness unless she is extremely uncomfortable. Truthfully I don't know what to do. I'd like to send to the village and ask the doctor to examine her."

Mr. Trembe shook his head. "She made me promise not to let you send for the doctor. Apparently she has no love for the local physician whom she says is better at treating horses than people."

"But what can we do? There doesn't seem to be a fever. I'm afraid to give her any medicine for fear it might be the wrong kind. I think we need to watch her very closely until we decide what to do."

"Yes, I think you're right. I'd like to stay by her bed during the night if she hasn't turned for the better before then."

"We'll share the responsibility," Margaret said as she squeezed his arm. "I don't know what I'd do without you."

He put his hand over hers where it rested on his arm. "We may have to send for the duke, my dear. I think he would want to know."

"Yes, I imagine you are right. The question is, how long should we wait before making the decision?"

"Therein lies the difficulty."

The decision was made for them the next morning. Mr. Trembe, having spent most of the night in a lounge chair beside her bed, looked tired and wan.

When Margaret asked the duchess if she would like to sit in a chair to eat her breakfast, the duchess started to rise, then fell back on the bed.

"My leg. I . . . I'm afraid I can't move it."

Margaret looked from the duchess to Mr. Trembe, then back again. She cleared her throat. "Your grace, I have decided to send for the duke. It is only fair that he be here at a time like this."

"Yes, Margaret, I think that's a fine idea."

Margaret was surprised at the strength in the woman's voice. Had she not known otherwise, she would have sworn that the duchess was perfectly normal. Apparently Mr. Trembe had also noticed the change. When they both looked at the duchess, her face turned slightly pink and her eyelids fluttered.

"Oh, dear. The room is tossing about. I think I'd like to be alone for a while to rest."

A maid was posted in the adjoining sitting room in case the duchess should call for help while Mr. Trembe and Margaret went downstairs for breakfast.

Margaret sipped a cup of very black coffee. "I asked Thomas to send a messenger to the duke at his London residence. He sent a man on horseback . . . much quicker than a carriage. It should only be a matter of hours until the duke knows."

"Um." Mr. Trembe appeared to be deep in thought. "Yes, I suppose that was the only thing to do."

Margaret looked at him sharply. "Are you having second thoughts?"

"No . . . no. I don't think so. It's just that . . ." He shrugged. "There was nothing else for you to do, Margaret. From the way she reacted when you suggested sending for the duke, I'm sure she will rest more easily."

"Probably. I was certainly surprised that she didn't

protest when I suggested we send for him. She is always so sensitive about causing unnecessary trouble for anyone."

"Yes, yes indeed. Well, it's done. I rather suspect he will arrive sometime tomorrow, assuming the messenger finds him at home."

Mr. Trembe's remark stayed with Margaret all through the day. She had counted on having the summer to rid herself of her hopeless infatuation for the duke. Indeed she had gone so far as to secure the duchess's promise that the duke would not be visiting the farm but would remain in London. Of course one could hardly hold to such a vow under the circumstances. The duchess had not suggested sending for the duke, but she had obviously been relieved when Margaret voiced her determination to inform him of his mother's illness. Was it possible that the duchess was more gravely ill than anyone suspected?

Doubts nagged at Margaret. Had she been wrong not to send for the local physician? Perhaps even the duchess didn't know the true extent of her illness. If only Peter would arrive. She needed him to make the decisions; she needed his strength. He always knew what to do. There was never a doubt in his mind as to whether he was right or wrong.

When Margaret took her turn at the bedside, she was amazed at the duchess's restlessness. She tossed and rolled, unable to find a comfortable position, sleeping only for minutes at a time. She refused a sleeping potion. Finally, late in the afternoon she dozed, and Margaret slipped away from her bedside lest she disturb her by an unguarded move.

Mr. Trembe was sitting in the study with a book of law propped on his knee. His mind was obviously elsewhere when Margaret entered, but he glanced up.

"Is there any change?"

"She seems to be sleeping now. I can't understand why she is so restless. There doesn't seem to be a great deal of pain. She complains of an inability to move her leg, but it is more numb than painful."

"Yes, that was my impression when . . ."

His words were interrupted by the creak of the ceiling overhead. They looked at each other in speculation. Margaret put her hand to her mouth.

"Isn't that the duchess's bedchamber directly above?"

He nodded. "I think so. Is the maid with her?"

"No, I left her alone, thinking she would rest better."

They both rose from their chairs and ran toward the stairway, reaching the bedchamber at the same time. Margaret opened the door and gasped at the empty bed. Flinging the door open, she rushed into the adjoining room as Mr. Trembe followed close behind.

The duchess was standing at the open window, her dressing gown billowing out in the cool breeze.

"Your grace!" Margaret nearly shouted. "Whatever are you doing? Get back into bed before you take a chill!"

The duchess whirled around, hands flying to her face. "Oh dear! How dreadful. You've caught me sooner than I intended."

"Caught you?" Margaret asked, reaching for her arm. "I don't understand. Can she be delirious, Mr. Trembe?"

The duchess pulled away. "Delirious my foot. Stop pampering me. I've had enough attention to last me a year."

"Please, get back into bed."

"Not for a week, if I have my say. There's nothing wrong with me. Nothing at all."

"What are you saying, Eleanor?" Mr. Trembe asked.

She gathered her dressing gown in front of her and sat down in a chair. "Haven't you sent for Peter?"

Margaret nodded. "Yes, of course. He should be here within a matter of hours, assuming they were able to locate him." She stared at the duchess. "Your leg. You were walking; you can move it."

"Indeed, I always could."

Margaret stared at Mr. Trembe. "Did you know about this?"

He shook his head. "No, but I was beginning to suspect. It was the restlessness. Keeping the duchess in bed overlong would be the worst possible punishment for her unless she was quite ill."

The duchess laughed. "Oh, John, you know me so well. Had it not been for your company during the night, I would never have been able to go through with it."

"But why? Why would you pretend to be ill, your grace? I can't imagine you to be deceitful."

The duchess had the decency to blush. "It seemed like a good idea at the time. I had promised you that the duke would remain in London. The only way to get you to stay here if I sent for him was to make *you* send for him. Otherwise you would have packed your bags and run. Am I not right?"

Margaret nodded reluctantly. "But I don't understand why. What did you hope to gain by bringing the duke here?"

"I don't know. What I do know is that nothing will be settled with him in London and you in the country." She looked up appealingly. "You've got to tell him exactly what happened that night at Hampshire House, Margaret. There is no other way."

Margaret felt the blood leave her face. "No. I simply cannot do it."

"Then I will."

She sighed in defeat. "No, it would be better if it comes from me. If you will excuse me, I think I'd like to be alone for a while."

The duchess stood and caught her hand. "Forgive me, Margaret, if I have interfered where I had no business. You must know how fond I am of you and that I would not intentionally hurt you."

Margaret nodded. Mr. Trembe had stood when the duchess rose. He apparently realized there was nothing he could do to ease the situation, so he simply bowed as Margaret left the room.

Margaret felt as if the walls were closing in around her. Everywhere she turned, there were reminders of the duke, things he had touched, used; they wouldn't let her thoughts turn from him for a moment. In desperation she went outside and down the steps toward the path which led to the pond.

A brisk breeze rippled the surface of the water which reflected the gray sky for the most part, but shone blue green where the clouds parted to let the sky show through. She closed her eyes. With a little imagination she could pretend she was standing on the deck of one of Peter's ships, her hair blowing in the wind, Peter standing at her side. He had promised to take her sailing. Now . . . it was useless to dream about such things.

How could she face him now that she had sent for him? Would he believe that she had no knowledge of the duchess's ruse? She had so much explaining to do. If only she had never met him. No! She took it back the moment she thought it. Whatever else she might change about her life, she wouldn't want to lose her memories of Peter. They meant too much to her.

The clouds moved rapidly, as if driven by winds high above them. The sky cleared, revealing the sun like a drop of molten butterscotch against a background of gentian blue. She shaded her eyes against the reflected glare and turned to let her hair blow back over her shoulders. Leaning against the tall pedestal of the sundial, she mused about its past. It had stood here for longer than she had lived, its butterfly paused in frozen flight to mark the passage of hours, days, weeks, years. It would be standing here long after she was gone. Perhaps his children would trace the numbers chiseled in the stone.

She squeezed her eyelids tight to stem the tears. This was no time for self-pity. There were decisions to be made, plans to be laid. It was odd that she had found the idea of being on her own so exciting a few short months ago. Now she thought of it with despair.

She blinked rapidly. Whether it was the sunlight shining against the pond or the glitter of tears still unshed, she wasn't sure, but through a mist she saw a man coming down the pathway toward her. As she turned to meet him, she lifted the paisley shawl and let the wind float it over her shoulders like a lover's caress.

It was Peter. Instinct told her so before her eyes gave recognition. She folded the shawl protectively around her as she waited for him to approach. His face was so dear, the craggy brows, the dark, deep blue of his eyes, the moustache that felt so good against her mouth. She waited for him to speak.

"Hello, Margaret." He bowed low, slowly, as if the movement hurt.

She curtsied. "Your grace. You received my message? Of course, why else would you be here? There's something you must know. Your mother is . . ."

"I know. I've already talked to her. What she didn't tell me was the reason for her pretense. It couldn't be that she was lonely . . . not with John to keep her company . . . and of course you. Even if she had been, all she would have had to do was tell me. I would have joined her at once."

"No, I think . . . I think there was something else she wanted you to know."

He looked up quickly. "I can guess. I've known it for a long time."

"Indeed?" Her lower lip quivered. "I didn't think you knew the whole truth."

"How could I not? One can't keep something like that a secret."

"No, I suppose not." She ran a tongue quickly over her lips. "May I ask what you plan to do about it?"

"What's expected of me, of course."

"You wouldn't . . ." She felt the blood drain from her face and was unable to continue, but he did it for her.

"Give a party? Of course I would. Well, that's not to say I'd do the work myself. The staff is well trained to deal with such matters."

Margaret clutched the sundial for support. "I'm sorry. I'm afraid I don't follow you."

He looked at her closely. "The betrothal, of course. Surely you must know that the duchess and John Trembe are all but betrothed."

"I . . . knew about that."

He looked at her and shrugged. They stood for a minute letting their gazes wander over the pond, neither one of them sure of their ground. More to fill the silence than anything else, Margaret spoke.

"I'm sorry to have caused you such inconvenience, but at the time I sent for you, I was convinced the duchess needed someone, family, to make certain she received proper care. Had I known her motives, I would not have interrupted your busy schedule."

"I was glad of the excuse to come. She had given me reason to believe I would be less than welcome here at the farm."

"My fault, I'm afraid. I was very angry when you refused to let me have the money due me."

"We were both angry. I'm sorry for that." He turned to look at her. "Just now when I came down the path you were holding your shawl away from your sides and letting the wind ripple through it."

She smiled. "Like this?"

"Yes. For a moment you looked so fragile, so delicate that I thought you might take wing and fly away."

She fluttered the shawl and smiled up at him. "Like a butterfly, perhaps? A paisley butterfly?"

He grinned. "I can't think of anything more beautiful, not even the diamonds and rubies of the Carrington coronet."

She looked into his eyes, and he returned her steady gaze. Margaret felt her soul rejoice with the love she saw shining there. Could it be true? Could he really have begun to care for her, beyond the needs of the body, beyond the heat that rose in his blood when he touched her? She yearned to reach out to him and hold him in her arms, but she was afraid to break the spell.

He looked away toward the pond for a few minutes, then turned to look at her. "I found the *Mariposa* with the name lettered on it. It was a splendid thing for you to do, and I thank you. How did you manage to hold it while you did the work?"

She laughed. "It was not as difficult as I originally thought. Instead of lettering directly onto the model, I drew the letters on tissue, then glued the paper to the model."

He nodded. "Very inventive of you. More sensible than it was for me to try to hold it."

She blushed at the recollection. "Yes, we didn't fare too well that way."

His voice was low and husky. "I've missed you, Margaret."

She looked up at him. "Have you? I thought perhaps Lady Alvira managed to keep you entertained. You seem to have taken to spending your nights there as well as your days."

He looked shocked. "You've been listening to the clack and gabble of the gossips. You ought to know better than to put stock in what they say."

She lifted an eyebrow. "Gossip is one thing, your grace, but your own driver told us the night when Liverpool resumed office that you had instructed him to tell the duchess that you would be spending the night at the Simpson estate."

He threw his head back and laughed. "My God, Margaret. Did that bother you? Her father and I, along with a dozen other men from the Tory party, were trying to pull the lines of the administration together again. I neither saw nor heard of Alvira all during that night or the next day."

Margaret felt her face go pink. "And the night of the party at Carlton House when she so easily spirited you out of the conservatory and left me dangling with her mother?"

"God help me, it was the same thing. She came to advise me that the Prince Regent wanted a few minutes to speak with some of his advisors. He had received rumors that, although Parliament had agreed to the American demands, word had not gotten through to them, and war was looming over the horizon. Since then the rumor has proved right. The Americans declared war on Britain on June nineteenth."

"Dear heaven, I didn't know," she wailed. Then, almost as if ashamed of her own selfishness, she continued, "But . . . but I saw you dancing with her."

"Indeed. But only one dance. She went out of her way to ask me in front of her father and the Regent himself. I could scarcely refuse her." He gave her a peculiar look. "Has this been on your mind ever since that night?"

"But you disappeared so quickly, without so much as a word."

"Alvira said it was urgent, that her mother would explain and stay with you until I could return." He looked incredulous. "Then you cared about me? Cared enough to be jealous?"

"How could you question such a thing, Peter? You kissed me. Surely you know the answer to that."

"Oh, Margaret. If I had only known. Ever since you left, I've been spending my time at the clubs in the company of one debutante after another. I kept hoping to find someone to measure up to you, but it was hopeless."

He reached for her then and would have kissed her, but one of the maids came running down the walk.

"Beggin' your pardon, your ladyship, but the man said it was urgent that he see you. Thomas told him to wait, but he's comin' down the walk."

The man introduced himself as the innkeeper. " 'Tis right sorry I am to be disturbin' you, Lady Margaret," the innkeeper said, "but the gentleman was firm in wot he said." He reached into his pocket and handed her a velvet box. "The count told me that you was to have this right away, and, in truth, I don't yen for the responsibility o' keepin it." He bowed.

She thanked him as she turned the box over in her hand. There was no question in her mind what the box contained, but she would have given a year of her life if it had been lost along the way. The duke had stepped aside when the maid approached. Now he stood grimly straight as he watched Margaret, his mouth drawn into a thin line beneath his moustache.

"Well, go on, Margaret. Open Dantoni's gift. I'll wager it's a ring."

# CHAPTER NINETEEN

Margaret's fingers felt wooden and stiff. She turned the box over in her fingers, then started to hand it back to the innkeeper, but he held up his palms in a gesture of refusal.

"No, miss. I canno' take it back. The count gave me orders that, should you refuse to wear it, I should say that you were to sell it an' buy a bookstore. It didn't rightly make sense, but them were 'is words. Beggin' your pardon, your ladyship, but that taken care of, I'd like to be gittin' back to the inn." He bowed, and Margaret inclined her head and thanked him. Neither Margaret nor Peter said a word as the maid escorted the innkeeper back toward the house. When they were alone, Peter turned to her, his voice harsh and grating.

"Well, aren't you going to open it?"

"There is no need. I already know what it is. He offered it to me before, but I refused it."

"Open it."

Margaret felt like a child being forced to reveal evidence of some unspeakable misdeed, but she was powerless to refuse. Slowly she undid the catch which released the lid, then handed it to him. He opened it up and held it, box and all, on the palm of his hand. Margaret was convinced she saw him tremble, but he snapped the lid shut and handed it back to her.

"You may consider yourself well paid, Margaret. The ruby is worth a queen's ransom." With that he turned on the ball of his foot and strode to the house.

It was a good half hour later before Margaret managed to compose herself enough to follow. A request to Thomas sent a messenger boy to the inn, but Count Dantoni had left the village before the innkeeper had visited the house.

The duchess and Mr. Trembe came into the study a short time later and confronted her as the duchess settled herself in a comfortable chair. "Margaret, my dear, what have you done to my son?"

Margaret looked at her in surprise. "I beg your pardon, your grace. I'm afraid I don't understand."

"Come now, I think you do. When he arrived, he was quite naturally upset, but as soon as he learned I was well, his mood became lighthearted and happy. Then, after a few minutes with you in the garden, he was ready to have the lot of us transported. I've never seen him in such a fettle."

Margaret handed her the ruby ring. "It seems the count can't take no for an answer. Peter and I were alone in the garden when the messenger chose that unfortunate time to present me with the count's gift."

The duchess groaned. "Oh, I daresay that would account for it." She turned the ring over in her fingers. "What do you plan to do with it?"

"The count has already departed. I have no desire to keep the ring, even though he suggested I sell it to finance my bookstore. Naturally I shall return it to him as soon as possible."

"You might be well advised to think twice, Margaret. That amount of money is not to be taken lightly, particulary in your circumstances. One must be practical, isn't that right, John?"

He nodded. "Indeed, Eleanor. But one must also de-

244

termine what is of most importance in life and hold to it."

She reached for his hand. "Yes, I have come to realize that, my dear." Turning again to Margaret, she gazed at her with a worried expression. "I perceive from both your attitudes that neither you nor Peter have come to understand each other's ways. What are you going to do now, Margaret?"

She rotated the ring in her hand. "I'm going to leave as soon as possible. The duke doesn't need me now. He will be hard put to find an excuse to keep me from leaving . . . not that he will try."

"Have you told him the truth about your relationship with Dantoni?"

"Not in its entirety."

"You're making a mistake, Margaret. Promise me you will tell him before you leave."

"To what end? Peter is blind where the count is concerned."

"Yes, that is certainly true. And if you care so little for him that you find it a waste of time to fight for him, then perhaps it would be best if you did leave."

With that the duchess got up and swept majestically from the room. Mr. Trembe followed, but he turned once to look back at Margaret, and his face betrayed his astonishment.

Margaret was shocked beyond belief at the duchess's outburst. Fight for him indeed! If he loved her, why should she have to fight for him? Love was supposed to be the most natural thing in the world, yet for them, if indeed that was what they felt for each other, love was as intricate as a Chinese puzzle. And more precious than an emperor's jewels, she thought as she remembered the fire that seared her veins whenever he touched her. She stood at last and went to her rooms where she would not be disturbed. Above all, she didn't want Peter to see her until she had a chance to think things over.

She had been in her room for several hours when Corrine came in to help her dress for dinner. The girl was bubbling with more than her normal share of mischief.

Margaret took one look at her and folded her arms across her chest. "What is it now, Corrine? I can tell by the look in your eye that you are planning something."

The girl tried to feign an innocent air. "Go along wi' you, miss. It must be your fancy." She pulled a straight face. " 'Er grace said you was to wear the blue dress wi' the flower trim at the hem when you comes down to supper."

"Indeed? Are we having guests?"

"No, my lady. Cook's plannin' for four, I know that for certain. Shall I get out the blue?"

"You're sure that she said tonight? I'd feel a fool if I were the only one to dress. After all, this is the country."

"Yes, miss, she said tonight."

"Very well."

"Will you be wantin' me to put yer 'air into a French twist wi' a bit o' flowers at the back?"

Margaret hesitated, remembering the duke's face as he saw her hair blowing in the breeze, then shook her head. "No, thank you. I think I'll wear it long."

When Corrine didn't object, Margaret knew something was amiss. She put her hands on her hips and faced the girl.

"All right, Corrine. Before you do another thing, I want you to tell me what this is all about."

Corrine flopped down on the chair and stretched her legs out in front in a position of absolute abandon. "You'll never believe this, your ladyship, but my

Harvey has up and popped the question. 'E wants me to be Missus Grover as soon as we kin post the banns."

Margaret was taken aback. She hadn't guessed that Corrine's news was going to be personal. She quickly reached over and held the girl's hands. "Corrine, I'm so happy for you. I know this is what you've been wanting."

"Aye, miss. But 'e sure took 'is good time about hit. Him wot thinks 'e's the cock o' the barnyard."

"What made him suddenly decide to offer for you?"

She grinned. " 'E knows a good thing when 'e sees it. I'll make him a good wife in every sense o' the word. Besides 'e needs me as much as I need 'im."

Margaret nodded. How simple she made it sound. Maybe life was less complicated for the servant class. No, she was looking for an excuse for the disorder in her own life. Her short foray into the working world had given her enough insight to know that lack of funds was the original complication. She pushed aside her thoughts. It was enough for the present to wonder why the duchess had ordered them to dress for dinner.

An hour later Margaret was dressed in the blue faille, her hair brushed to a glossy sheen.

"Will you be wearin' the ruby, miss?" Corrine asked, a devilish light shining in her eyes.

Margaret squelched her with a look. "I hope Mr. Grover is a strong man. It will surely take one to manage your impertinence."

Corrine laughed and danced off into the other room.

Going downstairs, Margaret felt as if she were walking toward the gallows. Peter would be at dinner. Nothing short of a catastrophe would excuse him; she would venture a wager on that. They were gathered in the salon when she entered. Mr. Trembe was dressed in his best white waistcoat and breeches with white cravat. The gold braid on his shoulders swung forward as he bowed.

The duchess approached and, to Margaret's surprise, kissed her on the cheek. She looked radiant in a pale pink gown overlaid with pearls and tiny silk flowers in a deeper pink.

"Come, Margaret. We've been waiting for you. Peter, would you do the honors?"

He stood in the shadows, isolating himself from them. Reluctantly he came forward, and Margaret was distressed to see the tired lines around his eyes. He was here because she had sent for him. The country was caught up in a new war with America, a fact which no doubt demanded a large portion of his time. He had ridden on horseback to get to his mother's side, and the moment he arrived he become immersed again in Margaret's association with the count. Her heart went out to him. Perhaps it was right that he should know all the facts surrounding her friendship with Dantoni. Perhaps the questions which plagued his mind were worse than anything else that could happen to him. She vowed then and there to have it out as soon as she had a chance to be alone with him.

He came toward her and gazed at her briefly, long enough to be civil but not long enough to expose himself to further hurt. He bowed. "May I offer you a glass of sherry?"

"Thank you." It was odd that Thomas was not present to serve the wine, but the reason was soon explained. The duchess gathered them all around her with a motion of her hand.

"My dears, I wanted the two of you to be the first to know. I have decided to accept Mr. Trembe's kind offer for my hand in marriage. We plan to be married as soon as possible, after which, the war and other conditions permitting, we shall take a tour of the Continent."

The duke looked surprised for an instant, then smiled and bowed. Taking his glass from the table, he raised it in a toast. "To the two of you. May your years together be many and may they be filled with the joy and contentment you both so richly deserve." They drank their toast, but it was followed by an awkward lull in conversation. Mr. Trembe tried gallantly to fill it with an appropriate remark.

"This must certainly be one of the happiest days of my life. I had begun to wonder if, as they say, love triumphs over all, but I question it no longer."

The duchess smiled. "Indeed, it took me long enough to make up my mind. I think it was seeing you sleeping in that wretched chair beside my bed all through the night which finally decided me. I suddenly realized that a coronet would be little consolation had I actually been ill. My only regret was that it took me so long to come to terms with myself."

Mr. Trembe reached for her hand and kissed it. "Never fret, Eleanor my dear. We have a good many years ahead of us in which to make up for all the time we've lost."

The rest of the evening passed quickly, with dinner taking second place in order of importance to plans for the wedding. The duchess left no choice to Margaret when she made it clear that she expected Margaret to stay on long enough to get her safely married. Margaret agreed that nothing would give her more pleasure. It was strange, but Margaret could have sworn the duke relaxed considerably after that. Maybe it was the wine. She too felt less tense knowing that her departure would be delayed yet another month or more.

Knowledge of the reprieve did little to help Margaret fall asleep. After an hour of pacing her room, she decided to go down to the library in search of a book to read. She knew the one she wanted and exactly where to find it on the shelf. In addition the moon was so bright that she needed no candle to light her way. Pulling her shawl over her dress, she went downstairs.

The house was quiet. The wind had died to a mere ghost of itself, halfheartedly lifting a corner of the curtain where the window stood open a crack to ventilate the room. She traced the edge of the table with her fingertips as she carefully made her way toward the shelves in the corner of the room. The book was on the third shelf down. It was a slender one, about a third of the way over from the corner. She found it without trouble, but as she started to turn, someone entered the room. It was Peter.

She should have said something immediately to let him know she was there, but she had waited too long and was left with a feeling of having been caught.

He, too, had chosen to forgo the nuisance of a candle. Coming into the room, he slumped down into the chair behind the desk. Breathing a quiet oath, he folded his arms on the desk and dropped his head down upon them. Margaret thought she could leave the room without his having known she was there, but he stopped her before she reached the door.

"Who is there?"

"I . . . it's Margaret. I came downstairs for a book."

He swore softly. "I might have known. You always were a night prowler. I hope this time you didn't stub your toe."

"No, not this time. I hope I didn't startle you."

His tone was dry. "Being startled by your actions is

a way of life. I keep thinking I'll become accustomed to it, but so far the score is in your favor. Sit down, Margaret. I'll light a candle if you like."

She sat down at one end of the love seat and tucked her legs under her. "Don't bother about a candle unless you prefer one. The moonlight is fairly bright."

He relaxed again into his chair. They both sat there for a time without saying anything. Then Margaret stirred.

"I should think you would be exhausted after your horseback ride from London."

"I am, at least physically. My mind won't stop working long enough to let me sleep."

"Are you distressed about your mother's betrothal?"

"Not in the least. She is happy. That's the important thing." He sighed heavily. "Don't pretend, Margaret, that you don't know what is bothering me."

She caught her breath as he continued. "Since the day I first saw you and kissed you, thinking you were Alvira, I haven't been able to get you out of my mind. You seem to delight in tormenting me."

Margaret was appalled. "You can't possibly mean that. Above all, I am honest about my feelings. Never would I choose to deliberately taunt you for any conceivable purpose."

"Then why are you doing this to me? You surely must know by now that I want you more than I've wanted anyone in my life. I'm determined not to force myself on you, but if you keep this up, I'll not be responsible for my actions." He got up to pace the room. "What kind of woman are you, Margaret? You and your confounded independence! I want to believe that you are as innocent as you maintain, but I keep seeing you lying half clothed on Dantoni's bed. On top of that you have the temerity to tell me you went willingly to his room."

He came close to the love seat and stood looking down at her. "And the ring, Margaret. Even a man like Dantoni doesn't give such baubles away for no reason."

Margaret felt his closeness as he stood over her, but she was afraid to look up. Instead she thanked the darkness of the room for hiding the agony on her face. She clasped her hands tightly on her lap.

"I had no wish to torment you, Peter. Indeed, I've been living in my own special purgatory since that night. But I dared not tell you the truth. Now it seems there is no other alternative."

He came over to sit beside her, leaning forward with his arms on his legs, his fingers knotted between his knees. She would have felt less vulnerable had he remained behind her. As it was, the moonlight provided just enough illumination for her to see the anguish on his face above the deep V of his open shirt.

She ran her tongue over her lips. "That night at Hampshire House you had disappeared with Lady Jordice and I was feeling . . . left out, I suppose. When the count invited me to see a collection of ivory, I agreed. But instead he took me to the gazebo in the garden."

Margaret saw his fingers stiffen, and she hurriedly continued. "While we were there, my dress became torn and Dantoni suggested I go to his room where the maid would repair it for me."

He turned to look at her. "Why do I have the feeling you left out a very important point? Just how did your dress manage to tear, Margaret?"

"It was purely accidental. He reached for me and, as I moved away, his hand caught in my gown."

The duke made a sound of derision. "Of course it was an accident. I find that hard to believe."

Her voice was level. "Indeed? You of all people

should be able to recognize the logic. I have in my closet at this moment a dress which is beyond repair thanks to a similar encounter with you."

He stammered in embarrassment, then managed to ask her to continue.

She sighed. "The maid took me alone to his chambers. While I was waiting for the gown to be repaired, I drank a cup of tea. Unfortunately the tea contained a potion of sorts . . ."

Before she could finish, he snapped to attention. "A potion. What the devil are you talking about? Are you telling me that he drugged you?"

"It . . . it was not enough to harm me. I . . . became drowsy and when I awoke, he was sitting in the chair near the window. He thought that I would want . . ." She bit her lip in frustration. "But my senses were only blurred."

The duke was so close to her that she could see the tiny moons reflected in his dark eyes. His breath was ragged in his throat as he searched her face.

She continued. "At first he tried to force me to submit to him, but when I managed to convince him that I was untouched, he let me alone. I swear to you, Peter, Dantoni didn't hurt me. It was only because he assumed I was unchaste that he tried such a move."

"He deserves to be hung. God help me, I'll make him pay for what he tried to do!"

"No! Why do you think I was loath to tell you what had happened? I would have told you that night that I had been drugged, but your good judgment falls short of your temper. I knew you would have gone off, ready to call him out. And what good would it have done, pray tell? Dear Lord, Peter. He could have taken me without a struggle. Give the man credit for some sense of decency. Don't let your hatred for him blind you to the truth."

He grasped her by the shoulders. "Why must you constantly defend him? Wherever we go, Dantoni manages to be there. I thought I would surely be free of him here in my own duchy, but instead I find he has preceded me and is plying you with jewels. Just what did he expect from you, Margaret, that he should be so generous?"

"I grant you that originally he had hoped to become my protector. When I refused, he asked for my hand in marriage."

A spasm began at the corner of his mouth, ending at the edge of his temple. She felt her heart go out to him in compassion.

"No, Peter. I told him I could never love him. Once before I returned his ring. I intend to do it again."

"Do you swear that's all there was?" His voice was filled with an agony too great to bear.

She turned to face him, a sweet tremor of heat running along her leg as their knees brushed. "By all that is holy. How could I go to him when I feel about you the way I do, the way I have since I first met you?"

"What are you trying to say?"

Her eyes entreated him. "Don't make me humble myself, Peter. Must I tell you how much I care for you?"

He groaned. "Dear God, it's true, then. You do love me the way I love you?"

She smiled. "I love you, Peter. More than anything in this world."

He took her face in his hands and smoothed the fine brows with the pad of his thumbs. "I never thought to hear those words. From the moment I saw you in the bookstore, I was drawn to the way you looked and to your courage in the face of your misfortunes."

"And to my independence?" She smiled.

He breathed an oath. "Yes, my lovely witch, your

independence. Much as I will strive to dominate you, I can only love you the more for your strength of will." He took her in his arms and held her as he buried his face in her hair.

"Marry me, Margaret. I don't want to spend another hour without you."

"Nor I, Peter. I'll marry you whenever you say."

He kissed her gently but with growing passion. Every fiber in her body was attuned to her need for him. She molded herself against him, yielding to an urgency born of love.

After a while they walked to the garden to watch the sun come up over the distant woods. A tiny breeze lifted her shawl and fluttered it about her face. He smiled as he pulled her close. "My lovely butterfly, my own paisley butterfly. Enjoy this last sunrise because never again will we have to prowl the night in search of sleep."

She smiled and leaned her head against his chest.